'The Scattering'
'Jaki McCarrick tells a chilling tale

'The Sanctuary'
'…a tender story of mourning and longing.'

*writewords.org.uk*

'Of particular note… Jacqueline McCarrick's "The Sanctuary"; a
tender portrait of a lover dealing with the death of a long-term
partner.'

Mark Brown, *The Short Review*

'The Badminton Court'
'I was totally knocked for six by this story. It is an incredible piece
of writing… The spare, sinewy sentences had me going over and
over them; and such economy of writing! I must, simply must
see more of her work…'

Alex Smith *The Frogmore Papers*

'The Visit'
'"The Visit" takes the reader deep into old sadnesses and life-
changing feuds which still burned under the surface of Irish
society at the time of Bill Clinton's visit.'

Susan Haigh, *The New Short Review*

'By the Black Field'
'My highlights to date would be: Jaki McCarrick's "By the Black
Field"… it has such an understated menace running through it
and the writing is so subtly coloured, it reads like looking at a
painting."

Brian Kirk, *Wordlegs*

*Leopoldville* (play)
'A superbly dark, taut thriller…. A fascinating piece of theatre.'
Deborah Klayman, *RemoteGoat*: 4 Stars

'Impossible to shake off, the effects of this show plaster themselves
on its audience… a stellar script… Expect to leave shaken.'
Naima Khan, *Spoonfed Theatre Journal*: 4 Stars

'A sharp, well-observed piece of writing that is performed beautifully by this young, ensemble cast. The tension builds and builds throughout the play culminating in a harrowing twist that both excites and disgusts in equal measure… Fantastic work.'

Phil Tucker, *Broadway Baby*, 5 Stars

'A fantastic, haunting, terrifying play… very strong, young cast & tight direction. It's the winning entry for The Papatango New Writing Competition 2010 and rightly so…'

Shenagh Govan, *The Group*, Theatre Royal Stratford East

'All the familiar ingredients are here: rustic eccentricity, colloquial lyricism, the Troubles. Yet fine performances and a subtle handling of the shades of morality lift this above the ordinary.'

Kieron Quirke *Evening Standard:* 4 Stars

'A powerful play'

Nina Steiger, Soho Theatre

'I love her voice'

Simon Reade, Bristol Old Vic

*The Mushroom Pickers*, Gene Frankel Theatre, New York
'There's a great deal to admire in new Irish playwright Jacqueline McCarrick's debut work "*The Mushroom Pickers*"… a compellingly dark and difficult play… steeped in the dialect and lore of Co. Monaghan… one of the play's major strengths is its strong sense of place – the local landscape is presented throughout as both beguiling and dangerous – and McCarrick knows how to sift drama from the tensions and realities of everyday border county life… McCarrick's play is unique in that it presents a part of Ireland rarely seen on Irish stages, and the playwright presents the realities of that region with courage and rare honesty… (the company) is also to be thanked for bringing this challenging new production to the New York stage for the first time.'

Arts Editor, Cahir O'Doherty, *New York Review*

# The Scattering

For my father,

and in memory of Pamela Von Hunnius

# The Scattering

*a collection of short stories*

by

Jaki McCarrick

Seren is the book imprint of
Poetry Wales Press Ltd
57 Nolton Street, Bridgend, Wales, CF31 3AE
www.serenbooks.com
Facebook: facebook.com/SerenBooks
Twitter: @SerenBooks

ISBN: 978-1-78172-032-5

The Badminton Game, 1972 (oil on canvas), Inshaw, David
(b.1943) © David Inshaw / The Bridgeman Art Library
Typesetting by Elaine Sharples
Printed by Bell and Bain, Glasgow

quote from Jen Hadfield, *Night-no-Place*, with thanks to
Bloodaxe Books

The publisher works with the financial assistance of
The Welsh Books Council

# Contents

Each of us is responsible for everything and to every human being.

DOSTOYEVSKY

# By the Black Field

Angel was building a fence right along where his land cut down to the river, not because the river might burst its banks, which it was prone to do in the rain-heavy months, but because he or Jess or the child might accidentally fall in, especially on a moonless night when they might not be able to see. He was concerned because the ground was too soft now for the poles, and he was convinced that what he should have done was rebuild his grandfather's wall as far as Henry's.

A pleat formed between his brows. He was bothered and his eyes hurt. He lacerated himself for his persistence – and for wasting good money on the poles.

He looked up at the swaying pines as if seeing his wife's face: no doubt she would be disappointed in his efforts. He turned to the newly ploughed field. Soon it would be ready for sowing. He thought of summer when there would be knee-high potato stalks with their purplish and white-wheeled flowers filling its black space.

He heard a woman talking on the road. It was Margaret, the frenetic, spindly woman who lived round the turn on the other side of the ring fort. He could never say what, exactly, but something troubled him about her. She and her husband Jack ran a computer business from their blue dormer. She was nice enough to him and Jess when they first arrived, and when they'd meet her on the road she would say hello and sometimes ask them about themselves. But still, Angel disliked her; he saw in her a kind of desperate and cold ambition and it reminded him of London. Her mustard-coloured MG would regularly screech to a halt out in the road. She'd have forgotten something that the small, wiry Jack would invariably be asked to retrieve. Or she'd pull over to take or make a call, and talk so loud the birds would fly out of the trees. And there she was now, Angel thought, at it again. Though this time she seemed to be alone, and was walking.

He was heavy with depression: a feeling of length in his stomach as if a fist was inside him pushing down on his breath. He set about methodically collecting the poles then stacked them against the side of the house beside the turf.

There were times when Angel thought that the land communicated with him. He knew that this was irrational, and probably due to overwork, and to the fact that he had not yet lost his city-born infatuation with green fields (and also, possibly, because he'd spent his childhood summers in this place and had fond and lively memories of it). He imagined that after a few more years on the farm he'd be as hardnosed towards the land as every other farmer he knew. Still, he could not dispel the sense he had that wherever he went on his six acres he was not alone. He would feel guided towards sowing this or that crop, doing this or that farm job. Sometimes he would just put his 'delusion' down to the voices of men and women at work in nearby fields being carried on the breeze or downriver. That's what he told himself. He said nothing about the experience to his wife.

As he closed the door behind him, Jess brushed past carrying his grandmother's large blue-flowered plate (that she had left to him) filled with steaming vegetables. He quickly washed his hands and changed his clothes then tucked himself into the table.

'The poles are all wrong, Jess,' he said, his mouth full of food.

'How come?' Jess asked.

'It's too wet. I should have hired some help and built the wall.'

She was strong, like a thick white lily in the sunshine. And now, in the eighth month, more unavailable to him than ever. Since they moved here she seemed to fall into an ever-deepening daze, Angel thought. He knew she had no love for this land. Not everyone was able to engage with nature the way he could, he knew that. He had not expected her to love the place, just to appreciate something of its beauty and charm, as she had seemed to do at first. But lately she'd begun to talk about London and how she missed it, and the talk had annoyed him. He felt as if he had failed her. He looked at her across the table from him. She was beautiful with her long white hair, and eyes that were as pink as his own.

The house, lost on the end of the long road before the turn towards Carrick, was set into a wide, elder-protected circle, further shaded by pines and a large oak. A dead beech stump, host to clusters of oyster mushrooms, sat behind the front stone pier. It was one of the few restored cottages of its kind in the barony. All the other homesteads of a similar age in the area served as a source for walls, or were used as rickyards or byres – or were simply abandoned. While he had rehabilitated the old house, his neighbours – the Dalys, Cassidys, Conlons – had all set up in the soulless, heavily mortgaged piles they'd had built alongside stone cottages (in various stages of dereliction) in the same way the Church had established itself throughout the land on pagan sites and shrines. Before they had come, the house had known no modernity, though latterly, with electricity, his grandmother had had 'the wireless'. And up until now it had been shelter (during the summers, anyway) to only one albino child (and how he got into the works nobody knew), and that was Angel.

In the autumn there had been a rat in the barn and it was this, Angel believed, that had triggered Jess' mistrust of the place. At first they thought it was a mink; a neighbour who had come home from Australia had begun breeding Swedish mink for fur and all the mink had escaped. A rat, however, was another story. Angel had stalked the rat for three days. Then, one morning, he found it on the barn floor, sleeping, and took a hammer to it. His frenzied attack on the creature disturbed him, and he knew then that he, too, had begun to change in the place.

After the meal, he cleared the plates and sat by the fire. He watched his wife as she walked to the window and looked out. He wondered if, after the child was born, she would want to stay.

'Will we go out and watch the weather, Jess?' he asked, hoping she would stand with him on the porch and look up at the stars as they had done when they first came.

'In a bit,' she replied, and went to lie down in the back room. He pulled his chair into the warmth and thought of the fence. It was important to get a barrier erected. A partially sighted child could not be allowed to wander a farm left unguarded to a deep river. He'd call in some aid and build a wall. He'd call someone tomorrow. There was more than enough stone; round the sheds there was plenty, and it was all free.

He must have fallen asleep. There was a heavy rap on the door and when he awoke he had thought for a second he was back in the flat in Willesden and was confused. He went to the door and opened it.

'Terence O'Hanlon?' the tall garda asked. Angel could smell cigarette smoke off the man's breath.

'That's me,' Angel replied.

'Can I come in?' Angel hesitated. He'd heard stories about people calling to remote homesteads under all sorts of pretexts, then looked out and saw the squad car. He asked the garda in, shut the door behind him and dropped the latch. Jess came out of the room, slowly tying her hair. He watched the garda staring wide-eyed at Jess' long white hair flashing around the low-lit room.

'I'm sorry to have bothered you both,' the garda said.

'No. It's fine. What's the problem?' Angel asked. The garda seemed nervous.

'Terrible storm forecast,' the garda said.

'I heard.'

'Messing it up terrible these days, aren't they, the weather people?'

'They are.' Angel laughed, thinking of his poor day with the poles.

'What can I do for you, Officer?'

'Patrick is fine.'

'Patrick. What can I do for you?'

'Please. Sit down,' Jess said, and gestured to the garda, who took Angel's chair by the fire.

'Look, I just have to ask you both not to go far, at least not out of the local area, if you don't mind. For the next couple of days anyway.'

'Why? What's going on?' Jess asked, alarmed. The garda seemed put out and wiped his mouth with his hand which, Angel observed, was as wide and thick as a brick.

'I suppose you'll know soon enough, but a body was found this evening up there in the bog. The other side of the ring fort.'

'A body?' said Jess.

'Aye. A woman. A dead one,' the garda replied.

'Who is it?' Angel asked.

'Your neighbour, actually. Margaret Murphy. Lives, or lived, I should say, up in the blue house. These are hard times now and people do crazy things. We need to make enquiries all around. Who knows what goes through a person's mind these days, huh? The figures are up.'

'The figures?' Jess enquired.

'Suicide,' the garda said. 'We have a mink problem as you know in these parts. But it is my belief she must have been dead already for them to have done that to her.' Angel sat Jess down into a chair.

'Did you know herself and Jack Murphy?'

'Only in passing,' Angel replied.

'Fresh over from England, Mr O'Hanlon, are you?'

15

'Well, yes and no. We've been here since last spring.'

'Keep yourselves to yourselves do you?'

'Mostly, yes.'

'I seemed to recall word of a fella with the look of yourself come to the old O'Hanlon place from London.'

'That would be me then,' Angel replied, curtly.

'Right. Well, I'll not keep you both tonight.' The garda stood up, nodded, and went to lift the latch of the door. Angel quickly aided his release out onto the porch.

'Is that it?' Angel asked.

'That's it. I'll call in tomorrow and we'll catch up then.'

'Patrick…' Angel called out before the garda had reached the hedge.

'I saw her you know. Margaret. Today. Out on the road.'

'What time would that have been?'

'Four, five hours ago.'

'She was probably on her way up. 'Tis a pity you didn't catch her first, huh?'

'Then you're sure it's…'

'She has previous. That's all you need know. Just keep to the village for the weekend now till the forensics are done. Goodnight now.'

When he returned to the house, Jess was curled up in bed. Angel quietly closed the bedroom door and went into the kitchen. He stood with his back to the fire and began to consider the day: nothing had gone right from the start of it. Maybe the whole project had been a mistake and they would have been as well to have sold the property when he'd inherited it. But they'd had this mad idea of a life in the country. Maybe it was he and Jess; maybe they were just wrong in the place, like the Swedish mink. Why had he not called out to Margaret when he saw her in the road? She was alone, and not shouting her usual venom at Jack. He should have guessed something was amiss.

He went out with his big stick to the side field. He walked along the lane-way to the edge of the land, passed the desolate-looking black field, all darkly ploughed and waiting to be sown, the tall grasses on the rim of it kissing in the crosswinds. He looked over towards Henry's and saw a flashing light from a television screen spill onto their flat dark lawn. He looked up at the black pines and turned to face the long width of emptiness over the ravine down to the river. In the water he saw his reflection and the transillumination of his eyes; they glowed. He took a gulp of the sleet-laden air and thought of poor gormless Jack who had now lost his wife. It racked him. He thought of Jess, and of all the precious time he'd missed with her this past year. The wall can wait a while, he told the land, and turned and walked quickly towards the house.

# The Badminton Court

The window of my room faces a tall hedge and an ancient oak, home to a kestrel and her two chicks. Beyond Redwood are hills, the edge of a winding silver lake. As I observe its gleam curl around the estate, I know instantly that I do not have to cross the lake to find what I need, that happiness is a small question, easily answered.

Summer. The smell of cut grass, the faint odour of plimsoles. Throughout the house the unmistakable bouquet of hemp. Fourteen acres of manicured gardens and lawns. The sky an azure spell. Clouds that are bird-shaped: an eagle, doves, buzzards. There is a palpable sense of waiting on the badminton court below, a silence soon to be punctured by bat whacks, whistling shuttlecocks and the swish of serge skirts.

I look down at the court, the sun scalding the lawn, the bullfinches gathering in the gods of the low, long hedge to watch the morning game. I know I'll be here for a while. Then music: Saint-Saëns, Joy Division. I know what she wants. I hear the front door slam. I go to the games room and change into the maroon-coloured gown. I am here to play. I am here to help her forget. I am here to help her die.

This is Redwood House, Suffolk. Constable country. Miranda is seventeen. She is thin with shorn blonde hair, and is altogether the most disarmingly honest person I have ever met. Reveals to everyone precisely what her illness is, gives them diagnosis *and* prognosis. Brain tumour. Malignant. Grade four. Three to six months. I am used to a more guarded (though perhaps 'duplicit' is a better word) environment. My father's cagey manoeuvres, his dubious schemes, his admired business acumen. My presence is itself the settlement of his debts to Miranda's father.

Apart from Frances and me, she is alone at Redwood. Her father is off on some protracted business trip; her mother, never discussed, is, I think, barely known to her. The herbal preparations, the meals, the thrice-weekly trips to the clinic, are left to Frances.

Further to the south of Redwood there is another property, with a small boathouse: South Lodge. Lavender hedgerows, saxifrage-covered rocks, an assortment of mangy cats and kittens. This is Inshaw's place. From this land he watches us. When we play he pretends he is out gathering mushrooms or repairing the corrugated roof of the boathouse. Sometimes I see his dark, deliquescent eyes follow the shuttlecock back and forth over the net. He is a presence in the game; triangulates it. She tells me to ignore him.

I have become, within weeks, father and mother to her. Father, mother and more.

Dinner. Frances has prepared salmon and marinated tuna and Miranda wants to teach me how to use chopsticks. She rises, comes towards me. The sick smell of her as she bends over my shoulder; death is in her breath. I have forgotten she is so ill. It is easy to do: that lightness of spirit, precision of play. She drops her head on my hair. Your beautiful hair, she says, your long, dark beautiful hair. I am aware of her bones against my own tumescence and curves. She comes away, stands before me, androgynous and stark, and for a moment it seems as if each of us has been called up from the depths of the other's consciousness. We go on like this. The days are endless, summer does not turn. Only I notice the chicks are bigger in the oak, and that Inshaw has finally repaired his roof and is sailing his boat, or I would hardly register the passing of time at all.

I bump into Inshaw in the village. I am surprised. Nice man, shy. We discuss Miranda. Poor Miranda. It isn't fair. It isn't right. He says he will look out for her when I leave at the end of September. I realise I do not want to leave, not ever. I think of my first night and the thoughts I'd had of escape, of secret instant escape onto the tall hedge; I consider how fortunate it was I did not give in to those thoughts. The encounter with Inshaw has startled me. The sudden reality of the situation, a splint of cold glass in my skull.

She says little at breakfast. The evening before she had been on fire. Rapid, erratic thoughts, unfinished sentences, sentences that unravelled, ending in lacunae, gibberish. She had been rude, her inhibitors obstructed by that thing, growing, multiplying inside her. Tumour talk, Frances calls it. She has some toast, a thimble of marmalade, tea. I know she wants a game because she is dressed in the maroon gown. Worn when badminton was played as formally as tennis or cricket, the serge gowns are almost a hundred years old. They belonged to her grandmother. Miranda had found them soot-soaked in the cellar, later began to wear one as protection from the sun. Long-sleeved, cuffed, mandarin-collared, they are oriental in design. Frances says they make us seem like twins. Miranda leaves the house and I go to the games room to change. She has left a sprig of something, eglantine, by my washed and ironed gown on the bench. The sight of it horrifies me.

Our last game. Her play is at half-speed. Her co-ordination off. She is all over the place, drops the shuttlecock. It is tragic to watch. She observes the weakness in her own swing. Summons all her strength and it is poor. Flails about with the racket, pretends there is something wrong with it, but her racket is fine. Essays an awkward thrust and teeters. She is being milked by that thing. It is unspeakable. Eventually she gets a whack. The shuttlecock is not so much launched as massaged by the catgut. She continues, laughs it off, but she cannot get the shuttlecock to cross the net. The sky is a bowl of darkest mussel-blue. Then rain. She runs inside. I hear music: Joy Division, 'Dead Souls'. The curtains are drawn. I smell burning herbs, cannabis. She is in pain. I know what I must do. I walk to Inshaw's. He offers to sail the boat for me but I assure him I am a seasoned navigator. It is untrue. My upbringing proves fruitful for something: Inshaw lends me his boat for the day.

Miranda and I sail on the silver lake. The day turns bright and humid; a heron wades through the dark-green mud of the bank, water lilies spin with the current. The motor is off and I oar through syrupy, calm conditions till we come to the bend, continuing through a wider willow-lined stretch, still on the estate. Here the wild flowers are in bloom, the eglantine, meadowsweet, great burnet. Low clouds of red admirals skim the side of the boat, their fat gravid centres covered in wet fur. In fields I see bales of hay, barley being harvested. Her face has tilted to one side. Her freckled, yellowing face is beginning to develop a pronounced drop, with drooped jowls, and she drools when she speaks. In her eyes some recognition of what is happening to her. I will always be convinced by that look. I try to tip the boat. It is a struggle. The boat shudders, takes a while to capsize. She screams, splashes about. I swim towards her, hold her, our bodies small and snug in the water. My plan is to swim back once she has gone under, but I can't leave. She clings to me, accepting and placid.

Twenty-four hours later I wash up against a bank. I am alive, and later wake up in hospital. Miranda floats to an island in the river, into a swan's nest. She is so white two diving teams fail to spot her wound around the reeds and tall red crocus.

Twenty-two summers pass. The world is a changed place.

Redwood belongs now to Inshaw. He grants me a walk through the estate whenever I come here. Around the mile or so of angular hedges, the ancient oak and badminton court, where, sometimes, I think I hear the wind fluting through plastic.

# The Badminton Court

Once he asked if I was happy. Before I had the chance to reply, he said his own life had been good and prosperous, but hardly happy. Mine was the same, I said. What is happiness? he asked, as if I knew any better than he. I pondered on this. For me, I said, happiness is two girls playing badminton under an azure sky with clouds that are bird-shaped. Those summers were best, he replied, when I used to watch you play. It occurred to me then, that for nearly a quarter of a century we had both been sustained by a few intoxicating memories squirrelled from our youth. I told him it was high time we lived a little. He agreed and told me then of his plans to flatten the court. I remember that as I walked towards my car, parked beside the silver lake, I had the distinct and certain feeling I was being watched.

# 1975

As the light weakened, Mr McCourt pulled open the velour drapes and lit the vanilla-scented candle. He had just said goodbye to his youngest daughter, and watched as she crossed the road to catch the airport bus. His children had been coming and going for a long time, perhaps twenty years, but he'd never gotten used to it, and 'goodbye' had become increasingly difficult.

'We're thinking of buying the white bungalow,' he had heard her say throughout the four days; he knew she hadn't even arranged to view it.

'You'll not be able to settle in if you leave it too long.'

'It's my town isn't it?' she had replied.

He watched her stand stiffly by her black trolley, her long red hair jetting out of a high ponytail. She did not look across at him standing behind the flame in the otherwise dark room. He must, he thought, be visible behind the nets in the dusky evening. Nor had she so much as glanced at the white bungalow. She reminded him of his wife with that hair and her petite frame, but something tight and of the city clung inelegantly to her. He had not fully believed her work-attributed reasons for rushing back to London.

He thought that maybe he'd talked too much during the days he'd spent with her; he thought of what his son, Francie, had said: don't try too hard with her, don't take time off for her. As far as he knew she hadn't even been near Crowe Street.

He *had* taken time off for her. Almost in anticipation of her visit, he had recently brought in two new girls to help Bridie, his chief baker. Bridie had come home after thirty years with big plans for her own shop, only to have her husband run off with a girl half her age after their first month home. (He had felt sorry for her; she was often sour-faced but good with the women.) It had been his hope, until recently, that Francie or one of his daughters would run the shop with him. It had happened at Daly's and Duffner's; siblings working together in their respective shops, both families exuding a soft and enviable pride. Once he had Francie with him for a whole summer; the girls came sporadically during holidays but that had been the extent of their working together as a family.

The bus was late. Perhaps she would cross to the house and stay another night. They could listen to the Lena Martell records, or to Geraldine O'Grady, and he could tell her the stories about the farm, stories about the Channonrock families and O'Hara and his own scrapes at the border in '69. He hadn't told any of them the stories in years, he thought. Nor had they asked for them. Further evidence, if he needed it, that they'd all managed to sever themselves from their past. The realisation had come as quite a shock to him, about five years ago.

In London, his wife had dragged the girls to Irish dancing on the other side of the city in Finsbury Park. He had taken all four of them to Irish language, flute and recitation classes at the Irish Centre in Quex Road in Kilburn, twice a week. They had done so in anticipation of returning, building a home and business back in the town; and he didn't want his children to forget and grow up English. (The South London accent was enough for him; had he had any say they would have been trained to adopt his own sharp Monaghan spurt.) It had taken much longer than planned to save in London, and by the time he'd brought them back, the so-called

'Irishness' they'd been inculcated with stood out as artificial; an outmoded thing in the prospering town.

'Irish culture is alive and well and living in Birmingham,' he would to say to Bridie, who knew exactly what he meant.

He watched his daughter haul on a cigarette. Of all of them it was she he worried about most. She drank too much, he thought. He wondered, as she stood in the road, looking to see if the bus was coming over the Dublin Street hill, if she'd ever forgiven him.

The Mother and Daughter Wards (as he called them) passed the window and looked in. He jumped back because he didn't want Margaret Ward to see him. She would think it peculiar, the lights off as he stood there looking out from behind a lit candle. He found her stern but also striking with her black-black bouffant hair and kohl-lined eyes, and he felt a little afraid at the thought of explaining himself to her. If she had caught sight of him she would probe him for sure. All the same, she was gracious, and uniquely considerate, too, in that she had had a memorial mass said for his wife in The Friary every year at Christmas on the anniversary of her death. But take-me-take-my-mother was written all over Margaret and he wasn't ready for that level of commitment. He moved to the side of the window and momentarily took his eyes off his daughter, now fretfully pacing, to watch Margaret Ward's pencil-skirted rump sway with maturity and confidence as she walked her mother into their own house, three doors up.

'Why don't you sell up, Mr McCourt? That's what you should do. Travel while you still have the time,' Margaret had said when he told her about his children's lack of interest in the business.

'Don't you think the town'd miss me, Margaret? Wouldn't they miss my buns?'

'They would, I suppose. I'd miss your Tipsys. Mother would miss your Chesters, that's a fact.'

'This is it, Margaret. I couldn't sell up even if I wanted to because I know there's no one makes as great cakes as *The*

*Home Bakery.* And until there is, I feel I just can't sell.' He had no intention of selling the shop and, at this stage of his life, had little interest in travelling beyond the town.

He checked his watch. The bus was now twenty minutes late. He thought he caught sight of his daughter looking over at him through the window. He waved but she didn't wave back. He saw then that the birdseed she'd scattered on the bird-table had attracted a host of peach-breasted chaffinches, bullfinches, some siskins and a pair of collared doves, but the family of robins would not come down from the juniper tree. He had known this would happen. *He* only ever laid stale breadcrumbs but, as she'd bought the seed especially, he kept quiet about it. The male at the front played sentinel as the brood waited in the nest making ticking sounds. They're cute enough, he said to himself. The robins would swoop down for stale bread because it was of little interest to the bigger birds that pecked at it as a last resort, preferring the berries, worms, gifts of other gardens. He liked to think that it was their closeness and joviality as a brood that impaired their ability to attack and mark territory. They were his favourites, and he made a mental note to go out and put down breadcrumbs once the bus had come and gone.

They had not always had such a variety of birds. When they first bought the house there had not even been a proper garden, just scrubland out the back, concrete at the front. He and Francie had rolled out a new lawn over the dug-up concrete. They had planted flowers, shrubs and a laurel hedge, and sowed a small area with vegetables.

After the garden, he'd put almost all of his time into the business, missing much of his children's growing-up. Somehow he thought they would understand his occasional moodiness, his silences, as the consequences of running a demanding, successful bakery. He would start at four in the morning with the breads. By six he would be ready to blend icing. He would then pour the icing into various spacklings and place these in the fridge. Black icing was required for the lettering; lemon, pink, blue, green and gold were used for the buns and birthday cakes; navy for the children's cakes – and this had to be prepared slowly as it was made from a delicate combination of black and red Wilton colouring. Sometimes he'd watch his over-heating hands ruin his handiwork and he'd have to plunge them into ice water. Then he would bake pastry: choux for the eclairs, flaky for the cream slices, short-crust for pies, tarts, followed by the mixes for the Madeiras, angel-food cake, gingerbread, lemon cake and various puddings. His creams consisted of mock, whipped, clotted, butter-starch and Chantilly, and an hour before the shop was due to open he made the pink and white meringues. His schedule was relentless, and though he experienced occasional surges of pride and satisfaction from his efforts, it was, in the main, a long, hard graft. That his children had never appreciated this punishing schedule was plain now. He had nonetheless been surprised to learn of their peculiar resentment towards him; they seemed to think he'd given too much time to the business during the difficult years after their mother's death.

The candle flickered, crackled on a fallen hair. He thought of the bomb. Planted in the blue Hillman Hunter outside Kay's Tavern in 1975, the year he lost everything. In 1975 he had handpicked all ingredients and supplies himself, baking the stock out the back and serving alone in the then staff-less shop. He bought some breads in from McCann's and McElroy's but mostly made his own: soda farls, brown sodas, white sodas, yeast browns and whites, and once a week a black rye with walnut and caraway seed. It was Mr McCourt's fervent belief that had he not been alone in the shop on the day of the bomb his premises would have been spared.

His thoughts drifted off to the unearthly light that had hung over Crowe Street that Christmas afternoon as he watched *The Home Bakery* melt to the ground like warm lemon icing.

'We're lucky the town hall didn't go too,' Jack Daly had said. 'Blew the doors clean off. Bits of them oak doors flying like leaves, so they were, Mr McCourt.'

'It's a horrible thing,' he had replied, 'horrible for someone to do that to people.'

'That's their response to Sunningdale* you know. You of all people, McCourt, should be doing something about that now.'

Daly's unsubtle call to arms still haunted him. What he had done at the border in '69 had been admired, but any man might have done that; the bombing of Kay's was different, for it signalled the escalation of a dirty and protracted *war*.

Mr McCourt recalled that it had been a strange, overcast day from the outset. He remembered the full moon that had hung ominously by the outermost tip of Cooley, as if it possessed some significant bearing on the awful proceedings below. For many, the day had become a blur; for McCourt, a detailed recording he could replay with exactitude.

He had tried hard to save the shop. *Over here, over here*, he had screamed to the firemen, indicating the fire raging in his kitchens and all along the outer wall. He had watched them carry out two bodies, and over twenty injured from Kay's. They had looked shattered: Joe and Jaxy. He knew them both, and he had never seen either of them look so bloodless and horrified. *We have you Mr McCourt. You're next*, they assured him. He remembered the flames finding fresh force in the pub, just as the Town Hall foyer exploded. He recalled the eerie smell of gas and the realisation then that he would probably lose the bakery.

With the detailed images of that day, came also its hellish sounds. He recalled the bells in St Patrick's rumbling dissonantly as thin cracks wired the plaster in the shop wall right in front of him. Within seconds of the first blast, large wedges of two-by-fours, complete with flames, nails, melting turquoise paint, had crashed through the pastry display and onto the marble counter, catching the thick pile of wrapping tissue. He had even tried to quench the fire with his own shop coat. Open tins of oil, lined up in a row against the kitchen wall,

* = Sunningdale Agreement (signed 1973, collapsed May 1974)

caught the flames with a heavy fizz, and the entry to the ovens area collapsed outright. He had used the small fire extinguisher he'd bought off the travelling salesmen, but it had been no good. The emission dry and wispy.

He seemed to be in a daze as he stared out at the street's glowering aftermath. Beneath the platform of the foremost engine, a red barrel had been rolling up and down a long stray plank. The barrel made a relentless, rhythmic din as it massaged the half-burnt length of wood. The rattle fixed in his ear, gave a rhythm to his thoughts: *look at that barrel, like a sea-saw rattling, will it ever roll loose.* Over and over, like some macabre rhyme. Beside the barrel oozed puddles of petrol with rainbow-coloured rims. Loose pieces of corrugated sheeting were strewn across the dark, wet streets, and occasionally gusts of wind would clatter them against the sides of fire engines. He recalled that water had dripped from eaves, even though it hadn't rained.

Nor would he ever forget the pervasive smell: wet smoked timber and ash mixed with the distinctly bitter smell of gelignite. He had smelled that combination before, and it was, he thought, by far the world's bitterest smell.

He recalled the devastation that had quickly collected around him: the pavements had turned pure charcoal. By the door of the shop lay the remainder of a white leatherette car seat. Two brown, soot-stained platform boots lay abreast by the drain. He remembered wondering how on earth two matching boots had come to be so conveniently together. A woman's black, feathered hat and one black glove lay in a pool of bubble-topped grey water, swirling in a pothole. Ahead, gardai were walking around the remains of the blue Hillman Hunter, taking notes and sealing the area off with yellow plastic tape. And then the bizarre sight of a man who had wandered out of the Town Hall with a blown-off hand, having to be taken to hospital in the back of a truck with a big blue sign for *Elliott's, The Fishmongers* stencilled on the side.

But, he recalled, the rattling barrel had continued to draw him that day; its hypnotic sound, its eye-catching shade – the colour of his wife's hair.

The doorbell rang. He had not even heard the clack of the garden gate. He quickly looked across to see if his daughter was gone. Twenty-five minutes had passed, and still no bus. He watched the jet of smoke rise into the cold air from her pursed mouth. She sat on her trolley, held her coat in tightly with one arm, as if her stomach ached. A man tried to speak to her, but she remained almost rudely mute. She had always been his least talkative daughter. The rest of them usually drove him mad with their chatter. He went to the door. It was Bridie. He was surprised to see her.

'I left the shop early, Mr McCourt,' Bridie said, quietly.

'Do you want me to go in to the girls?'

'No, not at all. It's near closing now. Anyway, you're off and that's it. We do need cornstarch though.'

'I'll see to it.'

'Grand. I just wanted to come up and ask if I could have the day off Monday.'

Something was wrong. Bridie was an attractive woman: pale as milled flour, but because of her persistently poor self-esteem, she did not radiate the beauty that was evidently hers. She wore no make-up, never seemed to get her wiry grey hair coloured or styled, and habitually wore thick beige nylons with small eyeholes stopped from cobwebbing entire legs by layers of clear nail varnish. One time he had noted a glittery blue by her right calf. He had laughed at the cosmetic tricks of his daughters, and knew that repairing nylons had long gone out with the ark. Still, he found her injured politeness magnetic.

'Is that alright, Mr McCourt?'

'Monday? Yes, of course. Take it off, Bridie. I'll take over. That's if I haven't forgotten what to do.'

'Ah now. You're too modest.'

'Planning a heavy weekend then, Bridie?' he joked, ushering her into the front room.

'No,' she said quietly, 'it's my divorce.'

His face reddened and he turned to the window. In the more energised atmosphere of the bakery he would have been quicker off the mark and able to respond to Bridie's frankness. But at home, this evening, his guard was down, and he couldn't think of anything to say. He stared into the darkening street.

'Warm fire you have going there, Mr McCourt. Would you not close the curtains and put on the light and settle up to that? It's dark now, you know.'

'I'm watching my wee girl, Bridie. Till her bus comes for the airport.'

'Righto,' she said, gazing towards the window. 'Maybe I'll bring you a pie then, later. Would you like a pie, Mr McCourt?'

'No. I'm not hungry at all.'

'I'll go so.' He let Bridie out of the house. He was sorry to see her leave, but glad that he could carry on by the window in peace.

The dark clouds were staggered in short strips across the horizon. His daughter remained perched on her trolley, her bus now almost forty minutes late. He considered going to the door and calling out for a cross-traffic conversation, but then thought this would embarrass her.

Theirs was an emotional, fragile bond. She was five when his wife had died. He had not managed to be both parents to any of his children, least of all to her. He had behaved badly. When the others had left for England and America, she and he had been left at home together, and there had been much drama. He had not known how to raise a child by himself. Francie and the girls did what they could to help (as the bakery was being reestablished) before leaving for work and lives elsewhere.

During her teenage years, he had switched tack, resorting to plain-talking force, and once had woken her up for school by pouring a bucket of cold water over her while she slept. He knew now that it was just one of his many cruel and unforgivable explosions of anger in the house; that he should have asked for help with his morose, introverted daughter. He'd not had much trouble with the others (apart from a brief episode with Francie), but she had left him exasperated. When she was fourteen she had suddenly become a vegan and began to object vehemently to his use of gelatin in the shop. He learned later that the protest came as a result of her membership of the Baha'i Faith, which she had clandestinely joined. There had been no end to her rebellion.

In her late twenties they had begun a slow truce. There was much left unsaid about the years he might have been more percipient, had he not been in such a prolonged mourning himself.

His eye fell on the mossed-over marble seat in the corner of the garden: the love seat. At least, that was what he and his wife had secretly called it. Engraved somewhere were their initials, and '1975', the year they had come home. He and his wife had behaved like kids in private, and he was often stunned to think that within the family there had been two of him. That the children did not know the man his wife had married amazed him, but that was how it was: one man, necessarily split. And when she died, it seemed that the man she had married went too. The dead take big bites out of you, he thought, so you'll never forget. Every day he had hoped the bombing of the town would receive a thorough investigation; there had been a few gestures, some well-meaning attempts to get to the bottom of it, but little had come of them.

His thoughts went back to Crowe Street. He remembered he'd been staring into the smoky, stinking streets for ages, stunned, unable to find his legs, or, after the mesmerising motions of the barrel, a modicum of voice. Understanding had come slow and hard: she had been waiting in Kay's Tavern, his red-haired wife, and they had been due to meet there at four. He remembered hoping she was as late as she usually was for him, or that she'd got caught up in O'Neils, Christmas shopping; he remembered he'd had a bad feeling. He recalled the wintry gust battering the red barrel down Market Street. It was then he'd looked up to see Jaxy and Joe walk slowly towards him, their peaked yellow hats held low.

The bus pulled in with a jolt. He watched his daughter stamp out her cigarette then press down the creases in her coat. She lugged up the bar of her trolley, wheeled it into the queue. As the long line of late and frustrated voyagers mounted the bus, he watched her quickly slip from the queue, pull a pen and scrap of paper from her bag, look towards the white bungalow and jot down the details from the FOR SALE sign. She mounted the bus and jostled into a window seat at the front. He watched her turn and peer out of the window towards him. He could see her nervous face light up as she caught sight of him behind the flame. She waved and kissed the window with her gloved hand as the bus drove off. He waved back and watched till the diesel trail cleared. He felt the breach that had been between them close a little. After pulling the curtains, he put on the lights and blew out the candle. Vanilla filled the room as he went towards the kitchen to make breadcrumbs.

# Hellebores

'Did you say *girls*, Bobby Jean?' Jessica asked, wondering exactly what kind of girls her friend was referring to. 'I'd love to take them. I would. But this is no place for… BJ, do you know what time it is?' Jessica held the phone away as Bobby Jean pleaded and hollered on about it being an emergency. 'I can't. It's Jules. First he washed up from God knows where, and now he's gone off again. I've just about got my hands full with him and the plants.'

But Bobby Jean worked on Jessica carefully, knowing Jessica wouldn't be able to resist when she told her the girls' parents had floated off somewhere down the swollen Mississippi; that when the levees had been breached and the bridges destroyed they had never been seen again, and that the two girls had been shunted from Pineville to Baton Rouge to Atlanta. Bobby Jean knew her wards' story would chime with something deep inside Jessica. Because it had themes that were familiar to her: losing the people we love and having to carry on all alone without them. Bobby Jean knew pretty much everything there was to know about Jessica May Lawson.

The day the girls were due to arrive Jessica had a clear-out of her house, which was really the living quarters above, and an extension of, her store. She cleaned the spare bedroom upstairs, and had Guy, a landscape designer with no physical strength whatsoever, help her bring into it a double bed and coat rail. She put fresh sheets on the bed, brought in a bedside table from her own room, placed on it a vase of freshly cut irises. Then she went into Tina's room, stood at the threshold and looked around at the dustsheets covering the furniture. She knew that the two girls could just as easily have had this room, or even a room each, except that it wouldn't have been easy for her. She closed the door and noted how expectant the house seemed, as if it awaited the arrival of the two young girls, hungrily.

The next day, Olivia and Ashleigh T. Williams arrived at Lawson's Nurseries with Bobby Jean over two hours late. Unpacked and seated at the table, the girls sat quietly and had hot chocolate and lemon cake (which Jessica had made especially). When they were done, Jessica showed them to their room.

'They barely said a word other than "yes Ma'am, no Ma'am",' Jessica said to Bobby Jean when they were finally alone together.

'They're traumatised, and why wouldn't they be? They've just seen the earth open up and steal away their folks. And they had to navigate some deep and mean floods, too, before they eventually got picked up.'

'What did you say the parents did?' Jessica asked her friend, a well-respected realtor who was always doing some kind of good in the community.

'Father a preacher, mother led the Pineville choir. There are relatives in Atlanta, that's how come the girls were sent there, but Atlanta can't find them. Not yet anyway.'

As the two girls slept, Jessica walked out into the warm air of the Panama City night. She went to the new delivery and brushed her fingers along the thick green shoots. She could hear the surf crashing on the sands and the sandpipers chattering. She thought she could hear, too, the start of new winds gathering. After a while she went to her chair and watched darkness race through her palms and bamboos like the tide. She pressed her face and neck up against the clear wide sky. This was how Jessica found her unity with the world: imaginatively, and in the dark. And sometimes, cast adrift in the night air, Jessica would think of the nights on the beach with Tina and Jules, back when they were a family. Sometimes she might even hear Tina getting in or out of her car, and it would make her jump. It would never be Tina, of course, but usually Jules with some beach girl. It would never be Tina because Tina had been gone a long time. Jessica's thoughts were just about to slip back to the days of Jules and Tina on the beach when she heard a noise out front. She was ready to chastise her son but turned and saw the taller of the two girls, shaking and crying.

'Are you alright, Ashleigh?' Jessica asked.

'It's Olivia, Ma'am, my sister,' the girl replied.

'What's wrong with her?'

'She's sick and we ain't got no medication with us.' Jessica stood up. She could hear thrashing noises coming from the room upstairs.

'What's wrong with her, Ashleigh? You needn't be afraid to tell me. In fact it's best you do.'

'Olivia, Ma'am, she's, well, sometimes she has these fits.' Jessica ran faster than she had done in an age. On reaching the room, she did what she had seen done in so many movies: she restrained the erratic motions of the child, who was half out of the bed, soaked to the skin in sweat and spit, by holding down a tight and twisted-up cloth between the child's teeth. When the shaking stopped, Olivia passed out, bone-rattled and exhausted, like the entire State of Louisiana in the weeks after Katrina.

*

'Jessica, I did not know. There was no time, and believe me I'm gonna give Atlanta shit on a stick for this.' Bobby Jean sounded furious. And Jessica believed that her friend would indeed give the Atlanta authorities 'shit on a stick'. Nonetheless, when she had agreed to Bobby Jean's requests for shelter for the two girls, Jessica had not planned on offering anything more than that.

'How come she didn't have a seizure until now is what I want to know?' Jessica asked.

'Well, you know how it is. I guess her body thought if anywhere was a good place to have a fit, yours was it.'

Jessica sat in the hospital waiting room with Ashleigh beside her. She was beginning to regret letting Bobby Jean get the better of her.

'Are you gonna give us back to Atlanta now, Mrs Lawson?' Ashleigh asked.

'Well, of course I won't be doing that,' Jessica replied, and looked furtively at the pale willowy child sitting beside her. There was something odd and overly mature about her, Jessica thought. She reminded Jessica of a hothouse flower, as if she'd gone from bud to bloom without much flowering in between.

Olivia was led out by a male nurse. The name on his badge said Eric.

'Sometimes it happens like this with children,' Eric said. 'They sort of tailor their suffering to the situation. They can just up and decide to feel it later.' Eric urged Jessica to get both girls seen by the hospital psychiatrist in the coming weeks. 'Standard procedure for Katrina victims. If they lost their parents the way they say, these kids are gonna hurt and pretty bad too.'

The girls were quiet on the way home. Olivia curled herself up against her sister's shoulder in the back of the car. In the mirror, Jessica could see Ashleigh peering out at every blown-away door, every broken window or house-frame, as if they were signs she alone was able to read.

'You alright back there, Ashleigh?' Jessica asked.

'Sure,' Ashleigh replied.

'When the hurricane made landfall here, it wasn't so bad, as you can see. It got worse towards Alabama. Panama City was pretty much prepared for what it got. You see my bamboos in the nursery?' Ashleigh nodded.

'Saved the whole place. Bamboo bends with the wind, see. Better than stone. And it protected everything inside. All the plants and flowers. All my stock.'

'Bamboo wouldn't have stopped the water though, Mrs Lawson. Coz nothing stops water. Water is real patient. I seen what water can do. I only beat it coz…' Ashleigh stopped short, flung herself back against the seat and sighed.

'Because what, child?'

'Well, because I got in touch with my own strength. I pulled it out of me. I had to.'

Once again, Jessica was struck by Ashleigh's grievous words and gravity of tone.

'What does the T stand for in your name?' Jessica asked, as if it might offer up some kind of clue to the child's severity.

'I don't rightly know. Troy, I think. I guess they wanted a boy,' Ashleigh replied.

\*

Night fell on Panama City in late September around six. After the store closed, Jessica would usually make a light supper then walk around the nursery doing jobs in preparation for the following day. She'd repot plants knocked over by the wind or by children running down the pathways. Sometimes she'd find a racoon or fox scavenging and shoo it back into the bamboo. The bamboo attracted a lot of rats, too, as they liked to bed down in the dense undergrowth. Occasionally, if Jules were home and wasn't drunk, he would come out and help her align the saplings and shrubs, and then, if the day had been dry, they'd water the plants together. Then Jessica would put on the garden lights and sit back in her favourite chair. She loved the night sky over the Gulf of Mexico. In the moonlight, the water was emerald green, the sky a deep lapis lazuli blue.

Jessica went to the trays of new shoots and began to carry them towards the store. Before she'd shifted the second crate, Ashleigh came out of the house and began to help. Jessica saw that the girl was strong, built like a boy, broad and thick at the shoulders. Ashleigh carried the trays to the porch where Jessica wanted them laid out in a line so that they could be priced up and ready for sale in the morning.

'Don't you have a boy, Mrs Lawson?' Ashleigh asked.

'I do, but he's out of town. You'll meet him soon enough, though *boy* he is not.'

'What's his name?'

'Jules.'

'If I had a place like this I'd never leave.'

'It's good to travel to places, Ashleigh. Jules – my boy – he likes to get out, that's all.'

'You travel much, Mrs Lawson?'

'A little. I wanted to do more. But with the business, I guess I didn't get the chance,' Jessica replied.

'Maybe you thought there wasn't much reason. I saw the way you like the evenings out here.' There she goes again, Jessica thought, spouting her insight and her wisdom.

'You got a daughter, too. I know coz I seen her pictures. That must be her room with all the covers in it.'

'It is,' answered Jessica, quietly.

'You waiting on her to come home, too?'

'I am,' Jessica replied, swiftly pulling on her garden gloves. She tugged at the tiny sprouts of weeds peeping up through the clay. She felt a surge of anger course through her that she could not reasonably explain to herself. Except that she knew this blood-rush always came whenever anyone would try and talk her out of waiting for Tina to come home. Not that Ashleigh had done that. But had she, Jessica would have sorely wanted to rip the child's heart out.

'What are these things anyway?' Ashleigh asked, turning to the crates with their inch-high shoots.

'These? Why these are my Christmas roses. Except they're not really roses. That's just a nickname they got.'

'What are they, then?' Ashleigh asked.

'Hellebores. They bloom early. Around January. They're poisonous. But I don't grow them to eat them,' Jessica replied.

*

Ashleigh and Olivia had been signed up by Bobby Jean for a term at Bay City High. Three days into term, Cole Spencer, the Head, called Jessica.

'No, it's not Olivia, Jessica May. It's Ashleigh. Look, I just think you should come down here, soon as you can.'

When Jessica arrived at Bay City High it was quiet. All the times she'd been in that school for Tina or Jules she'd never seen it as calm. It was like it was shut or Christmas. Cole Spencer rushed into the foyer and asked her to hush as he led her into the assembly hall. All the students sat around quiet as mice, the teachers behind them, arms folded. She noticed that Miss Quigley was crying. Miss Quigley was as stern as iron so Jessica thought that maybe someone had died. Until she saw who it was they were sitting around listening to. Up front, by the stage, on a small classroom chair, her long pale legs all tied up around each other like pea vines – Ashleigh, talking animatedly about the hurricane.

'It's not just Katrina,' whispered Spencer.

'What else is there?' asked Jessica.

'A whole lot of what else. She says… well… she says she's *the daughter of God.*' A cold shiver ran down Jessica's back. Mad as the words Spencer had just said sounded, they went a long way towards explaining the unnerving self-assurance she herself had observed in Ashleigh.

'Don't be crazy, Cole. She's a kid. It's just a turn of phrase.'

'Listen to her, and watch their faces. She's hypnotic. I'm telling you, the child is gifted. From the beginning of lessons this week she's been dazzling every teacher in her Grade. She says she got the gift out in the floods. From the hurricane itself.'

Jessica looked around at the rapt faces of the children. They were all engrossed in Ashleigh's tale. Which seemed to be about how, when the whirlpool started up in the river, Ashleigh had stood up and demanded it fall away, and how it did just that, and how when the waters parted she walked on dry land to the other side of the river to rescue her sister, Olivia.

In the following weeks the store was the busiest Jessica had ever seen it. People came to buy flowers and wreathes and winter shrubs, but mostly they came to see the girl who had been touched by God in the hurricane. Even when they didn't ask directly to see Ashleigh, or point her out to each other, Jessica knew that was why most people came to the store. (It had never been busy at this time of year.) On Saturdays, when Ashleigh would help out, Jessica would see old women or sick-looking people whisper into the girl's ear to see if she could help them. Sometimes they touched her arm, or brushed past her clothes, and Jessica knew it was so they could get something of Ashleigh into themselves. Some kind of hope or healing. Jessica wanted Ashleigh to settle down to a normal life, as much as she could offer the child while under her roof.

One evening Jessica asked Ashleigh to sit with her out on the porch.

'Sweetie, I know what you've been saying at the school.'

'I know, Mrs Lawson, I saw you.' Jessica lit up a cigarette. She hadn't especially wanted to discuss the matter. It was Ashleigh's personal business, and soon the child would be gone from the house and Panama City anyway. But after seeing how people were with her in the store, how they looked at her on the street and in the bank, Jessica felt she had to speak up.

'This has got to stop, honey. You don't realise how people can react to this kind of talk. It's dangerous.'

'You don't believe me, Mrs Lawson?'

'It's not about whether I believe or don't believe. Look – Eric – you remember Eric from the hospital?' Ashleigh nodded.

'Well, Eric said you and Olivia need to come by one day soon. He'd like you to speak to someone. Counselling it's called. You know what that is, Ashleigh?'

'I'm not crazy, Mrs Lawson. I already spoke to doctors.'

'You did? When?'

'In the 'dome. After a couple of days they had doctors talk to the children who lost their folks. They thought I maybe got hit on the head. But I didn't.'

Jessica looked long and hard at this skinny girl with the white braids and grey-blue eyes. She was convinced now that the loss of their parents had caused Ashleigh and her sister such inestimable pain that they were, most likely, as Eric had said, suffering from some kind of delayed reaction.

'Pineville is a long way from New Orleans. How'd you get to the Superdome?' Jessica asked.

'Red Cross picked us up on some dirt track,' Ashleigh replied.

'By then your parents had…'

'Yes, Ma'am.'

'The house went too?'

'Yes Ma'am. See, it came real early in the mornin'. I remember the air filled up with grey and dark, and pieces of our rooms, my dolls, my books, were swirlin' around, gettin' flung down onto trees and other houses. We ran out of the house and just as we did it folded up behind us like firewood. Olivia cried for Beau, our dog, and Ma and Pa went lookin'. They were just gone a couple of minutes when the river burst out of the earth and swept everythin' forward. We all got separated so quick. I remember my breath – coz it got took clean out of my body, and my nightdress swelled up and I thought I would take off and fly. But then I got swept along so I clung tightly to Olivia. We seemed to be in the water hours and hours. But nothin' fell on my head, Mrs Lawson. I just made up my mind to pull the strength out of myself, and I did.'

'And all of this "daughter of God" business?'

'Olivia got pulled to the other side of the river and this force started to build up inside the water and I couldn't cross. I tried and tried. That's when I heard a voice, and I recognised what it was sayin'. It was from Exodus: *And the children of Israel went into the midst of the sea upon the dry ground: and the waters were a wall unto them on their right hand, and on their left.* So I just did what Moses did, which was what the voice told me to do.'

It occurred to Jessica, then, that maybe Ashleigh was right. Maybe nothing had fallen on her head. Maybe she just hadn't been well to begin with. After all, what did Jessica really know about these young people now living in her home? So much data had been destroyed by Katrina; Ashleigh could be just as ill as her sister for all Jessica knew.

'Ashleigh, now Bobby Jean and me, we mostly go to Unity Church. And Unity is non-denominational. You know what that means?' Ashleigh nodded. 'It means a mixture of everything and nothing in particular. You see, we don't do much Bible study at Unity. And we don't believe hurricanes have anything at all to do with God. Maybe you believe it's his "wrath", do you?'

'What I believe, Jessica, has nothin' to do with religion.'

'Your daddy. Was he a Baptist preacher?'

'Episcopal.'

'Episcopal? Well, they aren't fanciful. So how come you got to thinking you're the daughter of God?'

'My daddy said.'

'What do you mean "he said"?'

'My daddy told me. He said I was the special one. He said it every night he come in my room. And it was only the moment I saw my sister on the other side of the water, that I truly believed him.'

★

Eric brought both girls out to the waiting room where Jessica waited with Bobby Jean. Then Bobby Jean stayed with the girls in the bright, sea-lit room as Jessica went into the consultation room with Eric. Jessica sat. The female psychiatrist entered and sat down opposite Jessica and opened a file.

'Olivia's epilepsy is congenital, but with the right treatment she will most likely stop having seizures by her teens. She is slightly traumatised, but it seems Ashleigh covered Olivia's eyes from a lot of the horrors they might otherwise both have seen.'

'Horrors like what?' asked Jessica.

'Well, there were a lot of bodies on the river. Drownings. A lot of loose animals, too. And it was hot, so you can imagine what state those bodies were in. Ashleigh believes she saw things.'

'What things?'

'Like I said. Drownings. Animals gnawing at bodies.'

'What else?'

The doctor hesitated: 'Well, if you must know, for instance, like a National Guardsman airlift a woman into a helicopter then drop her to her death. Like soldiers opening fire on a black neighbour of the Williams' who, Ashleigh claims, was procuring food from his own store. These are serious allegations. So for the minute it's Ashleigh we're mostly concerned about, Mrs Lawson.'

Jessica decided at that point not to inform Eric, or the doctor, that there were people in Panama City who believed Ashleigh had divine lineage. But somehow Jessica thought that perhaps they knew something about this already. The beach town was, after all, as provincial as any small village – which, indeed, it used to be and in a way still was – despite its recent sprawl out onto the highways of Wal-Marts, malls and Po-Folks restaurants. People on this part of the Gulf knew the exact movements of the tide; they knew when new retirees arrived into this or that complex, or when they died. At the Unity Church there would be a coffee hour after service each Sunday and everyone would talk. Jessica had the feeling that everyone in Panama City (including the people from Unity) pretty much believed she had the daughter of God living under her roof. So it would be a lot easier for Jessica if it turned out the child had concussion. Then everything could calm the hell down before the two girls finally left for Atlanta or somewhere else. Just about anything (except that thing Ashleigh had alluded to the night before) was better than the child going round with an inner power other people wanted a piece of.

'What's wrong with Ashleigh?' Jessica asked the quick-eyed doctor.

'I'd like her to have an MRI scan,' she replied. 'Just routine. To rule out concussion or brain damage. Before we assess her further.'

'You don't believe she saw what she says she saw?'

'We need to rule certain things out.'

'Well, what do you *think's* wrong with her?' Jessica insisted.

'I think the child is traumatised. Quite seriously. She assumed a lot of responsibility.'

Jessica mowed in: 'Has she been abused is what I'm asking you?'

'I don't know,' the doctor replied. 'It takes time to find out.'

Jessica called the hospital the following day for the result of Ashleigh's scan: all clear. Then she made an appointment for the following week for the commencement of Ashleigh's counselling. The evening Jessica got the news that there was no sign of damage or concussion, or any nascent tumours in Ashleigh's brain, Jules came home from Miami.

*

She had begun to organise excursions for the girls so they would see less of her unshaven son slouching around the house. Jules had been unusually quiet since he'd come home, broke, in debt, and deeper into the end of his bottle than ever. He didn't join them at mealtimes, and worked mostly alone in the yard.

One evening, Jessica asked Ashleigh and Olivia if they'd like to go to the theatre. The Bellevue players were to stage *Come Back to the Five and Dime, Jimmy Dean, Jimmy Dean* at the Martin Theatre, in which her friend Doreen was playing a waitress.

'Who's Jimmy Dean?' asked Ashleigh.

'A famous actor who died tragically in a car accident,' Jessica replied. As soon as she uttered the words she saw Ashleigh's face light up with understanding. She realised then that Ashleigh had somehow heard the story about Tina's car being left open with the radio on by the dunes and the lack of any body, or sign of it, for the best part of seventeen years. Before the girls had come, and before Ashleigh had stirred people up with her claims of divinity, Tina's disappearance had been the only story of note ever attached to the Lawsons.

After the play, Jessica brought the girls into Panama Java for hot chocolate. She looked at the two girls so joyous in the busy café with the fan swirling crankily above their heads like some kind of predatory bird. She knew that soon she would lose them both.

That night, Jessica heard screams and thought Olivia was having a seizure. She ran quickly to the girls' room and opened the door. Olivia sat bolt upright, frightened, white as a sheet.

'Where's Ashleigh?' Jessica asked.

'She ain't here,' said Olivia. The moans and cries continued as Jessica walked along the corridor. She saw a light on in Tina's room. She opened the door and saw her son standing by the window, smoking. Ashleigh lay on the bed. There was blood all around the girl's groin, and Tina's sheets were stained. Jessica put on the main light. So dazed was she by the scene before her she could barely make out a word Jules was saying. All she could focus on was the blood, and Jules' foul smoke-breath filling up her daughter's room. Suddenly Jessica's voice seemed to take on a life of its own and she began to shout. She continued until she felt her son shake her violently by her shoulders.

'Are you listening to me?' he said. 'I said, I heard crying. I thought it was Tina.'

Jessica broke free and went to the bed. She covered Ashleigh with her robe.

'It came just like a flood,' Ashleigh said. 'I got so scared I came in here so as not to frighten Olivia. I'm sorry about the blood, Jessica. But Jules never touched me, not like you're saying.'

'Why you just didn't let her have her own room, this room, I don't know. It's obvious what's happening to her!' Jules screamed.

'This is Tina's room. And you know I don't let anyone sleep here.'

'Well, why's that I wonder?'

'You know damn well why. Now shut up and get me some towels.'

'Tina's dead and she isn't ever coming back. And you know it.'

'How in hell do I know that, huh? Am I psychic or something? Are you? They never found a body. Case. Not. Closed.'

'Tina's case was closed the night she went out and…'

'Shut the fuck up!' screamed Jessica. 'She liked the nights on the beach. Just like we all did. You, me, her, your father – we often took you both out in the moonlight, you motherfucker. You know that. Now you just like the nights out drinking.'

'Come on, Mama,' Jules pleaded.

'She left the radio on in the car! Suicides don't leave the radio on in the car!'

'Yes they do!'

'She met someone and took off. She was like that. Flighty. She would just take off.'

'She's dead, Mama. I know she is.' Jules moved slowly towards his mother.

'Why d'you rush in here if you're so sure about it, huh? You said you thought you heard her.'

'I just wanted it to be true.'

'You still came. You're as unsure as I am, why don't you just admit it?' Jules left the room with his head bowed. Jessica curled up around Ashleigh on the bed and held tightly to the menstruating child. After a while, Ashleigh turned to Jessica and said: 'It seems to me you had two children and you never noticed but one. And not the one that stuck around neither. Jesus says to love all the children.'

'I know,' Jessica replied.

'Tina ain't coming back, Jessica May. Not ever. You jus' been clingin' to that radio.'

'I know,' Jessica replied.

*

When Bobby Jean came to pick up the girls, Jules was out in the yard taking the lights off the Christmas tree. He hadn't had a drink in over a month and Jessica was glad to see him busy. A couple of girls from Bay City High had come to say goodbye to Olivia and Ashleigh, and Jessica was leaving them to it. Then, as Jessica tended to the last of her hellebores, their five-petal heads all drooping to one side, Ashleigh came up quietly behind her. Since the night in Tina's room Ashleigh had not spoken again in assembly and had gotten quiet all round. Cole Spencer had even called to ask what had happened to the dazzling student. Jessica was just glad that the circus that had built up around the child had packed up and left. And now that the Atlanta authorities had tracked down a relative, an aunt, Jessica had no more cause (officially, at least) to worry about Ashleigh. The girl's counselling was to continue in Atlanta, the details of which would now pass exclusively to her aunt.

'Why do they droop their heads like that?' asked Ashleigh.

'I guess they're just protecting themselves.'

'From what?'

'From things that might otherwise destroy them. The wind and cold and such like,' Jessica replied, and looked up, puddle-eyed, at Ashleigh.

'I'm going to miss you, Jessica May.'

Jessica held her close. The scent of camomile from Ashleigh's hair hung in the air as she moved off. Jessica watched her stop by the Christmas tree and speak to Jules. Something electric passed between them, and she saw her son suddenly become younger-looking and less bound up with his own inarticulate feelings and thoughts.

As Bobby Jean's car drove off with Olivia and Ashleigh in the back, Jessica thought her heart would break. She cleared up the plates of half-eaten lemon cake and tidied up inside. When she went out into the yard to turn on the evening lights, Jules was there. He had a towel rolled up under his arm.

'Where are you going?' Jessica asked her son.

'I thought I'd go for a walk on the beach. Maybe take a swim.'

'You be careful. Don't go far out. Just as far as the rock.'

'I will, Mama,' he replied, and walked off along the side of the store in the direction of the beach.

After her evening tour of the nursery, Jessica sat on her chair on the porch and listened to the sea. In the lull between the waves she could hear the low thrum of the humming birds in the bottlebrush. She looked up to the tops of her tall bamboos. The slim, dark leaves bubbled in the breeze all along like a wave. Jessica closed her eyes and pushed her face out into the mild evening. In the darkness she felt herself rising up over all the plants, flowers and trees of her gardens into the warm sea air, becoming first part of the lapis lazuli sky, and then the whole sky that looked down on all the travelled and untravelled earth.

# The Scattering

As he stood on the shore gazing at the sea, water began to seep through the eyeholes of his boots. He could feel the weight of the year that had been, and wished by wishing it would slip away from him into the tide.

The coast drew in by the green mobile home up on the cliff. He looked up at the big grasses swaying in the wind, at the wooden gate set into the cliff steps, and at the curtains inside the home tied back neatly with bows. How he'd like to have lived by the sea in a caravan or a mobile home, he thought, kicking a gold stone out of the sand. He turned and walked in the direction of the cliff face, saw the mile-long stretch to Whitestown, white and quiet, strewn with mounds of silky, walnut-coloured seaweed.

He thought of September, when they had stood on the end of Carlingford pier and scattered Gerry's ashes into the harbour. At first he had hated the idea, but Eva insisted it was what Gerry had wanted. Now, three months on, on the first day of the New Year, the thought that his brother was out there in the sea began to reassure him about the whole grisly business.

Beyond the heaps of seaweed he saw the skeletal remains of an old boat and walked towards it. He stepped into the hull, pulled at some rotting wood, and in the gap noticed two small bottles on a ledge: one, a white plastic Our Lady of Lourdes with a blue crown cap, and the other, brown and medicinal-looking, tied round the neck with coffee-coloured string. Turning the brown bottle in his hand, he guessed it had contained a tincture for wounds, though it had no odour, except of salt.

Further along the beach he saw a car parked above the dunes. A woman was standing by the edge of the dunes looking at the sea. She was holding a blue plastic bag tensely against her cream coat. He thought of turning back as he was now alone on this stretch and did not want to alarm the woman, who had begun her descent to the beach. Suddenly a dog came bounding towards him. He had seen the exuberant three-legged collie on the beach many times, always alone, absurdly oblivious to its missing limb. When it ran towards her the woman shooed it, and it carried on in the direction of Carlingford.

As he passed the woman he said hello, but she ignored him. She was familiar. He turned and watched her stop at the boat, but could not place where he had seen her before. He walked on.

Everyone had been quiet on the pier. (Even when his father had nearly fallen into the water at his turn to scatter.) They had been led by Eva along the beach rather than the pier road, and he had raged at the sight of all these people made to traipse in the dusk across stinking lobster cages, stones and dark-green pools. There they were, this mass of family and friends, stepping over stones and pools – children, women in heels – to scatter Gerry's ashes, and, miraculously, the whole thing had gone off in fine style. A blazing pink sun had come out on a day filled with rain; the muddy shore to the steps of the high-walled pier was thronged with chattering sandpipers; the evening light curled around the edge of the Mournes onto the flat black stones of the harbour beach.

He rested the shells and stones he had collected on a tuft of sandy grass and, sitting on a rock, wondered if he should leave a note. What would he say? That he had slipped out of the scheme of things? That he had looked at his life after Gerry had died and found it a frightful mess: his job, his marriage, his house, his own self? That only a few moments of his existence here and there had truly belonged to him: last year's visit to Belfast, Aisha, the black-haired Polish girl, the hotel she'd brought him to, the one night of clarity? He checked his pockets: no pen or paper. He thought he heard Gerry speak his famous aphorism, *Never waste a journey*. At first it registered as a taunt for his lack of preparedness with the note, then as a kind of plea.

The whitish light over the sea had given way to a dark anvil-shaped cloud moving in from the north. He thought of his wife and the length of time they'd been married. Here, in the bracing air, he could honestly admit the years were only a number to him – he could easily walk away. Then why hadn't he? Instead, he went round in a state of permanent uncertainty. And this being so, Gerry's aphorism gave his quickly mounting doubts about walking into the cold sea something to cling to.

As he came off the beach at Templetown and headed for his car, he noticed on the side of the road a small shrine. There was a bright red poinsettia (with a blue plastic bag skirting the pot) on the ground in front of a low marble-engraved stone, together with coloured beads, dead flowers, holy medals. The stone read: *To our mother, Jean McConville, murdered by the IRA in 1979 and believed buried on this beach.* He looked up at the big signpost for Templetown advertising its recently acquired blue-flag status. A blue flag for a clean beach. The people of the Peninsula had worked hard for it; he'd seen them on Sundays lugging rusty beds with loose springs from the rocks under the dunes, plucking canisters of farming chemicals from the shore. They had made this beach, once so full of waste and death, clean and safe. They – and the industrious tide, which was like forgiveness and made everything new.

After shaking the sand from his boots he opened the car door then stopped to stare again at the sea. He had left the house, a few miles into the hills, to buy cigarettes for his wife. He'd have to hurry now to Lily Finnegan's who would shut her pub early on New Year's Day. But he was unable to rush. He slipped into the car and drove towards Lily's, thinking about Gerry out there in the darkening sea, far beyond his reach – and Aisha in Belfast who wasn't.

# Painting, Smoking, Eating

Patricia hurried nervously to the door and bolted it. The strangers peering in were far too boisterous; two of them had just inadvertently whipped Mr and Mrs Donnelly with their dreadlocks as the elderly couple passed them on the street with their dog.

She watched them enthusing about her Victorian dolls, her Gary Glitter shoes, the two Ossie Clark 'Twiggy' dresses. Eventually, she saw that their attention narrowed to her new collection of silver and gemstone jewellery, purchased a week previously at the buyers' fair in London. They like the citrine armlets and that amber choker, she noted, congratulating herself on the canny choices she had made at the fair. She saw that there was one of the three, however, upon whom the sparkling array of gems made no impression. The eyes of the blonde-haired girl were not drawn to the jewellery, the seventies shoe collection or the striking Mondrian designs of the dresses, but to a small hand-painted Japanese table-screen. She's looking at the Reverend's screen, Patricia thought, as she unlocked the door to let the strangers in.

'I have to keep the door closed,' she explained, brusquely, 'but do come in if you like.' The three entered the narrow room and fanned out to examine Patricia's prodigious display of retro-artefacts and fine vintage jewellery.

'It's like Aladdin's cave,' remarked the dark-haired girl.

'Like Mrs Haversham's living room,' joked the moon-faced man. Patricia hoped he wasn't referring to the lack of cleanliness of her artefacts; the task of keeping them free from dust and grime was an intricate and arduous one. For instance, she used *Silvio* on the chunkier silver necklaces, teapots and French cutlery, but some of the bead and diamante pieces were trickier to clean: hexagonal glass gems (usually inlaid with other glass gems) set into shallow clasps that had to be swabbed clean with cotton buds and cold soapy water. Dust motes hovered over the entire space, betrayed by the room's three sixty-watt bulbs half-robed by alabaster and stained-glass shades. Above the fireplace hung a creamy-white canvas appliquéd with a George Herbert poem. It read:

> *O that thou shouldst give dust a tongue*
> *To cry to thee*
> *And then not heare it crying.*

The display units and tables were tumbledown, and, where there were no linen or lace coverings, portions of what was once a bedspread that had belonged to Patricia's mother' served instead. Patricia was aware that the entire arrangement appeared as if it had been hastily assembled. It *had* been hastily assembled.

The blonde-haired girl reached in to the window display and picked up the Japanese screen. Excellent taste, thought Patricia, who was watching the movements of the three out of the corner of one big china-blue eye.

'Why?' asked the girl.

'Why what?'

'Why must you keep the door closed?'

'Because we had a robbery last week.' The other two turned in unison towards her and sighed sympathetically. The blonde-haired girl did not respond, as if intuiting Patricia's desire to elaborate.

'They came and took all my money. My entire year's profits. And most of my Japanese collection, too.'

'Who came?' asked the girl.

'I don't know. I wasn't here. My daughter was running the shop that day. They weren't from around here, that's all we know.'

'What did the cops do?' the moon-faced man asked.

'We'll see. Nothing yet.'

Patricia Millicent Urquhart was a woman of fifty-three, no longer shapely or beautiful, but attractive in a guileless sort of way. Men would no longer open doors for her in shops or hotels, and if they did, she would thank them, gratefully, as if they had made an astute and substantial purchase in her shop. She had a thin moustache and her two overgrown brows were knitted into a kind of permanent frown. Once, before she had married and settled in England, she had spent a year in Florence. There the Italian men had adored her voluptuous shape. Her rather chatty and spirited manner had made her more approachable than the other students of the Academy. She had been assured in herself, kept exquisitely groomed and, despite a love for the sun, always wore a hat. Then, she had a delicately pale and fresh complexion, and was unselfconsciously proud of her strong figure. It had been a definitive year. She often went to Florence in her mind, to its narrow, ancient streets and cafes, to the Academia Dell' Arte, and of course to Giovanni.

She drummed the marble counter with the fingers of one hand, resting the other on the bridge of the till. Her gnawed red fingers were incongruously adorned with rings set with moonstones, malachite and rubies, her thick wrists wrapped in a slew of thin gold bangles that jangled as she tapped.

'What's this made from?' asked the dark-haired girl, dangling a bracelet studded with squares of blue and port-coloured stone.

'Lapis and garnet.'

'It's very exotic.'

'An early-seventies design. You can tell by the geometry. They loved all that, the Moroccan look,' replied Patricia.

'Cool!' said the man, scrutinising the bracelet. The dark-haired girl and the moon-faced man began to compare the garish colours of the sixties' collection to the mellow earth-tones of the seventies', and the debate broadened out to the sixties versus the seventies in all things. Patricia was glad to see her pieces provoke such interest in history. All the same, she kept her eye on the dreadlocked two as they motioned towards the end of the shop, gleefully examining the trends of a century.

The robbery had brought back memories of her husband, Gordon. He had been a generous but violent husband. His rages had exhausted her, had left her self-confidence ebbing and flowing like the tide. Giovanni had told his students that as guardians of artistic souls they were to protect and nourish them. She knew she had failed to do this. Her marriage had been a colossal mistake, and, since the robbery, she had begun to think she'd made yet another with the shop. She'd not run a business before and had gotten into antiques purely by accident, having inherited so many.

Gordon had had complete control over all their furniture purchases in their London house. His choice the Louis Poulsen lamps, the Hitch Mylius sofa, the Le Corbusier recliner, the two red Arne Jacobsen egg chairs. And his choice the commissioning of artwork to match the modernist furnishings. And so, when Patricia found herself drowning in clutter in her dead mother's house on the northeastern Irish coast, she decided the best way to dispose of it all was to sell it, and within months she had developed the kind of dealer instinct that takes some brokers a lifetime to acquire: she knew what would sell, she bought cheap and nurtured her top clients. This world of antiques was the antithesis of her previous life, and that this was so made her very happy. But now it was clear that if she did not find the funds to replace the stolen stock and repair the displays (which the thieves had levelled with a hatchet), until her insurance came through at least, there would be no business. And what would she do then?

'Were they of great value, the things they took?'

Patricia took a long look at her blonde-haired inquisitor. The girl seemed to understand the distress the robbery had caused her. Not even the police had realised it had near enough plunged them into poverty.

'Yes. Some were irreplaceable.'

'I've not seen you here before,' the girl said, pressing a crimson moiré-silk corsage into the fat of her cheek.

'We've only been here a year or so. From London. But I'm from here, originally.'

The girl wandered closer, stopping to smell the perfume off the pumps and thick glass tips of the scent decanters.

'What's your name?' she asked.

'Patricia,' Patricia said.

'Mine's Jean.'

*Pat's Curios* was centrally placed on the street so that it had a clear, unhindered view of the Irish Sea. On a good day much of the low-lying Cooley Peninsula could be seen from within the shop, its swathes of heather and gorse sweeping down to the shimmering water. The sea here was tame, and until the arrival of winter, possessed no real force. It was a seaweed-smelling sea, thought by many to have been poisoned over the years by Sellafield. Scuba divers continued to visit all year round, but generally people no longer came to Dundalk's elegant coastal village to collect cockles, as they had done, or to swim. It was a sea that had to be fought off in winter with sandbags and towels, as the brown, sand-heavy water would rage over the promenade wall, under doors and into houses. All the same, it possessed a predictable temper, to which the locals were well attuned.

Behind the lighthouse, on the far side of the Peninsula, was Templetown beach, where the police had been digging for months in search of a woman's body. The beach had been named by the IRA as the vicinity of her burial place, but Templetown beach was two miles long and so the searching had seemed interminable. In the mornings, Patricia would look out at the helicopters and the flashing lights of the diggers, a chilling reminder of the old tensions of the place. In the afternoons she might see O'Neils horses stride out from the headlands to the shallows, just as they would when she was a child. Sometimes she would stop what she was doing in the shop just to watch the cargo ships pass on their way to Greenore harbour.

In recent months she had begun to gaze out at the black rock in the bay; as a child she had played in its grassy loft. She would momentarily catch sight of sea creatures and sirens, formed, she concluded, from the sun-reflected foam and driftwood that would gather by the rock. At times it seemed to Patricia that only this sea understood how disorganised and fractured she felt. This sea, George Herbert – and now, perhaps, the blonde-haired girl.

'How much is this?' asked the girl, returning to the Japanese screen.

'It's not for sale.'

'Oh. I thought…'

'It's an accessory. For the shop. To divide the pieces.'

'It's very pretty. Was it part of your collection?'

'Yes. A gift. I'm grateful they missed it.' The girl returned the screen to the podium.

The sight of the screen recalled to Patricia her recent trip to Earls Court. She had broken briefly from buying to visit the church where she and Gordon had married. At the end of the lane-way, by the black railings of the cemetery, she had stopped, surprised by the sound of water. She had turned in to the courtyard and found a fountain humming its soothing water-music for the dead. Once, in place of the fountain, there had been a large diseased cherry blossom with a seat inset for pilgrims, mourners and escapees from the relentlessness of

# Painting, Smoking, Eating

Kensington High Street. She had been relieved to find that Reverend Kent had had the sense to replace it. A beautiful touch, she had thought, passing her fingers through the water as it trickled down a miniature staircase onto bonsai shrubbery. She had tiptoed to the door, peered into the Reverend's kitchen; the peachy evening light spilled onto the blue terrazzo floor tiles. It had all changed inside too. The windows had new yellow curtains. Her heart sank as she thought Reverend Kent might have married. It was he who had encouraged her to make the break, to stand up to Gordon. All the times she had sat with him under the cherry tree. She had wanted to thank him for his kindness and advice (he had told her 'drive – don't drift' and it had made all the difference). Irresolutely, she took a step forward. The brass plate on the wall read: *Reverend Craig. Please do not ring after 8pm*. In that moment she felt desolate. She had wanted to retch. She'd had such a run of bad luck: a strained and difficult divorce, the robbery, now the only person in the world in whom she might confide had disappeared without telling her. She said a prayer for the shop in the church then toiled back to the hotel in the rain. Surely Reverend Kent would find her if he wanted to.

The door of the shop flew open, the bell reverberating loudly. A tall, shorthaired girl of about seventeen stormed in wearing headphones and a backpack bulging with brushes, pallet, a folded-up easel and a rolled-up canvas with frayed edges. She grunted something at Patricia, waded through the shop till she got to the end of the room curtained off to a small kitchen, then snapped the drape closed behind her.

'Natalie, my daughter. Home from an exhibition,' Patricia said to the blonde-haired girl, who seemed bemused by the whirlwind entrance. Natalie quickly re-emerged, minus impedimenta, and loped towards the till. Patricia kissed her daughter on the cheek.

'How was the exhibition?' the blonde girl asked, passing her hand through the bristles of a coral-backed hairbrush.

'Great,' Natalie replied. Patricia noticed her daughter leering at the stranger who seemed so casually authoritative in their shop.

'I told this lady about the robbery,' Patricia said.

'Whose work did you see?' the blonde girl asked.

'Oh, it was a Guston retrospective.'

'Ah. The clenched fist. *Painting, Smoking, Eating.*'

'You know his work?'

'Oh, indeed. I've even been to his house in Connecticut.'

'You have?'

'Sure. Guston believed his studio was filled with all sorts of angels and ghosts, did you know that?'

'No,' Natalie replied, dismissively.

'He used to have a poem, Auden, I think, on his wall. Just like you have here. Let's see… it said *the ghosts that haunt our lives are handy with mirrors and wires.*'

'What does that mean?' Natalie asked, perplexed.

'That, maybe, sometimes, they're there to help.'

'The ghosts?'

'Sure.'

Patricia wanted to ask where the ghosts were on the day of the robbery, but thought better of it.

The three women huddled together in the centre of the shop discussing Philip Guston and painting, while at the furthest end of the store, by the World collection, the couple with the dreadlocks tried on Patricia's much-prized African war-masks.

\*

Patricia stared out at her daughter smoking a cigarette on the promenade wall. 'She has been a different person,' she said with a sigh, 'since we came. She has bloomed. But the robbery shook her. She thinks I'm going to have to close.' The blonde girl pulled out a dark opal-like stone from her pocket.

'Have you seen this before?' she asked, and placed the stone in Patricia's hand.

'What is it?'

'It's called seraphanite. Chanellers, healers use it. I know that sounds a bit, well... but the vibrations are very strong, don't you think?' As she turned the stone around in her palm Patricia wanted to laugh – and went to return it to the girl.

'No, I want you to keep it,' the girl replied. 'Please. Hold it close. It will protect the shop.'

Patricia saw how sincere the girl seemed, how genuine in her insistence she keep the stone.

'Won't you have something in exchange?' she said, 'like a bracelet?'

'No, it's a gift. I don't want anything in return.'

Patricia held the rock up to the light. Thin flecks of silvery quartz glistened in feathered ribbons of white. It radiated an intense heat. Immediately she thought of Giovanni. Once, before she'd finally left England for Ireland, she'd opened the door of their summerhouse in Devon to the frail figure of her old art lecturer. She had ushered him in and tenderly held him, noting his dank, sour smell. 'Why did you go my little Patricia?' he had said, over and over. (She had always loved how he called her 'little'.) She had never given him an explanation for her sudden departure from the Academy, nor did she tell him at the house. Patricia saw herself with Giovanni on that sultry evening, watching the light fall on the yachts and trawlers of Salcombe Harbour as they sailed out towards the English Channel. It had been so warm they had eaten on the porch and listened to the waves lap the low chalky cliffs. She never heard from him after that visit, and read some months later in *The Times* that he was dead.

'I have to be getting back now. But please, keep the stone. And remember, you must never give it to anyone else. I'd rather you hurled it into the sea. What has been taken from you will come back.'

Patricia felt a tremulous shiver in her stomach. She knew the girl was right. Her luck would change. It had to. A renewed sense of trust in herself and in her destiny filled her.

'Thank you,' Patricia said.

As the doorbell resounded, Patricia watched the blonde-haired girl walk eastwards towards the rocky part of the coast until she could no longer be seen from the shop. Patricia saw the Japanese screen and grabbed it. She rushed up to the other two, who were about to exit, and offered them the screen.

'I can't leave the shop, but would you mind giving this to your friend?'

'Which friend?' asked the dark-haired girl.

'Jean! The blonde girl that was in here with you.'

'No, you are mistaken. The blonde girl was not with us,' the moon-faced man replied.

The door closed and the two dreadlocked strangers walked hand in hand towards the sands. Patricia looked out at them, then at her daughter, who was on the promenade wall, laughing at a chattering seagull.

# The Congo

When I awoke the first thing I did was check my bag. I took from it what I needed then tucked it back under the bed, placing my father's slippers neatly in front. I went to the window and opened it, amazed as I did that I remembered the bottom pane was loose. A grey cloud hung over the town, and three mallards the colour of barley flew in a line towards the Ramparts River. I wondered if I had been away at all, for everything was as it had been when I had left, twenty-odd years before, except I could no longer hear the lowing of cows from Quincey's field, which was home now to a new housing estate. It had been like this since my arrival: encounters with my old self, a strange sensation of continuum, of picking up where I had left off. As if my London self was there still, walking through Richmond on his way to Kew, while my younger self, that ghost, was here in this damp house, staring out at the dawn weather.

I closed the door behind me, the smell of the eggs I'd fried for my father's breakfast still clinging to my nostrils, and walked to the corner of the tree-lined Avenue. The edges of my holster chafed at my ribs and sweat beads formed on my forehead making my face feel cold. I carried on down the Echo Road, past the freshly mown playing fields, on towards the Grange.

The place was as tranquil as I'd ever seen it. In the pale morning light even the houses with the smashed-in windows and weed-run gardens looked serene, so that the ragwort passed almost for daisies. There was a fabulous assortment of colours too, from the many flower baskets, filled as they were with petunias, begonias, violets. There had always been people in the Grange who would try to pull themselves up; always a mother or father prepared to stand up to the gangs.

From where I stood, I could see Devlin's place. The house seemed much the same: the satiny fuchsia hedge, the faux-Tudor windows gleaming like mirrors, the tall palm soaking up the rays of the early sun. Had he really returned, I wondered? Or had he gone, upon his release, to Kilburn, as some had said he had, where it was possible he'd been living under my nose all these months?

Grace had always been proud of her home. I'd always considered it a testament to her resourcefulness that when she'd found herself stuck in this estate on a widow's pension with six sons (two of them gang members), Grace had still managed to keep an attractive house. Fortress Devlin, she would call it, as she'd felt so safe within its walls. Built in the seventies, the Grange had promised the families that came to live in it – modernity: bathrooms, spacious bedrooms, central heating. But within a decade it had become a festering sprawl, filled with gangs, drugs, violence. And her husband's death before her boys were full-grown, ensured that Grace and her sons remained there, such is the quicksand nature of the ghetto, which requires money, time and strategy to get out of (and none of these had been much available to Grace). The air up on the Avenue had always been rarified and easy, while here, even now, I could feel the deadweight of Grange air in my lungs.

As I proceeded to the corner of the car park for the new Dunnes Stores (where once there had been a hill – 'the clump' – where gangs such as ours would meet for prearranged fights), I saw a figure walk towards the bottleneck opening of the estate. I moved in behind a van and, for a second, thought I might have been seen for the figure did not pass. A match was struck and tipped to the ground, a cigarette sucked upon. The man continued past the van and a row of wood-panelled houses, stopped at the end of the street by the tall palm, opened the gate. It was Devlin. And apart from the close-clipped hair and greying sideburns he'd hardly changed: the same casual self-assurance, the almost effeminate gait.

I became perturbed by something: my heart, pounding against my ribs. This was not how it was to have gone. Think of The Congo, I kept telling myself. Think of The fucking Congo. I closed my eyes, and for a few chilling moments supposed I was actually there.

*

'Where d'yez think you're goin', you lot?' Staunton leaned into the car and thumped the glove compartment open. He rummaged inside, probably looking for drugs or drink, and pulled out my book. '*War and Peace*,' he read out, venomously. Devlin stared straight ahead. None of us spoke. 'Yez have been drinkin', am I right?'

'Aye. We're all under the affluence of incahol, Sergeant,' Devlin replied, deadpan, at which the rest of us cracked up. Staunton bit his lip. Devlin reached out, grabbed the book, threw it back to me. At this I knew the cop would do one of two things. Either pull us over and quiz us, maybe roughly, with a slap to the back of Devlin's head, or he would leave it, sensing what so many others had: the stirring power of this young man with ink-black hair and obsidian-like eyes who spoke with alarming authority. Then Devlin drew close, whispered something inaudible into Staunton's ear. Something he had on him, something we could tell was sexual. The cop paled, was breathless, his appointed authority gone like a mirage, so much so that when he asked what had happened to the missing wing of my Hillman Hunter, I confidently responded that it had 'flown away'.

'Well, go on. To wherever you're off ta, but yez can't stop here,' Staunton said, oblivious to the fact that we had just left the publican in a torrent of blood, his rooms upturned, his cash register emptied, his skull in pieces under a corn-yellow canister of gas.

We had not gone to bed that night. Under Devlin's orders, the twins had taken the simpleton, Gascoigne, into the cemetery and tied him with rope to a stone Celtic cross. Devlin had wanted to teach Gascoigne a lesson. To get him to keep his mouth shut about things he'd seen in his mother's B&B: somebody else's girl, somebody's wife. Mikey peeled the bananas while Joe forced them, one by one, into the lad's mouth. It was my job to watch over all of this. Watch, as the Crilly twins pissed on the poor wretch, bound and stuffed like a pig on a spit, the piss-steam rising off him like smoke. Under Devlin's orders we left Gascoigne in full-dark, wailing and crying for his mother. Then, later, when I'd slipped back to let the boy go, I saw Devlin walk him out of the cemetery, his arm around the boy. I imagined Devlin saying to Gascoigne that it was *he* who had saved him, that he would look out for him, like he'd done to me. That was how Devlin operated. Like all bullies, he sought out the feeble-minded, misfits and outsiders, who, having experienced the ferocity of his power also knew its narcotic warmth and radiance.

Later, after we'd left the bar and its publican for dead, I drove to the Cooley hills. All the way up the meandering lane, Adamski's *Killer* boomed (as if accusingly) from the car stereo. I parked the car by the gates. We clambered out and walked into the bog, sat high up on the plum-coloured heather.

I looked down at the town, all amber in the evening light, at the Irish Sea below us winding around the stark blue Mournes across the border. I felt cold. The hills filled with an icy sea-wind that closed around us like a cloak. I thought immediately of the Russian winter and the frostbitten Napoleonic soldiers of my book. And for the first time I doubted Devlin's leadership. Why had he let it go so far? The reality of the murder we'd just committed under his feverish spell suddenly hit me. I looked around. The twins had felt it too. They were both pale and slumped, huddled together on the mizzling day, like two spent sunflowers in October. Then Devlin walked up to us. I will never forget the way he did that. He churlishly took the twins' knives and twisted them into a bank of turf, hard and skinned-over since the Council had prohibited cutting it a few years before. (The knives had not even been used that day.) Then he said he was *hungry*, that the cold mountain air had made him ravenous. I wanted to puke when he said that, and suddenly what we had done down there in the town began to seem as real and terrible a thing as Devlin's hunger.

I cannot remember exactly why he chose The Congo. I just remember that after the cemetery, Devlin said he wanted *to do some damage*. I had no idea he meant 'people damage'; I thought he meant burning something, or trashing some old house up, and I was ready, as ever, with my car.

'Where you thinking of goin'?' Mikey asked.

'Park Street,' Devlin said.

'Class!' Joe said, and went on about being in for a day's drinking.

'No. No drink. That's not what I meant,' said Devlin.

'What did you mean?' I asked.

'Well, somethin' will come. Somethin' will come and we will know.' That was Devlin all over. So damned enigmatic. As if he had commune with someone other than his own present self. I would learn in court that this was a trait common to the likes of Charles Manson and Ian Brady, a means to avoid all guilt: *blame it on the voices, the signs, some force outside oneself.*

He was younger than me by two years, so by rights we should never have been friends. Only he saved me once. One night, up the alley by MJ's (where he and the twins drank), he'd stopped me from being kicked to death by a bunch of shit-kickers from Ardee. Only for that night I'd never have been part of the gang, or come to know him or the Crilly twins, or any of the lads from the Grange. (After all, I went to the Grammar, and lived on the Avenue.) I remember looking up, half-expecting the tall, dark-eyed interloper to join them, and, instead, he flung them off me like a wild cat. Then the twins charged in, dragged my two hick assailants towards the river. I never asked Devlin why he pulled me from that beating. I presume he saw in me what he later saw in Gascoigne: an exploitable weakness, such as the shame I wore like a badge as son of the town's most notorious drunk.

I sheltered in, and even came to like, the 'hard' reputation the Grange boys had. I hoped that by association it would rub off. Until my involvement with Devlin, I'd had to suffer all manner of quips about my family's change of fortune. From millionaires to hungry up in the big house (followed by the passing of my mother, who did what she did, some said, because she had felt so disgraced). So, by the time I fell in with Devlin, I was that fed up I no longer cared if people thought me a chip off the old block or not (and they definitely did). I began to justify their thoughts, became well and truly Mad Mansfield, the Drunken Solicitor's Son. I began to drink heavily, mindlessly sometimes; to gamble (anything – cards, horses, dogs, the slots*), so that I must have seemed like rich pickings indeed to Devlin with the amount of insecurities I had. Whatever way it happened, the way two people find their fate in one another, I was a troubled young man from the Avenue one day, and the next bewitched by a lout (albeit a beautiful lout).

Devlin called in to the bar. No one answered. The signs he'd been waiting for: no one around, middle of the day, cash register open.

For the first few minutes inside, the twins joked and pretended we were in the bar of a Western. The Congo was high-ceilinged, had never been updated. The wooden floors

* = slot machines

were dull and decorticated in places. The bar itself was breast-high with a gleaming brass rail hanging just beneath the rim of the bar top. Devlin sat on one of the red leather seats and lit up in his usual girlish way, slow and light, his little finger apart (erect almost), and watched the twins as they fooled around. I have never since met anyone, however duplicitous or skilled in the craft of acting, who could smile as sweetly as he – the smooth white baby-fangs, the gentle crescent dimples – yet possess a simultaneous deadness in the eyes. It was, I understand now, the overlapping of two people in one. He was night and day in one, and it was, for me, I recall, a hopelessly magnetic contrast.

'Mikey leave it!' Devlin said.

'But Jesus man, the place is fuckin' empty!'

'You're tanked up enough. We might need to run for it. Use your head.'

'Well, come on then!' Joe said. 'We've got the money, what we waiting for? Let's go.'

Devlin placed his long legs on top of the table, and crossed his feet. He put his arms behind his head, wrist to nape.

'Why would someone leave a place like this for scumbags like us to come and fuck around inside it, hah?' Devlin said.

'Maybe he's gone to get somethin',' Mikey replied.

'Who's he?' Devlin asked Mikey, who was now scared.

'Who's he?' Devlin repeated.

'Prentice Black he means,' I said, 'the owner.' My father had known Prentice Black. People who came to the bar thought Prentice a survivor from an Irish UN battalion massacred in the Congo in the 1960s, and Prentice would let them think it. The truth was Prentice had bought the pub from a man named Cyril White in the same year the Congo had gone from being a Belgian colony to a Democratic Republic. Prentice (who had himself been a member of the 'old' IRA, i.e. pre-Bloody Sunday IRA), could not resist what he saw as a parallel between his purchase and the establishment of the African state, hence the pub's name. (There was even a map of Africa in the shape of Patrice Lumumba's head in the men's toilets.) When I suggested that Prentice might be over in the bookies opposite, it set something off in Devlin.

'Well, then we'll wait,' Devlin said, coolly.

'Fuck's sake, why?' asked Joe. He and Mikey had become bored and restless in the dingy veneer-panelled lounge, the light a muddy olive colour from the stained-glass tiles above the windows. They had begun writing, with a black felt-tip marker, obscenities, on the wide mirror at the back of the bar.

'Hey, we'll wait, fuckwit, because a man that'd leave his bar in the middle of the day is a careless man. And in my experience, a careless man always has easy access to money.'

It was then I started to become afraid. Mikey and Joe had between them taken over fifty pounds from the till. My pockets were stuffed with cigarettes, crisps, a bottle of Bombay Sapphire. We could have walked. That's what I wanted to do. Even the twins looked worried. For Devlin had implied something way beyond our usual messing. Even beyond the worst we, as a gang, had done up till then (which, apart from Gascoigne, had been the bottles we'd stolen for the Provos for petrol bombs). Yet we remained. Compelled as ever by that smile, by those black unforgiving eyes, by the magnetism I loved but had already begun to resent. And so minutes passed and we waited. I remember the silence. I remember wondering what he would do and how he might do it. I remember not knowing if I should run, or throw myself down and bathe in his glow. The room was like a theatre, all hush and darkness, as we, the actors (chorus and lead), waited in the wings for our audience to enter. And somehow I knew, through some inner sense, that when Prentice Black returned to his bar from wherever he had been, he would never leave.

Disturbed by a flapping sound, I quickly opened my eyes to find that I was a long way from those dark, unforgiving days of

my youth: it was the leaves of the tall palm whipping at the air
as if they would break loose. I watched the ravens caw over the
rooftops of the Grange on their way to the Avenue's tall cedars
where they nested. Again, I noticed it: the sensation of
continuum. A trickle of smoke from the chimney of Devlin's
house – though it was a warm morning, and I imagined Devlin
in there looking after Grace.

I'd gotten seven years for my part in the murder of the
publican. Devlin and the twins mandatory life. I'd blamed
Devlin for all that had gone wrong with me since: my discovery
of opiates, my involvement in importing scams. I'd even learned
how to use a gun; there are many such places in London. But
standing here at the edge of the Grange, despite my anger, my
hand would not reach into my holster, nor would my legs (as if
in some kind of physical rebellion) carry me to his house. The
dreams of retribution that had seen me through the years in
London seemed suddenly impotent here. There was a sameness
to the place that was obdurate, and I saw that my rage belonged
entirely to the man who walked to his job at Kew each morning,
whose only deliverance from this self and that, was time spent
with the flowers and plants of the hothouses.

Of all the chilling details of that afternoon in The Congo bar,
one image in particular stands out for me. Crossing the lounge
to exit, I recall I'd looked across at the mirror, covered in the
twins' spidery scrawls, and seen a skull-like face: eyes bloodshot
from crying, blood on the hair and cheeks. I saw that the face
belonged not to me, but to Devlin, who was looking in horror
at something, or someone else, who or what, I could not fully
see, for the light was poor. Perhaps, he looked at nothing in
particular. Perhaps, he looked at me. I have often suspected as
much. I remind myself on such occasions that though it was I,
in the end, who had dropped the canister on the publican,
neither Devlin nor the others had tried to stop me. In fact
Devlin had screamed 'down, Mansfield, down'. His claims in
court that he had meant for me to place the canister out of

harm's way did not stand up under cross-examination. (My own lawyer, a long-standing associate of my father, had emphasised my vulnerability, 'the fragility of one so young without a mother'.)

Finding solace in Devlin's greying hair, and in the fact he now lived an obviously uneventful life in the same wretched council house in which he had grown up, I walked back to the Avenue. But I felt bereft, too, knowing I would never again experience the intoxicating spell he had cast upon my youth. Grace had blamed 'the middle-class boy from the Avenue' and claimed that if anyone had been the protégé it was her son. But Grange people have always been (understandably) jealous of the affluent suburb that looks down upon them, and, I suppose, with all the harshness life had meted out to her, Grace is no exception.

# 1976

*'Maggie's was a troublous life, and this
was the form in which she took her opium.'*

GEORGE ELIOT, *The Mill on the Floss*

I sit on the back step topping and tailing the peas. It is a warm day for May, the sky white and high, and already there is a watery haze over the fields. I split the pods and empty them into the ceramic bowl Dada makes cakes in. The peas are soft and shiny and smell of the earth, and without thinking I put a few in my mouth and bite down. Dada makes a sound behind me that I know means he wants me to stop eating the peas, so I do. He is watching me like a hawk this week, making sure, he says, I stay far from the contents of the medicine cabinet.

'Dada says to leave that cat,' I call out to Francie, who has been trying to lure one of our neighbour's kittens over the wall with a piece of rope.

'I saw Daddy do it himself last week, didn't you, Daddy?'

'No!' my father bellows. 'Listen to Claire,' he says, 'listen to my wee Claire,' and he scoops me up into the air, peas scattering to the floor.

'Go now, the two of yez, and tell the others to come, the wee scuts,' Dada says, and sends me out to Francie. By this break in his watchfulness I think that maybe he has forgiven me.

We pass the sheets drying in the yard and go towards the gate. As I hold open the gate for Francie, I look up and see Dada smiling. Then, despite all Dada has said, Francie walks on and neglects to bolt the gate after us. I see Dada shaking his head and the two of us share a glance about Francie and I go myself to bolt the gate. I might be bold for taking my brother's pills but Francie is older and should know better than to go against Dada's wishes.

We know where the others will be. When first we moved here Dada helped us uncover a den in the ruins of Roche's Castle, half a mile into the fields at the back of the house. Dada says the castle has tunnels beneath it that go on for miles ending at Ice House Hill at the far end of town. It was built for a Norman lord, he says, who had wanted an escape route to the Castletown River which flows through the town into the Irish Sea.

The entrance to the castle is via a winding, quartz-flecked staircase, down which the sound of footsteps echoes loudly. The bottom chamber – den headquarters – looks up to a row of black bars arranged in a half-moon on the ground outside. I lie down with Francie as we watch Nora and Isabel below. Francie reaches out, buries my hair in the tall grass. He screws up his face, whispers: 'We'd always find you in a crowd, Claire,' and brings his mouth to the bars.

'Oooh,' he says, low and deep.

'What's that? Isabel, you hear that?'

'Oooh,' Francie repeats, then presses his fingers to my mouth to stop Nora and Isabel hearing me laugh, pleads with his eyes for me to be quiet. I want to bite Francie's hand but I know no harm can come to him or Dada will get vexed.

'Nora, Nora, I think we've a ghost, what'll we do?' Isabel says. Francie is shaking with laughter, and Isabel, who has slipped out from the den, jumps us from behind.

'You didn't scare us. We're invincible to ghosts we are.'

'We did, we did,' Francie insists, then skips off in a whirl of excitement to the banks of the Fane, a few yards behind the castle. Immediately Francie picks up stones, skims them with great precision across the water. Isabel shouts over to him that he's not supposed to leave us but he pays no heed. Francis likes to pretend there's nothing wrong with him. This is all our mother's fault, Dada says.

Isabel pivots back towards the den with me behind. As we close into a tight triumvirate, I become rigid with anticipation.

'We found something,' Isabel says.

'What you find?' I ask.

'Promise you won't tell Daddy.'

'Or *Dada*,' Nora jokes, and makes a prim-looking face.

'Right,' I say. Then Isabel, who is fifteen and the eldest, grabs the crumpled noisy thing off Nora and hides it behind her back.

'You can't ask Claire not to tell Daddy something, Isabel, as she tells him everything. Claire go on over to Francie,' says Nora, who's twelve and plump and sounds the most English out of all of us.

'I won't tell him, honest I won't,' I reply. Isabel and Nora look at each other. Nora tilts her neck to the breeze filing through the bars above.

'Say you swear on Daddy's life.'

'No.'

'Isabel, you shouldn't ask her to swear on Daddy's life. That's bad,' Nora retorts.

'Well, then she can't see the thing.'

'Why can't I swear on your life?' I say.

'Oh here it is, but you better not bloody tell.' Then Isabel produces from behind her back a dirty brown paper bag. She reaches in, delicately, and fishes out from it a yellowed and bloodstained needle, like the ones I've seen used on Francis in the hospital.

'Jack Duffy sticks this in his arm,' she says. Then we all fall about, laughing, pretending to stab it into each other. Finally, Isabel wraps up the needle and proceeds to hide it by standing on the long corroded nails that are staggered into one of the castle's walls, placing the bag high up under a moss-covered brick.

We have been begging Dada for a television. But he says he has seen the other families on the Littlemarshes sitting in silence, eating meals off their laps, glued to the flashing screen in the corner, their exhausted fathers asleep on sofas – and he doesn't want that life for us. Aunt Sarah says she will get us a television for Christmas if Dada doesn't. Isabel says a television will stop us being bored, as we are most Sundays waiting for Ed Molloy. The arrival later of Dada's best friend means that Francie and Isabel have to close up their books, as the men will want the front room to talk in.

'Go into the kitchen,' Dada says, packing Francie and Isabel out of the room. 'We won't be long.'

'I don't want to be with the girls,' says Francie, who wants to carry on with his schoolwork, just not with all of us.

'Well, go to the room upstairs,' Dada says, 'can't you use the dressing table?' The look on Francie's face, I know well what it means. Before Christmas, Francie – who has his own room at the top of the house with a bed and no desk – would do his homework at the long dressing table in Mammy and Dada's room. But now we only go into that room if we want to stare at Mammy's pictures, or pick up and smell the scent off her perfume bottles or spread our hands across the coral and black hairbrush with her hairs still inside it. None of us would use that room for studying in. Not now.

'I'll read outside,' Francie says, 'it's warm enough.'

We are excited to see Ed Molloy as he always brings sweets. When he arrives we all stand but say nothing about the big bag he holds out in his arms like a baby. Dada allows us the Curly Wurlys and Fry's bars, I think, mainly as a distraction so he and Ed can go into the front room to do their talking. When Francie goes out to the yard to read, and Isabel and Nora are doing their homework in the kitchen, I go to the front-room door and listen, though my father's and Ed's conversations are not much to report as they are always the same: about the days they lived in London. Ed had lived on the same road as Dada and Mammy in Kilburn. They went to dances and to see showbands together. The photographs of Mammy in Mammy and Dada's room, and the one that was in the paper in January, were all taken by Ed. Through the door I hear Ed say England is a godless country that allows unborn babies to be murdered and that we are well out of it. I hear my father say he misses London and that he only ever came home because it was what 'she wanted'. I have heard my father say this before.

Ed is tall, with dimples in his face. When Mammy would show people our photographs they would often say, 'who is that handsome man,' and say nothing about our father. Ed often tells us about his days as an actor in a group and he knows everything there is to know about films. Ed came home from London first, before Mam and Dada, and I remember Mammy saying it was because London had made him sick. I think of this every time Ed says something in the room bad about London. I would like to say to my father he should know not to praise a place that made his dearest friend ill, only he'd know then I was listening. Once, when I asked Mammy how did London make Ed ill, she said it was to do with something that happened to the three of them in a dancehall one night but that it affected Ed the most. She never said what it was. I suppose if I really want to know now I will have to ask Dada.

When they finish, Ed comes out to the yard. Isabel wants to show him the den but Dada says Ed must be getting off home. Ed says he would like to see it though he has to leave after because he has an early start. As Isabel and Nora tug at Ed's jacket, dragging him towards the gate, I turn towards the kitchen and see my father watching us. He waves and I wave back.

Francis walks ahead of us, acting like he is a stronger, bigger boy. He is shouting out to Ed, telling him that we are in acres of bogland known as Cox's fields, that to the left are Haliday's Mills and a small indigenous wood and he gives detailed descriptions of the plants and birds Dada has taught us about since we moved here. Ed seems to know nothing about nature, and when Francie shows him the falcons circling above us and the raspberries ripening along the hedgerow, Ed is fascinated. All along our trip to the den, Ed wants to listen to what Francie has to say. Francie is clever and he knows it. Because Mammy wouldn't let him do chores, he has spent more time with his books than any of us.

Ed has brought his camera and he takes photographs of things that Francie points out. Ed wants us always to be in the shots, making big grins. Where it is most parched in the bog there are swarms of ladybirds on the rocks, and Ed suggests we pick up the ladybirds, let them crawl on our skin while he photographs them. Ed says he loves ladybirds as they are sacred to Our Lady, which is why they are named so. (Ed is awful religious.) So we put them on our arms and legs and Ed says a rhyme as he takes photos of the ladybirds crawling up under our skirts and T-shirts, and we all laugh as it is so ticklish. He says the rhyme, and we all repeat, like as if we were in a school play:

> *Ladybird, ladybird, fly away home,*
> *your house is on fire and your children are gone.*
> *All except one, and that's little Anne*
> *for she has crept under the warming pan.*

When Francie tells Ed about the tunnels that lead under Roche's castle to another part of town, Ed tells me and Nora and Isabel to wait by the river. He says we are to skim the stones across the water to see who is best at it while he photographs the castle, which, he says, is so interesting it should be in the history books. We don't mind; we are glad to keep cool on the hot evening.

The river is so still and I am distracted from skimming my stones by the quiet that is in the air. A willow tree is being tugged at by the water coiling around the tree's light-green branches and this is the only movement I can see apart from the ripples from our stones. As Isabel and Nora battle it out, skimming further and further down river, I look over at the castle, and I think about all the years it has been sitting there, and how it will probably still be there when I and everyone I love is dead. The thought makes me feel sad, as I have never imagined myself not being on the earth before. I wonder if Mammy ever had such thoughts.

By the time Ed and Francie come back to us, the sky is darkening and Ed says he has to get home. Francie looks pale and I think that maybe he did too much talking and tired himself out, that he will be needing a blue pill when we get back to the house and I feel instantly bad that a few weeks before I'd stolen half his supply.

*

When the school holidays come, Francie does not go out with us to the den but stays in all the time in his boxroom with the window open, listening to his transistor. Always the music he listens to is loud and angry. He says it's the music young people are listening to now in London. He also says he wishes we never came to this country because everything has gone wrong since. He secretly cries sometimes, too, and I think it must be over Mammy because I often cry for her as do Isabel and Nora. Then one evening there is a big row. Dada says he has found something in Francie's room in a toffee tin. It is a small lump of something that when he found it had been wrapped up in plastic. Lying out on the kitchen table it looks like sheep shit to me though it is herby smelling and oily. When Dada starts to bang his fist down on the table, I tell him to stop.

'Mammy would not be happy,' I wail, 'you shouting at Francie.' Dada looks at me then and he straight away stops the shouting and banging. Mammy had always protected Francis; sometimes it was like he was the girl, while me, Isabel and Nora were the boys – and I think Dada is finding it hard to protect

Francie the same way Mammy did. The word 'drugs' is said and I know what this means. Then Isabel comes in and Francie takes the opportunity to run out of the room, so I say: 'There's a thing, Dada, in the castle. A thing in a paper bag that Jack Duffy does stuff with.' Isabel looks at me as if she would kill me. Dada sees this look on her.

'What stuff and what thing?' Dada asks, and Isabel turns to leave when she sees how annoyed he sounds.

'Isabel, come back. Explain to me what Claire means,' Dada demands, but Isabel won't answer.

'A needle thing,' I say, 'in a bag under a brick. Isabel says Jack Duffy sticks it in his arm whenever he goes there. Nora says you put drugs inside it.'

'Duffy? The councillor's son?' Dada asks. Isabel nods.

'Fella you been chatting ta up there sometimes?'

'Yes Daddy, but he's very nice,' Isabel says.

'Jesus, Isabel. That's it. I forbid you, all of you to go up there again. Do you know what that means, that needle?'

'No.'

'You do, Isabel, you do!'

'But he's nice. Kind. He gives me…'

'He gives you what?'

'Books. Music.'

'Come on,' Dada says, 'you both lead me now to that brick. Put on your coats, the two of you.' He then leads Isabel and me through the bog at the back of the house towards Roche's Castle. We are not even fully dressed. We have our pyjamas on with coats thrown over and Wellingtons on and it is sticky and dark and we can't see the warrens and rocks in the high vetch even though Dada has brought a torch. When we get to the castle, Isabel finds the brown bag and hands it to Dada.

'Why d'you want to take it, Daddy? Jack will know it's missing when he comes.'

'Evidence,' he says to both of us, 'for fucken evidence.'

Dada brings me to the barracks with him because he says the others are too stupid to mind me. He is annoyed with all his children. He bangs loudly on the little shutter so that the sergeant will not keep him waiting. He jumps a queue of two women waiting with forms. They fan themselves with the forms and say things under their breath. My father says nothing about his pushing in front to the women, which makes them say more things and look at me with tilted heads and eyes that are full of pity. He bangs on the glass until two sergeants show up at once, both chomping on biscuits.

'I want to report a crime,' Dada says.

'What crime would that be?' the slimmer of the two sergeants says, and he winks at me.

'The crime of plying drugs to a boy of fourteen years with a heart condition. That's what.'

'Is it your boy?' the sergeant says and my father nods. The sergeant goes to open the doors.

'Come inside now for a chat, man, and you tell me what it is you're claiming was done to your son.' As we walk through the offices of the barracks, the guard beckons to a ban gharda* sitting at a desk.

'The wee one will have to wait outside, Mr McCourt. Don't worry, she's in good hands,' he says, and my father stops and hunkers down to me. He looks hard-eyed at me, like a sparrowhawk, and gives me a hug.

'Be good for the ban gharda now, won't you Claire?' he says, and I say: 'No. I won't be good. I want to come in with you.' The two guards look at each other and I hear the other guards in the office laugh. The ban gharda brings me in to the room where my father is and we sit by the wall. Perhaps she brings me because she sees the distress on him. Perhaps they all know here that our mother was one of the people who died in the bomb at Christmas and they want to help us. It seems everyone

* = Until 1990 in Ireland a female garda/guard was referred to as a ban gharda

has wanted to help us since that time. The ban gharda holds my hand all the while and I let her.

I watch my father pass the brown bag over to the sergeant. He makes a complaint about Jack Duffy and the sergeant writes it down. As Jack, Dada explains, is eighteen, he should go to jail for giving drugs to our Francie who might have died had he taken stronger. I see the sergeant raise his eyebrows when Dada tells him Jack Duffy is the son of Eoin Duffy, one of the town's councillors.

'Good luck,' the sergeant says.

Dada is pale and quiet all the way home. When we get inside the house he sends me into the bed with Isabel, who has her eyes closed and is clutching a photo of Mammy. I curl up beside Isabel but she shrugs me off. She is annoyed, I think, because I told about Jack's needle. That night, I hear Dada climb the stairs to Francie's room and speak softly to my brother.

Two or three days pass and things get calm again in the house. Dada has gone back to the bakery and everything seems normal – with him getting up early and coming home in the afternoon. Nora is in charge when Dada is away as she is the only sensible one among us, he says. Then on Sunday morning there is a heavy knock on our front door. Dada goes down to answer and I hide on the landing with Nora and Isabel. I peep my head round the wall of the landing, see Dada usher in a small man with greying sandy hair to the front room. I have seen this man before. His face is on every telegraph pole in our part of town and on the roundabouts towards the border. He has a pug face, which Mammy used to say reminded her of a Hollywood film star, such as James Cagney or Mickey Rooney. Some of the posters have things written over them. One in our own street had 'a vote for Duffy, is a vote for murder' written across Mr Duffy's face – before it was taken down. I go close to the door. Eoin Duffy is pleading for Dada not to press charges against Jack, but Dada won't listen. I hear our father shout: 'Ya can't believe a word comes out of an addict's mouth, do ya not know that, Eoin, hah?'

Then Eoin Duffy charges out of the room like a bull. As I run back upstairs to Nora and Isabel I hear Mr Duffy say to my father: 'I can afford good lawyers. You can't. And another thing: your boy went to a lot of others in this town. Not just to Jack, who is a fucken easy target, the mess he's in. Maybe you need to look closer to home, McCourt. Francie told Jack a thing or two about what happened him.'

'What do you mean, what *happened* him?' Dada says.

'Speak to your son,' Eoin Duffy says, and he opens the front door and bangs it as he leaves. Obviously, Mr Duffy is referring to our mother and the bomb, I think to myself – so why doesn't Dada see this? When Eoin Duffy is out of the house Dada looks up and is vexed to see us on the stairs. He says he wants us to go out – either to the public pool in Blackrock or to the cinema in town – while he speaks to Francie. For the first time ever, I do not trust my father. I think he will do something bad to our brother.

He gives us money for the film in the Adelphi, but we don't go: we want to see what Dada will do. After we leave the house he comes out, stands on the stone seat he and Mammy used to sit on together and sees we are not on our way in to town. He tells us to go on or he'll walk us there himself. We concoct a plan to hide behind the fir trees that jut out from the garden a few houses down so that when he looks out next time he won't see us. We hear the door open, close, and we stay still. Just as we are about to back up to slip over our neighbour's wall, the front door opens again and Dada leaves. We come out from the firs and follow our father, who is walking a long, straight route up the tree-lined Dublin Road.

'He's going to the Duffys',' Isabel says.

'How do *you* know?' Nora asks.

'Because this is the bloody way,' Isabel replies.

As we walk along the steep road in the dry heat, the sky the colour of Francie's pills, I feel sad. The last time I walked this road I was with Mammy and we were going to the shrine at Ladywell. That day, there had been throngs of people gathered around the statue of the Virgin by the well, waiting for it to overflow – as it is supposed to do every August 15 – and it didn't happen. Mammy had taken me because I'd wanted to see 'the miracle' with her, and so now as I walk with Isabel and Nora, past the Littlemarshes, past Ladywell and on toward the big plush houses of the Dublin Road, I feel my mother's absence keenly. It seems permanent in a way it hasn't felt before: she is not walking beside me, telling me about her dreams of moving to this road one day. Many of the people who own the shops and businesses in the town live on this road. Some of the houses are supposed to have swimming pools. As we pass the large imposing properties, I feel myself become more alert, as if the long tidy lawns, the cars in the driveways, the absence of any kind of wildness along the road has woken me up. I see a boy and girl my age dressed in riding gear, their shirts crisp and white as the shirts in the Daz adverts; across the road two older girls are running around in pink swimsuits, whacking each other with towels. Dogs with shiny coats are slumped on doorsteps. Isabel, Nora and I say nothing about what we see as we walk so as not to alert our father who is only steps ahead. But I think Isabel and Nora must also see how different this road seems, how it is a world of money and comfort, one that is not only alien to us but sort of frightening, too, in that it is all so dazzling, like intense sunlight, or the flash of a camera, which creates a glint and obscures the thing you're looking at. I think how unsuited to Mammy, who never hid anything – and yet, when I think about it, was herself sort of hidden – this road would have been.

Eventually Isabel stops. She says the white and turquoise bungalow on the southern edge of Cox's fields is Eoin Duffy's house. I am glad, as the soupy air has made me breathless. Though we are so sweaty from the walk the midges swarm around us when we do stop. From the shade of a chestnut tree opposite the bungalow we watch Eoin Duffy let Dada into his home. We talk then about maybe going back as there is no point hanging around now Dada is gone, not when we could all be instead in the cool darkness of the cinema, when suddenly, Isabel spots Jack. He is walking slowly down a slip-road from the fields. He turns for the road to his house, picks at leaves along the hedgerow, his long legs loose and ungainly, like a beautiful young giraffe. Isabel calls to him with a whistle he recognises. When he comes over she starts pulling at him, sort of taunting him about giving our Francie drugs. The way she does this reminds me of the way Dada gets angry. Intensely, with lots of tears and fury. And because of this, I see that Isabel likes Jack. I can tell. He seems to be telling her that there is something else to the story Francie told him, which seems not to have much to do with Mammy at all.

'He made me promise,' Jack says.

'And what's your promise worth, you big shit?' Isabel replies. She is crying and Jack is touching her hair.

'He said, Francie said, someone had done something to him.' Nora is trying to pull me away from the two of them now but I think of the ban gharda and how I stood my ground and so I do it again.

'What do you mean?' Isabel asks. Jack stiffens, shakes his head as if he has said too much already.

'You need to spill it love, come on,' Isabel pleads, and she becomes all soft with Jack. 'What did Francie say? He's not talking to us so you need to spill it. Or Daddy will take you to court. You understand? He's in your house right now, probably waiting for you.'

'Ah Jesus, I can't…' Jack says, and he keeps looking at me. 'Francis said… ah, Jesus… he said that someone *touched him up, like… held him against a wall…* and.' And then he whispers to Isabel who whispers to Nora who does not whisper to me. Then they all look at me and I can see shock on their faces, almost like the time when Mammy died.

'You go home now Jack Duffy and you tell this to my father, you hear?' Isabel says. She sounds very strict and Jack is nodding his head. We watch as he goes to his house and lets himself in.

'What happened to Francie at the wall?' I plead. My sisters, both of them, are welling up and shaking and Nora calls for Mammy who is dead now not even a year and I break from them and run towards home.

*

Dada has put a sign in the window of the shop saying that someone he knows has died in England and he will open in a week. He asks his customers to go to Joe Gallagher's bakery on Bridge Street while he is away. But this is not true. Dada is not in England. When Sunday comes, Dada makes the meal like he always does. A roast and a pudding. Usually he makes a trifle or a crumble, something simple, but the pudding today looks different. It is deep, fleshy, has berries all over. It smells spicy, cinnamon or allspice. I ask what sort of pudding it is and Dada says it's a celebration for 'the great long summer of '76, the best since '59'. I ask if I can help and he teases me about the cake I tried to make blue from Francie's pills and that he is better off by himself. We ask if Ed is coming this Sunday and Dada says no and that we are to go to Sarah's to celebrate the great summer with our cousins on Patrick Street. Nora and Isabel are looking at each other the whole time Dada is getting ready the dinner, talking about the amount of tayberries and raspberries he has used.

The day goes slowly at Aunt Sarah's. Our cousins take Francie, Nora and Isabel to the Castletown River to show them where our great-uncle drowned in a whirlpool as a child. I would like to see this whirlpool but Sarah says I'm too young. To keep me occupied, Sarah brings out the albums that have photos in them of her and my mother when they are my age.

She says I am the spit of my mother. 'It's the hair,' she says, 'real lobster-red,' and I smile though I have never seen a lobster. As Sarah pours herself a glass of wine, I look through the photos all neatly pasted into the album, and I see one of Mammy, Dada and Ed. Straight away I ask Sarah a question. (And I see once I've asked it there is something heavy in the air, some secret.) 'What was it, Aunt Sarah, made Ed so sick in London?' Sarah bites the corner of her lip, looks up at me.

'Well, your mammy, daddy and Ed were all at a dance one night in Kilburn,' she says. (I know this bit already.) 'And during it a group of men burst into the dancehall and told the band to stop playing, and the crowd they were looking for a John McGinnity, who they believed to be in the room. They said McGinnity should come outside as they were certain sure it was he who had betrayed them to the English police.' She sighs then, remembering this story of Ed's illness. 'But as no man by the name of McGinnity would come forward, the men decided to keep the crowd locked inside the dancehall until he did. Your father kept quiet because he thought the men might have guns and because your mammy was pregnant with Isabel. But he – yer man, Ed, started getting annoyed with your mammy and daddy. Well, what happens next is this: Ed huffs and puffs, breaks into a terrible sweat, becomes like a cornered rat. Starts flinging himself, wildly, at anything resembling a door or a way out. He just completely – *snaps* – is what he does.' Sarah clicks her fingers when she says this so I will understand what she's trying to describe. She is thirsty on the hot day, gulps down more wine. Then she puts on a voice that sounds like Ed's: 'Ya can't bloody well hold us like this,' she says, all manly and deep.

'And who in blazes are *you?*' she says in the voice I take to be of the hostage-takers, and laughs. Sarah describes then, in a way that both excites and scares me, how Ed grabbed the leader of the pack by the head and smacked it so hard on the floor Ed had to be pulled off the man, who along with the other hostage-

takers was soon turned out by the priests running the dance –
but not before telling Ed he'd come one day to kill him. Sarah
says it was after this night Ed began to think someone was
following him; all times in the mornings or on the train, on the
weekends about London or at the dances in Cricklewood and
Kilburn. Even the few girlfriends Ed had he believed to be
spies, 'and for the IRA, too, if you don't mind,' she says. 'So
that's how London made Ed sick. Up here. Not like Francis.' I
sense that this story is too wild for me to be told it, and is
something of a transgression, but I also sense that Aunt Sarah
tells it on purpose because she doesn't like Ed Molloy. She
shakes her head, drinks more wine. 'He really did that, ya know,
child,' she says, 'rocketed around that dancehall, went up the
walls. Shocked your father and your mother. Even the fellas
holding the place up were afeared of him. Your mother always
said it wasn't like he was caught or trapped, more like he was
*caught out*. He put them all at risk with his panic.'

That evening Sarah drives us home. Whoever my father has
had lunch with there is no trace of them now in the house. The
kitchen is scrubbed clean and aired, the smells of meat and
baking are gone. Dada is not in the mood to hear about our day
but when we ask again for a television he says yes. We jump
around, talk about the programmes we will watch. We ask if we
can go to the den to play but Dada says no to this, that we're
not to go there for a long while yet. Everyone agrees because
of the television. And because of what was found in the den.
And because of Francie.

Later, I come down from my room. I am feeling confused
about Francie and Mammy and even the summer pudding. I
want to ask Dada more questions about what Aunt Sarah told
me but I think it will only annoy him. Everyone is quiet, alone
in their own space in different parts of the house. Dada is in
the front room and has been there a while. I go into the kitchen,
the hum of the fridge the only sound, which makes me think of
Mammy who would sit at the kitchen table alone sometimes

when everything was done, giving herself a treat – a cigarette or a bag of peanuts or a small bottle of stout. And then I see it. Walking a slow, uncertain path across the counter. Fluttering her wings with the fragile black undersides, pulling again to a dead stop, as if listening for predators. Black-headed. Polka-dotted. Hard metallic red, like the postboxes I can still remember from London. I go to bring her outside, but she scuttles off towards the wall. I follow her trail and it leads me to something hidden behind the bread bin. I tentatively pull the object out. It is black and chrome with small silver letters spelling the word Minolta on the side and a long, thin buckled strap wrapped around it. I recognise it: Ed's camera. I wonder if Ed has been here today and why Dada has not told us. As I turn the camera around in my hands, I know instantly that I cannot mention it to my father, not now nor for a long time yet and I return the camera to its hiding place. I see the ladybird then, gather her onto my palm, bring her out to the garden.

In the morning the camera is gone. Dada is home for the day and the others are at school. I ask him if Francie is recovered now from his drug-taking and Dada smiles, says he is, that now everything will be like it was before the big row and that everyone needs to take care of Francie, especially for Mammy's sake. I do not mention the camera, as I know deep inside that to do so will expose my father's lie, and ruin the calm Dada says is to return to the house.

In the days that come after, we are visited by the guards and others looking for Ed Molloy. Always Dada mentions the same story, about Ed's fear of being hunted down by the men he'd met in a dancehall in London. 'He went peculiar after it,' Dada says. Sometimes, even months later, I hear Francie crying alone in his room and I wonder if maybe he misses Ed as well as Mammy for I remember then that Ed had always liked Francis the best.

Eoin Duffy would be re-elected that autumn. His pledges to the people who voted for him would be kept. He would ask questions of the politicians in Dublin about the bomb at Christmas – but get no response – and have a park built in Cox's fields for the Littlemarshes children to play in. He would declare the ruin of Roche's Castle to be of special archaeological significance (just as Ed had said it was), and have a group of men come to the fields one day to erect an enormous iron grate around it, 'to keep the castle safe'. It would occur to me, seeing the men padlock the heavy black chain around the castle's enclosure, that despite the great long summer of '76, the world I was growing up in was filled with things that ended in sadness. Our beloved den locked away in an iron cage, Ed getting so sick in London (or so I believed) that we would never see him again, our mother blown to smithereens (or so Isabel said) in a bomb, the Ladywell miracle that didn't happen. Shortly after I found the camera, I would stop calling my father Dada, call him Dad instead, a word that would always feel awkward and blunt in my mouth.

# The Burning Woman

I didn't stop to read it, just turned it over and saw that the signature was unfamiliar. A John someone, whom I did not immediately know. I bundled it, together with the two bills, something from the bank, into my bag, and drove to the station, making it just in time for the Dublin train.

Once out of the sidings the train sped across fields darkened by the floods of the past week. I took out the Alex Katz card, which, in a black spindly hand read:

Dear Tony and Anne,
Bad news. Quigley is dead. He'd developed diabetes and when he refused to take his insulin they locked him up. Terrible end. He's being buried at Kensal Green next Friday at 3. Be great to see you, but understand if you can't make it.
John

The woman beside me had been embroidering a piece of silk. A short pressured entry into the dust-coloured material, a drag of the thread upwards then over and back to begin the next stitch. As I watched her deft and repetitive movements the message on the card began to sink in.

The John of the card was John Traynor, an ex-pat artist living in London for the past forty years or more. Nowadays he eked out a living teaching in Adult Education and, before I had left London, I would occasionally see him in the library, temping. He painted guns and baseballs, was obsessed with the Beats and Jack Kerouac. He'd had nothing to do with the whole Goldsmiths scene of the nineties, though he could have done because his work had a Sensationalist quality, and he had taught there once. But he was a cantankerous character and, as long as I had known him, had refused to ally himself to any group that might have been able to help or develop him. Anyway, I never thought he was much good. Quigley, on the other hand, was entirely different. His talent was immense. In the new house in Dundalk I'd made the most fuss about where I would hang the Quigley triptych.

The card had shaken me. I could not believe Quigley was dead, yet I'd made no contact with him in the past ten years. I'd been in London several times and not gone to see him. Even though I knew he was broke and living in Victoria Mansions, a decrepit Gothic folly only a short walk from the flat we had retained in Brondesbury. We could easily have visited. I knew about the diabetes. On one of my visits I had bumped into John on Staverton Road and he had told me about it. The card suggested he had forgotten about that meeting, or at least was pretending to, perhaps so as to give me a chance to pay my respects without feeling too guilty.

Staring out at the still spring morning, I thought of the time Tony and I had first arrived in London. We had just graduated from art school in Dublin (and remaining in Ireland had not been an option, racked as it was then by recession and the Troubles) and we were very naive.

We had been given the keys to view a flat on Portland Road by an agency. Once inside, we had discovered it had been used for some kind of occult practice. A five-pointed star had been painted crudely with black paint on the living-room floor. Photographs with the eyes of women and children blacked out were scattered around, and there were two or three large books, written in Latin, filled with cabalistic drawings. I remember there had been a foot deep of a glutinous red substance in the bath, which made a fizz sound when I stirred it with a coat hanger – probably some kind of acid. Having speedily departed that property, we soon found ourselves homeless and with nowhere to go. Until a friend suggested the squats where John and Quigley lived in Maida Vale.

They had met at the Slade. Despite his name, Quigley claimed no Irish heritage, and John's Irishness was meaningless to him as he had left Limerick at fourteen and had never returned. To find as neighbours two young Irish 'artists', was, John told me later, an enormous relief to him. We gave him hope, he said, that a gay man with no interest in hurling, in Leinster vs Munster, or the Irish language, might be able to go home one day without fear of being strung up. On the basis of our mutual disregard for any particular nationalism, we four formed a strong friendship, avoiding Irish haunts in London like the plague. John made us welcome but it was Quigley who was the mentor, the guru – whatever is the correct term for an individual who teaches you the big truths of life, quickly and selflessly.

When I first saw him I thought he was a member of the National Front. His thick bald skull sat squat between his muscular shoulders, his back and neck covered in tattoos. A closer examination of these and you saw sea images: the pearly inside of an oyster-shell, shrimp, a bone-coloured conch and a pair of olive-skinned sirens on rocks with blue eyes and red lips, waves, boats – as well as numerous small birds and butterflies. And in the centre of these, from his neck to the base of his spine, was one prodigious poppy-red moth with intricate black markings. Quigley had got the moth done in Jamaica, where he said he had been happiest.

The two Edwardian squats belonged to a housing cooperative that had gone bust, so were in some kind of administrative limbo. This meant that the properties were in bad condition. And over time I came to believe that the top floor of the house we occupied was haunted. We would hear sounds at night, and, from the moment we arrived, there was a faint but distinctly bitter smell of smoke. We rarely used the top floor, though when people came to stay we would sometimes let them sleep in the top back room. I certainly remember I never liked to go up there; I would get a creepy feeling, and it was always cold even though the windows were kept shut and an electric fire occasionally left on.

I recall that once there was a loud manic rap on our door at about four in the morning. It was Quigley, frightened, white as a sheet. He said he had seen a gossamer-like outline of a woman passing through the wall of his top floor to ours. Tony ran up, but of course there was nothing at all. Only the vague smell of burnt sticks that had been there since our arrival.

As the train pulled in to Drogheda, I was jolted from my thoughts about Quigley and the days of squatting in London, about which, over time, I had become a little ashamed. The woman beside me had fallen asleep and the needle of her sewing stabbed the flesh of my thigh as the train pulled up suddenly. I passed the embroidery and needle back to her, and gave my leg a rub, glancing again at the Alex Katz card on the table. I thought of how the endless cycle of administering insulin must have bothered a man who had loved his freedom as much as Quigley had done.

He had always painted women. Not nudes or glamorous women, but the faces and bodies of working women; older women – damaged women. He said he found their worn faces beautiful, and had won himself quite a reputation for that kind of realist work. But his encounter with the ghostly figure on the top floor led to a growing obsession with a particular face.

The Burning Woman triptych depicts a dark-skinned woman of about fifty. She is staring out the window, sitting on a suitcase, as if waiting for someone to take her home, wherever home is. In the last picture she has hacked up the floorboards and built a fire, no doubt ready to leave her circumstances one way or another. The woman is herself full of colour: pink silk slips from under her black, jet-fringed hijab; her shoes are gold and embroidered, and she has thick red lips and kohl-lined eyes. Yet the room is grey, as are the skies. The series is clearly about displacement of some sort, and made Quigley a lot of money. But no sooner had he made a real mark on London's art world, than he took to drinking, and began to pile on the pounds, and generally tried to avoid work altogether.

Quigley said he had based the Burning Woman figure on the ghost he had seen. He said she had followed him, 'clung to his soul' were his exact words (I recall them so particularly because they had chilled me), and that he was unable to relax knowing she would follow him from house to house. Wherever he went he would find her, or she would find him, as if she were not outside him at all, but inside him; an unshakeable phantom that had taken up residence in his imagination, eventually taking possession of it.

From Connolly I walked into the IFSC* where I was to meet with an investment bank to discuss the expansion of my company. As I passed the new EAT restaurant on the corner, with its four brown awnings sheltering the clientele from the icy winds coming off Dublin Bay, I thought of the card and the insecure world of painting I had long ago left behind. I thought of John and how his was the lesser talent though he had proved the better at life. John believed in small things and getting through. Tony and I had parted for this very reason, for he was the same. I made a mental note to let John know Tony's address in Leitrim.

That I had sold the Burning Woman triptych before Quigley had died rankled me a little as I walked towards the riverbank: the paintings, which had been placed first in my bedroom, then in the hall had begun to disturb me. The sight of her fragile expression as I left the house could ruin whole days.

* = International Financial Services Centre

I walked by the Liffey, admiring the gleaming glass of the new bank buildings, restaurants and apartments. John would not recognise the country he had left, I thought. My phone vibrated. A reply to a text I had sent Tony from the train. He would go to the funeral and wanted to know if I'd go with him. But I simply had too much to do. And anyway, I knew how it would go. There would be John and Tony, some old girlfriends and children to whom Quigley had not spoken in years, perhaps the Hell's Angels that had shown up many times before at the squats with their harem of women and Harleys. No, I no longer fitted into that world. Even Quigley, in truth, had left it behind and only fell back on it again due to his ill health and poverty. I had 'risen above the horde', as Quigley used to say, and it had been a very long time indeed since my heart had ruled my head.

Outside the bank I stopped to smooth down the lapels of my jacket and, glancing across the river towards the docks, beheld an unnerving sight: a dark-skinned woman in a black hijab, sitting, slumped, on a suitcase. She was between two far-apart boats being unloaded of large green crates by a crane. Behind her, a pale, dusty wasteland of bulldozed houses, no doubt awaiting some new development (though it was unusually quiet, suggesting that the rumours I'd heard of an approaching slump might have some substance). Before the woman was the river, dark and deep, slowing as it opened out to the sea. She looked out of place, like a figure left behind in an empty bazaar, and I wondered if she had come off one of the boats. In her hands she held kindling, and below her I saw that there was a small black pile of the same, a line of pearl-grey smoke filing from it into the air.

# The Sanctuary

She wanted to go into the bedroom but was afraid. She knew what she would do if she could not find him (and of course she would not find him): clamber into the bed, burrow under the thick white duvet and the Foxford throw, there since winter, when they had left, when the pain had so tellingly returned. She would turn on her side, clutch at his side of the sheets, at his pillow, attempt to pull something of his life back. Maybe she'd find a hair or a fragment of skin, something. But she would not go in just yet; she did not want to know, for certain, that he was not inside, sleeping, or reading his book with the lamp on.

She straightened the six Paolozzis in the hall. She was aided by the small pencil marks he had drawn on the wall around the corners of the brushed-chrome frames. His eye was always so precise, a spirit level. She looked up at the sun-filled skylight he'd built to frame the North Star: dust motes swirled in the long rays. She went into the living room and pulled up the coffee-coloured blinds. He had wanted to redesign the windows so that the glass met in a geometric point; a jetty out to the sanctuary during the day, and to vast black skies and the stars at night. He had wanted to schedule the work for May. She expected it would have been finished by now.

It was as if they'd just left. A black leather glove lay palm down on the coffee table. She picked it up and put her hand inside, half expecting to find his. There was a sense that the house had been waiting for them to return. For they could just as well have been gone for the afternoon; gone for a stroll down Cotter's Lane to her father's like they had done in October. They'd picked blackberries along the Lane then, eaten them as they walked. Even at the time, she remembered, she had not wanted to be here in this borderland wilderness, where, she considered, a life could pass without making a mark, become slight and pathetic like the tiny silver moths that came out at dusk and were dead by morning. She wanted to be in the flat in London, helping him with the Practice, shopping in Marylebone on a Saturday (there was meaning for her in that life), and she simply could not understand his love of this place. It was not picturesque like Kerry, nor fabulous and strange like Connemara. It appealed to him, she decided, partly because it was unlikely. He always saw what others could not, what was hidden in a thing, its numinous potential. Living in this house had softened him, and here she had watched his once uncompromising modernism give in, ever so slightly, to the pastoral.

In the sanctuary a hare squatted tensely behind a rock. She knew it was a hare by its legs and ears and long hay-brown body. (They had come to know the different species of birds, rodents, plants and flowers; had become alert to bird cries.) The hare halted, watching something intently beyond the rock, and she was reminded of him. Ever since the service she'd noticed how certain things, for no particular reason, brought him to her mind. The pink and red pansies in the flowerbed outside Kensal Green crematorium; the grey-haired stranger's face on the Edgware Road; words in books and newspapers her eye would randomly fall upon. ('A characteristic of grieving' somebody had called it, this revelation in quotidian things; though far from bringing her comfort she found the experience disturbing.) Now, it seemed, even the sanctuary reflected him, as if he, with his magnanimous life force, had returned to nature and was down there influencing its flow, whipping up arcane schemes and intrigues like Prospero.

The hare moved on under the hedge towards Ramsey's field. She wanted to warn it, to tap the window and shout: *don't go in there, you'll get yourself killed.*

She went into the kitchen. All those jars of vitamin pills and miracle cures: dried seaweeds and mushrooms, B17 (a banned vitamin she'd had to buy on the black market), sealed packs of bark from some obscure tree. Cupboards of pills, rows of cancer cookbooks. All that hope and promise of hope: over, over, over. She plunged the books into a black rubbish bag, then gathered the glass jars of beans and pulses – anything that could still be eaten – onto the island. He had built it in November: a solid pine work board atop grille-fronted beech cupboards. Driven, when he shouldn't have, to B&Q in Newry for the materials and built it himself; a place for her to prepare his coffee enemas, his organic juices, his vitamin cocktails. November. That's when the pain had come back. That awful pain that she could not truthfully imagine having in her own body. For someone in such a fragile remission, he had done far too much.

She checked the sell-by dates. Dad might be able to use some of these, she thought, then packed the jars of rice and pulses into the green cloth Superquinn bags.

He'd come to love her father, had been responsible for her and her father's truce. (Their move here had brought them into daily contact with him, a familiarity that, over time, had caused her to forget a little her father's faults; in particular, his drinking.) The old man had been quiet lately up in the house; on his best behaviour. She had decided to stay there with him rather than here, as she didn't want to be alone.

Eventually she must go into the bedroom: she needed clothes. When they had left in January, she had not wanted to make a fuss about how long they'd be gone; they'd flown to London with two suitcases, one each, containing no light clothes. But his pain was such, she thought, that he must have known the trip would be for longer. And if so, what was he thinking as he left this house – did he sense he would not be back? Had he come here to die, she wondered? Had that been the point of it all, the hurried relocation, the mad search for a rural idyll? Perhaps he did have such a presentiment; their conversations in the last year had been oddly elliptical, and she had not probed his fears should such talk spoil their fight, for it was always *their* fight. And so she insisted they take little: a few warm clothes, shoes. That way he would be bolstered into thinking: *this new pain is a small thing, a glitch, and look, she is not preparing for the worst, she believes in me and my ability to conquer this, and soon we will be home.* She hoped that in his mind it had gone something like that.

She went into the utility room and opened the door to the back garden. The high grass almost obscured the garden furniture. All the plants were overgrown and dry. Some had died. She'd have to get the gardens seen to before the estate agent came to view the house; maybe her father would do it if he'd time.

As she walked down the steps she noticed, on the ground, wrapping around the corner of the house, a trail of yellow rose petals. She turned and looked up at the rose bushes grown tall in her absence. A bird or animal must have caused the petals to fall in this long curve, she thought.

The trail led towards her own fence, to a small bone with ants marching around it. Pink flesh hung off the marrow. Perhaps it was a hawk or one of the kites, or a ferret that had ruffled the bushes and set down there to eat. She turned around to the trail before her, long and gold, and was suddenly struck. *Oh no, no. Not now, not now.* The tears, the heaving chest, the throb in the heart. There was no reason rose petals should have had this effect on her. There was nothing about roses that recalled him.

But she had just glimpsed him. In this lemon-coloured trail, laid, perhaps, to say good morning, how are you today, I am free, I am happy, I am indeed *in the next room.* She took a deep breath, returned inside and walked resolutely towards the bedroom.

She entered quickly, looking over at the bed (he was not there, sleeping or reading). She saw head and leg indents, where, she remembered, he had gone for a nap before they had left the house all those months ago. She went to pull up the blind. As light poured into the room, she caught a glint of light refracting off the golden Buddha on the dressing table. From the window she could see the side of the sanctuary, the Cooley hills, Ramsey's tall trees crowned with crows' nests, the rocky tufts of Ramsey's field. Sometimes from this window they had watched men with long guns roam in and out of that field looking for grouse or rabbits. And sometimes, during the day, young hawks would be trained with string around bits of meat. The two fields looked so similar. An uneven gorse hedge with lots of gaps seemed to be the only divide between life in one, and death in the other. (Just how this ramshackle wildlife sanctuary had ended up beside fields where men would come to hunt, members of gun clubs, was an eternal source of conversation for the visitors who came to stay with them.) How they wished they could have erected warning signs for the animals that might wander in the wrong direction.

She turned to the Buddha, touched its golden head. He had never practised. He claimed to have forgotten, too, the rules of his two birth religions (Catholicism and Islam) so, instead, followed a simple bespoke ceremony. He laid out rosary beads on a white linen cloth, placed a black and white photograph of his father (sitting on a prayer mat in Cairo) against a miniature of the Little Child of Prague given to him by his mother, and lit candles. Certainly he spoke to something or someone when he came in here and sat by the dressing table. She never thought to ask him what, or whom, exactly. She knew only that she would find him in deep commune with it, or them, and that he would cry with his eyes closed, rocking back and forth then reach out and touch the statue or beads or photo as if reaching for a life raft.

Someone had been in. There were two thin drinking glasses filled with mayflowers on either side of the statue, and a tealight that had burned out. She touched the buds and put her fingers to her nose: a pineapple smell. Immediately there they were, on cue, the burning tears. She blinked, forced them back. It must have been Mrs Ramsey. She had asked her to check the place, given her keys. Perhaps Mrs Ramsey had (through the window) seen him sitting here, and known completely what he was doing hunched over the statue, clutching at the beads and the photo of his father. It was the one part of their fight she had not shared; she did not know how to pray, nor what it was that one prayed to (the Humanist service had been her idea). Mrs Ramsey must know, or else she would not have left the flowers, now wilted, their heads almost bald. She collected them up, threw them in the black plastic bag she'd brought in with her, carried the bag into the hall.

She managed to fill three bags with out-of-date cosmetics, food products, wastepaper from the office, junk mail. She packed a crate with things she could recycle: newspapers, tins, bottles (a reminder of her heavy consumption of wine that winter). She would bring the bags and crate to the recycling centre in town. She lined up the green bags filled with pulses and rice and vitamin pills to give to her father. She was convinced now that she would put the house up for sale and return to London. It would be impossible to remain and carry on a life here. He was not here. He was not anywhere. Not in the bedroom sleeping or praying; not in the office drawing; not in the living room staring out at the grouse and peacocks; not in the garage imagining its conversion into a room with a spa. He had vanished. Truly, he had passed away. Into that sweet jar-shaped canister of ashes held in the office at the crematorium (waiting for her to make up her mind – to scatter or to keep). And she'd better stop this looking, this being-revealed-to business, because it was only a step away from stopping strangers on the street, to see if he had gone there, into the body of another man.

# The Sanctuary

She picked up her handbag and rummaged inside for the keys to her car. She clutched at the cold bundle, placed them down on the long iroko shelf in the hallway (the brown-black colour of his Mediterranean eyes) and dropped the bag. She could not stop looking. If she had seen him in the rose petals then he must be here. He would come to her. She needed a place to lie down. Her legs felt weak. Weightless and frail, she drifted from side to side along the hall, aimlessly brushing up against the walls, mindlessly touching the edges of paintings – the Patrick Caulfield, the Paolozzis. She knew where she would end up: in the pit of tears that would tear at her ribs and rip her throat. She opened the bedroom door, glided towards her side of the bed, slipped under the duvet and the folded-down throw, and turned to cradle the indents.

An hour must have passed this way. When she woke she recalled she had not seen his face (as in a dream), or had any memory of him, but had been overcome by, bombarded with – colours: blacks and blues, deep greens and golds. She'd been tossed from one shade to the next, had emitted fluctuating levels of cries, until, at rest, jaded and empty, she landed on *yellow*, and here she breathed easy, stroking his pillow, rhythmically, till her mind cleared, whereupon she fell into a deep sleep.

A voice came from outside, by the window. She was sure she could be seen curled up on the dishevelled, tear-soaked bed like a child. She went onto her knees and looked out and saw that Mrs Ramsey had begun her retreat towards Cotter's Lane. She jumped up, ran out of the room and opened the front door.

'Mrs Ramsey, Julia, Julia – I'm in, it's me. I'm home.' Mrs Ramsey turned and walked towards her with her head bowed.

'I'm sorry love, I'm so sorry.' Mrs Ramsey reached out and hugged her, then rubbed her arms vigorously up and down, passing into her skin from hard warty hands motherliness, and a heartfelt sympathy. Then, with tears in her eyes, she asked if there was anything she could do.

'No. Not for the moment.'

Mrs Ramsey said nothing when she told her Chalfont was to be sold, that she could no longer see herself living in the place now her husband was gone. Mrs Ramsey seemed to understand.

'Thank you for the mayflowers.'

'Oh, that was your father. I saw him pick them along the Lane. He's awfully put out. He wanted to go over but the journey would have been too much for him, you know that.'

She closed the door. She looked in the hall mirror, at her face, lined and black-streaked, at the slate-coloured weariness around her eyes. Fixing her fuzzy hair, she remembered she had not pulled down the blinds. Inside the bedroom she straightened the duvet, folded down the throw, removed the damp pillow. She would place the pillow on her bed tonight; it still had his smell, clean and powdery, of the woods after a night's rain, and there were a few grey hairs still clinging. She pulled down the blind and closed the door, brought the pillow to the pile of things in the hall, ready to be loaded into the Jeep. She went into the office, pulled down the blinds, brushed her hand along the row of tall, dusty books on modern architecture as she exited, and closed the door.

She stared out at the sanctuary; it rustled in parts and she thought she saw the hare, but couldn't make it out amongst the rocks and deadwood. She had become out of step with the movements of the place. Once, they were attuned to the darting of a grouse here, a rabbit there. The animals were so quick, so adept at camouflaging themselves (except for the flagrant prowling of the white ferret who would steal in without caring who or what observed him), that only a kind of hawk-eyed seeing could follow their progress through all that scrub. After months of such looking even the nightlit grass would become penetrable.

She knew if she stared long enough the green undulating veil would lift, and she would see that wild world once more. Maybe tomorrow. Tomorrow she would come back to this house whose name he had not wanted to change, sit in this room with a cup of tea, and look out at the fields. Or, if not tomorrow then the next day, whenever she was ready to look steadily into things, for she was not able to do so now. She thought of her father, and wondered what he'd like to eat for lunch. There would be things to do for him; she would need to go to the shops. Today, if he let her, she would treat him to a meal in a restaurant in town. The day was fine. It would be really lovely, she thought, to walk.

# Blood

Fred Plunkett walked around her in his mind like an invisible wolf. She was thin and gazelle-like, had a creamy retrousse nose, and wore a brash perfume that tingled the back of his throat. There was also an arrogance to her, as if she were accustomed to other people's submission and was rattled now by having to explain herself.

'Didn't Louise say? I'm Lara. I've come to use the library. I'm researching a book. I've come especially.' As she went towards a bulging black satchel resting by the pillar, Fred thought, *Damn, she's got some sort of letter. Proof. From Louise herself. Now I shall have to say*:

'Ah yes. The friend from London.'

'Yes!' the girl replied.

'Come in, come in,' Fred said.

The girl entered the hallway, removed her sunglasses, hooked them over the lapels of her military-fit coat. She refused Fred's offer of Nescafé, but allowed him to take her coat (whereupon she placed her glasses on her head). On her way towards the stairwell, Tomas welcomed her with a leg rub from his moulting ginger torso. Fred watched her look down at the cat and smiled.

'Louise has such a wonderful home,' she said, stopping to view the artwork on the stairwell wall.

'How do you know her, exactly?' Fred said.

'Oh. From University. She was my Professor,' the girl replied.

Fred's aunt had taught at University College, London for almost twenty years. An authority on the archaeology of the Eastern Mediterranean and Middle East, Louise Foster had turned thousands of students on to the poetic and imaginative brilliance of the Koran (mostly via NJ Dawood's 1956 translation). Despite her retirement, due to recent world events (and her expertise) she was regularly asked to advise political organisations, think-tanks and journalists the world over. Hence, she was often away, and this is how Fred, who hoped to complete his thesis in his aunt's spacious Victorian house (with its substantial collection of rare books, local newspapers, archaeological journals, and tranquil setting between the Cooley Mountains and Irish Sea), found himself caretaker of it, and of his aunt's cat, a role that had not come without its complications.

'Here we are,' he said, once inside the library, 'a good view of the hills,' and placed the girl's bag down on the desk opposite his. The small cemetery at Faughart could be seen from the window. Here, the remains of Edward the Bruce had lain interred in a sunken vault marked by an iron Celtic cross since 1318. When she got to the chair, the girl angled it away from the window towards the large echoing heart of the room. She then turned, reached over and closed the shutters.

'The light,' she said, 'it bothers me. I'm somewhat photo-sensitive.'

He noticed that indeed the girl's eyes were watering in the sun's glare. Not until both shutters were closed did he get the full impact of them: sensitive and transparent like a calm June day in Greenore.

*

'I'll be taking a break soon,' Fred said, quietly, his head bowed over his book-burdened table. 'I've a bit of a job to do downstairs.'

# Blood

'Oh, yes,' the girl responded, sniffily. Fred immediately felt a strange pang in his chest, and wondered if, perhaps, Lara knew the full extent of his arrangement with Louise. He blushed and pretended to work. Furtively, he watched her lay out two large leather-bound books on the reading table.

'What are you researching, Lara?' he asked.

'Oh. Settlers to this area in the fifteenth century.'

'From Britain?'

'No,' Lara replied, scanning the huge ivory pages. As she did not elaborate, and as he was afraid to enquire further, Fred turned to his wastepaper basket and began to sharpen his pencils. The room seemed to fill with small, intrusive noises: the trembling chalky sound of the ivory pages being turned, the pencil shavings hitting the screwed-up balls of paper like rain, the swish of Lara's dress each time she moved, her assured slow breathing. Fred longed to speak, if only to divest all of these increasingly troubling and *arousing* sounds of their unwarranted power.

Slyly, he watched her remove a small cardigan and wrap it around the chair at the reading table. He took in her tight lampblack dress, the tiny buttons down the front, the sheer chocolate-brown tights with a seam, and shoes that had *high plastic heels*. Christ. How had he not noticed those before? At first he thought she looked like a Forties film star. And then decided that, no, that wasn't quite right: she looked like a Goth, but a much more glamorous Goth than the Goths he was used to seeing in Belfast. Her lips were a matt dark-red, her skin white as jasmine, her hands adorned with silver skull-decked rings. And there was something else about her that he liked, though he could not decide what it was. Was it this dark style of hers? (Though what did he know about women and their styles? He hadn't so much as touched a woman in six years. It was far too complicated: women, sex, relationships. It *was* rocket science. Fred had immersed himself in the much more certain world of academia, and had for the past six years, been utterly, inescapably celibate.) Or was it some more hidden quality she had that impressed him?

At Queens, Fred liked the Goths. They intrigued him with their Marylyn Manson T-shirts, dyed black hair and black lipstick. They formed an *underwelt*: the girls with their white faces and sleek hair, the men in their high-heeled rubber shoes. In a feeble attempt to ally himself with what he thought of as a kind of tribal subversiveness, Fred had had his mother sew PVC patches onto his tweed jackets and cardigans, and though he fantasised about wearing substantially larger amounts of PVC than that (like a gimp suit), he never did. Between seminars and symposia he would sometimes visit Gresham Street with its seedy hotels and flyblown glamour, or linger in the Arcade on North Queens Street delighting in the wares of Gemini, MissTique and Private Lines. He loved to stroke the PVC tops with their chains and cut-away breasts, smell the rubber T-shirts, cast his eyes around at the exotic, shiny blackness of it all and lose himself in this slightly seditious but alluring world. A world that far from belonging to the realm of 'fantasy', was a hard reality in Belfast. For Fred had found the city to be full of S&M clubs, fetish clubs, groups such as Transsexuals United Against Sectarianism, not to mention the bondage parties he had heard so much about but to which he had never been invited.

'I do hope you won't mind, but I'm intrigued. What is your book about, Lara?' he asked. 'I mean, what is it that interests you about these "settlers"?'

'Well, it's sort of about vampires,' she replied, pronouncing the 'v' softly, and the second half of the word as one syllable, so that in her cut-glass accent it rhymed with 'far'. Seconds later the ridiculousness of what she had said hit him with particular force.

'But there's no such thing, surely. I mean there's no such thing as *vampires!*' he said. 'Vampires! *Children of the night!*' he added, in mock-Transylvanian.

# Blood

'Have you read Dracula?' she asked. Fred glared.

'Then you know that while Mina is saved the Count is destroyed. But this is Stoker's fiction. In reality, Count Dracula's body was never found. I have reason to believe he escaped Romania and came here to the Irish borderlands in the fifteenth century.'

*Here? Dracula? To the Cooley Mountains?*

It immediately occurred to Fred, then, that a flake, albeit an extremely good-looking one, had interrupted a crucial day of study. 'So how did Dracula get here, then?' he asked, sarcastically.

'Probably through the Black Sea, through the Bosphorus and Sea of Marmara, then into Istanbul and around the Mediterranean. It would have been a terrifically tough journey and must have taken months. Oh, and I've just found here a number of references to a family with exotic origins that arrived in these parts at exactly the right time. Just think – there could actually be people living here in this area directly descended from the Count.'

Fred Plunkett sat back in his chair and laughed. It was rude he knew, but he couldn't help it. In fact, rather like his feline charge, he could hardly contain himself. As he guffawed (and guffawed) he could see the girl sitting composed on the edge of her chair, seemingly oblivious to the racket he was making; she had opened slightly one of the shutters and was gazing toward a darkened Faughart cemetery and the grave of Edward the Bruce. Fred stopped laughing and cleared his throat.

'I'm sorry. I've been terribly rude. Perhaps I should leave you to it.' He gathered up his papers, neatly re-piled his books, plugged his chair into the desk, and walked towards the door.

'I hope you brought an umbrella, Fred,' Lara said.

Fred looked to the window by his desk. It wasn't raining, but yes, she had observed it: the dense black cloud coming in off the sea on its way towards the house.

'I imagine that will have passed by the time I'm done downstairs,' Fred said.

'Oh yes,' Lara replied, 'Tomas.'

She knew! The deal with Louise! No doubt, she was on to him about his perving too, his afternoon of languorous looking.

All the way along the corridor, and down the stairwell, Fred convinced himself he'd been ousted from his favourite place, from his one place of real privacy, in a most devious manner. Lara had overwhelmed him with *strangeness*, with some fantastical belief that Dracula, like Edward the Bruce, had come to settle in the Cooley Peninsula. Hold that thought. Dra-*cul*-a. No. It couldn't be. The origins of the area were in the Gaelic, in 'Cualaigne'. It was pointless even to consider the girl's daft hypothesis. As if a legendary, largely fictitious character, played by both Gary Oldman and the great Klaus Kinski, would come and set up house in this inhospitable hinterland. It was far enough from anywhere now (an hour from both Belfast and Dublin on the train), but surely a lot further five hundred years ago.

Fred went into the living room and immediately saw the green cloud-shaped stain. He placed his knapsack down, removed his tweed jacket with the PVC elbow patches and placed it on the arm of the divan. He tugged at his aunt's Persian rug and turned to Tomas, newly awake. Sensing his minder's displeasure at this latest befouling, the cat launched himself over Fred's right shoulder and scratched the side of Fred's neck before scuttling off to some dark recess of the hall.

Blood trickled onto Fred's collar. He wiped it off with his hand and sat down. 'Little bastard,' he shouted after Tomas, and returned to the stain. He then rolled up his shirtsleeves, neatly, mechanically, and trudged towards the kitchen for a basin of hot water. Halfway there he stopped. What *was* he doing? Moreover, what was he doing with his *bloody life*? Such thoughts came to Fred Plunkett often in moments such as this. Moments when he caught himself doing mean, odious things like cleaning up cat's piss. And why was he cleaning up cat's piss in exchange for using his own aunt's library from which

# Blood

he'd just been so subtly ejected? Who said he could do such things, make such deals? At thirty-one he'd been a student forever. He had no girlfriend; he slept in a room, in which, at night, he could hear his own mother breathe and sometimes gargle on her own phlegm. It was pitiful. To others, his mother, his lecturers, he was a dedicated student. But what of the *real world*? (He hated that phrase.) This was the last year of his thesis, and what was he to do when it ended? After Queens, the only road open to him was research, at any institution kind enough to hire him. Other than that, the thought of 'employment' terrified him. Cat-sitting was one of the few jobs he'd ever had, that and a brief stint as a bookie's clerk. Neither of which he included on his CV.

He checked the gash on his neck in the mirror above the fireplace, then sat down into his aunt's swampy leather chair and opened a small gilded box on the coffee table. He took out an all-white Egyptian cigarette, and lit up. This was bad. Very bad. He inhaled, deep and slow. Why had he never listened to *the voice*? The voice that throbbed inside him at times like this. The voice that said: *that black shiny gimp suit is for you, and this tweed garb is so over*; the voice that said *leave with the books and papers you need, and fuck cleaning the rug*. No, he had never listened to that voice, and look where it had got him to date: he was lonely; he'd made a humiliating deal to mind an incontinent cat in order to use his own aunt's library. But for Fred it was always in such low moments that things made most sense. He would be flooded with understanding, as if before he'd been unconscious. He had respect for him, this rebellious creature, and wished as he sucked pensively on the fat cigarette that he could meet him more often, knowing that to do so would be to spend more time in the bass-register moroseness that had revealed him. For this was the real Fred. The Fred without the constructs. Man of his blood-memory. In such moments, Fred Plunkett would encounter the full force of the manqué rubber-clad deviant buried within him.

He threw the butt into the fire and lit up another cigarette. Hearing a floorboard creak, he turned to find Lara standing by the door, watching him, Tomas luxuriating in her arms. There was an intense look in her eyes. He had noted it earlier in the library. It was the look of someone who, over the years, had made themselves remote and icy, not so as to repel other people, but so as to be reached only by those as clear and direct and honest as they. He realised then that it was that, more than anything else, which he liked about her.

She moved towards the fire, teetered slightly on her high, glassy heels, at which Tomas jumped from her arms onto the rug, and positioned his rump as if to relieve himself once again, whereupon Lara gently shooed him from the room. She laughed loudly. Beautiful teeth, he thought. He watched her walk slowly to the coffee table, coolly open the gilded case and slip her hand inside for a cigarette.

'What were you thinking, Fred, when I came in?'

'Oh. About the rug, about my thesis. In fact, my whole life flashed before me.'

'Such a strange look. I barely recognised you.'

'I was about to clean that mess, and, suddenly, now, I cannot. I don't know why but I cannot. Perhaps you will apologise to Louise for me, tell her I will phone tomorrow? Would you do that?' Fred said. Lara nodded, then stood back and examined the cloud-shaped stain.

'Louise really should keep Tomas in the yard. She can hardly expect *family* to do something like that.' He drew hard on his cigarette. Lara was assuring him, and he was enjoying it.

'I was only supposed to cat-sit. You see, he's incontinent, poor thing. Some kind of infection. Louise never *asked* me, you know, to clean the crap up. I just felt it wasn't right the cat should soil the house on my watch. Now, well, I feel like a fool. I should never have assumed such responsibility.'

'You've been *asleep* Fred, haven't you, hmmm? Asleep to yourself.' Yes, that was how it was. Exactly. He was so bound up in a sense of duty, of what was proper and right, that in recent years he had been *asleep* to his own needs. He watched her yank together the two blue velvet drapes.

'Hope I didn't intrude upon your studies today, Fred.'

'No, no. Of course not.'

'By the way, I forgot to ask. What's your thesis on?' Lara asked.

'Oh, it's a study of various kinds of leukemia,' Fred replied.

'You find the library useful for that?'

'Of course. For the past twenty years we've had abnormally high levels of cancer and blood disorders in the Northeast. Sellafield being the main suspect. Louise has kept excellent local archives.'

When Fred left the house it was raining. Clouds raced across the sky and he stopped to see an alternately blue and yellow haze veil the moon, which otherwise shone like a perfectly round silver button. He was cold. He considered turning back for one of Louise's umbrellas, but the recalcitrant voice within him that had earlier risen up in a rage urged him to carry on into the full force of the silvery light, now turning the bay emerald. He found himself thrilling to the heavy droplets of rain sinking into his skin, and enjoyed this new sensation of defiance, of cutting loose.

Turning right at the bend by the cemetery, Fred walked towards the house he shared with his mother at the edge of a hazel wood. (All around, the land here had long belonged to the Fosters, and though his mother was one of their number, she'd not flourished as her sister had done and had only the small house.) There was an unfamiliar bounce to Fred's step, and his legs felt sinewy and strong as he strode up the narrow path. Before he entered the gates, he stopped. Something soft and thick was in his mouth, a strange taste, warm and bitter. It wasn't rain but he recognised it. He put his forefinger across his bottom lip and felt the torn flesh, then placed his finger inside his mouth, made a circle of his teeth. He looked up towards the moon, now high over Greenore, and checked his finger in the moonlight. Fred Plunkett did not know what to do. Should he find a way to reverse the transformation? Retrace his steps, go back to the house, find put-upon, tweed-wearing Fred and continue his life as before? Or, now that he had evidently developed a pair of long, smooth *fangs*, together with a ravenous desire for blood, should he forget about that Fred (that husk) once and for all, and obey the latest bizarre instruction of his booming inner voice?

# The Visit

It had been a day of weather: snow and wind, sunshine and rain. Water dripped from the overhanging hedges in the drive and the path was thick with pine needles. Brendan made a mental note to sweep them up once Pat had gone. He stopped before the gates and pulled his trousers up by their creases to check his shoes and thought that maybe he should've worn his boots. He walked on. Pat would make him forget. Pat could make you forget all kinds of silly woes. He glanced over at Coogan's and noticed the stars and stripes flag, still and wet on the pole.

After McCaughey's he looked over at Joy Callan's neat line of laundry crowning her raised side lawn: a small satin-rimmed blanket, black stockings, two blue ballroom gowns, a pair of orange nylon pillowcases. As he approached her house he saw her in the yard, bright and chic in pink slacks and a tight white jumper. She was raking up leaves. He watched her part the dresses then yank the wet leaves into a pile. It made him smile; she might have hung the gowns out after she'd raked, but Joy always seemed to do things differently from others. And anyway, he was glad, because she made the task so mesmerising. He recalled how after her husband had gone she had kept body and soul together by moonlighting, rather originally he thought, as a mushroom picker in Clones. Otherwise, as a relief teacher she had taught both his children in the Friary, though she had not been popular. He waved and wondered would she be at the Square tomorrow. He made a mental note to call in one of these evenings with the picture of Sean's wedding in the paper.

Walking on, his thoughts returned to Pat. He looked forward to seeing him. There would be much talk of the 'great adventures' as Brendan called them, the London times, the days of the Black Lion where he had been manager for nearly a decade and where Pat had been its most notorious barfly. He was proud to think he'd organised some of London's most celebrated lock-ins, booked musicians from Dublin and Doolin and Donegal, and had the likes of David Bailey and Donovan in attendance. Soon he and Pat would be reminiscing about those times, about the dog races at Hackney and White City, the times they'd played poker in Holland Park with Jack Doyle.

He walked up the cobbled lane towards the station. He could see clearly on the cold day the sprawl of the town towards the hills. The trees by the church were draped in ropes of white lights, and a flurry of flags hung from Carroll's Apartments. He was amazed to think that here, in this small dot on the face of the globe, he and Pat would stand together tomorrow evening and see the President of America.

The big station clock said ten to three. He had a few minutes yet to gather his thoughts, stare over at the glass wall of the brewery. He sat outside on the iron seat. The gulls hovered above him, filling the air with their cries. The sweet wort's more pungent today, he thought, as his gaze fixed on the huge copper kettle glistening through the glass. It had been his first job in the brewery to wash the kettle out once the sweet wort had been siphoned off. He would then prepare it for the following morning's shipment of hops and grain. He had spent the best part of five years inside that copper drum, up to his ankles in the remnants of fresh hops, proteins and sticky clumps of caramelised sugar. It had given him time to think; to put into perspective all that had happened in '74.

# The Visit

There was a rumble on the tracks. He turned and saw the sleek green body of the Enterprise stack up like a metallic snake along platform two. He walked over and watched from the ticket office. The doors of the carriages swung open. Women with pull-up trolleys, young men in dishevelled suits, Mrs Little and her daughter, Edel. As the crowds dispersed he saw a ghost, the tall, hulking frame of Pat Coleman standing stock-still on the busy platform. The springy hair was all white, the once firm chest now visibly lax. Brendan watched his friend remove a cigarette from behind his ear, ask a girl for a light, then take three or four concentrated puffs before flicking the stub behind him onto the tracks. Pat's short-sleeved shirt seemed frowsy and unironed; the thick brown arms with their blue tattoos recalled to Brendan Pat's nickname on the sites: Popeye. Popeye Pat had had the strength of ten men, and once, in a drunken rage, Brendan had seen him flatten as many.

He followed Pat's gaze. Up to the pale, elusive sky of the North; out to the striking sweep of the white-capped hills, the green spire of the Protestant church peeping up against them. He began to feel unfamiliar pangs of pride for the town, as if through Pat's languorous impression, he, too, was glimpsing it for the first time. The town was his wife's town, and he had always found it hard to appreciate its people with their wariness, their industrious, practical approach to things. His wife had been right; he *had* put up a resistance. She had accused him often of hiding away in the brewery kettle like a genie. But the friendships he had formed here had been without the closeness of his London bonds. The men he knew from the town were nothing like that famous man on platform two.

He watched Pat follow the crowds as they exited the platform via the wooden ramp. He'd forgotten about Pat's hip. The two of them would seem a right pair with their battered bodies, their war wounds, struggling up the road to the house. They'd have to get a taxi.

At first Pat walked right past him, then doubled back, grabbed his hand with a warm, heavy shake and twirled him round in the air, both feet dangling. The familiar horseplay made Brendan feel warm and young inside. He suggested they take a taxi but Pat said he wanted to walk.

'What d'you think?' Brendan said, turning onto the prosperous-looking road.

'Looks good,' Pat replied in his reedy voice, the rapid Limerick lilt fully intact.

'You know you're to stay as long as you like.'

'Well, I'll see. It'd be something to hear Clinton. After that, I've a whole load to see in Kilkenny and Limerick.'

Pat's sallow, tight face spoke of his abstinence. No beads of sweat across the brow or lip, no dank odour. Gone were the umber circles and the frantic eyes. *If you don't stop drinking you'll die*, Brendan had said quietly into Pat's ear on his last visit to Guy's. Pat had often said it was those words together with his friend's insistence he *could* quit that had saved his life.

Past the Texaco garage, Pat stopped to watch Nick O'Hare sort through a trailer of wicker goods. 'That's Nick,' said Brendan. 'Used to be a coach with the town's football team, now runs a type of yoga place in that house.' Pat seemed enthralled by Nick's wares. There were fusions of weave and dried flowers, shopping baskets with long handles, knee-high linen boxes stained in a dark cinnabar, as well as a small Lloyd Loom-style chair. Bowls of felt sunflowers, papier-mâché apples and grapes littered the tarmac drive. Pat went up to the brass sign on the pillar and mouthed the words engraved on it: *Vipassana Centre*.

'How are ya?' Pat shouted over to Nick, who was down on his hunkers editing strands of grass from the baskets.

'Well, Brendan,' Nick replied, thinking it had been Brendan who had hollered. 'I'm making these for the President. I'll bring one up to you.'

'Do,' Brendan replied, waving, and carried on hurriedly, hoping Pat would take the hint and move on with him.

# The Visit

'D'you ever go in there?' Pat asked.

'Jesus, no.' Brendan replied.

'I'd love one of those baskets for Fidelma.'

'Haven't I a dozen in the garage?' Brendan said.

Walking on, he tried to turn the conversation towards London and the Black Lion. He asked Pat if he'd heard anything from the old gang, from Mocky Joe in particular. Mocky Joe's success at cards had enabled him to live in London for over a decade without working. One night, weeks before Brendan had left London, the flame-haired Mocky Joe had been picked up under the Prevention of Terrorism Act and held. Of all the men he and Pat had known that had been stopped under the Sus laws or questioned under the PTA Mocky Joe was the only one the police had ever charged. He'd served twelve years. At first Pat seemed to have no recollection of him, but eventually put a face to the nickname. 'The poor fucker,' Pat said, 'I went to see him and he didn't know me at all.' Then Brendan thought of the time of his own arrest, the long night of questioning in Harrow Road police station, and of the lie he had told there.

Pat stopped to look over the bridge. 'The kids used to walk all the way along that one time, trying to catch frogs,' Brendan said, realising he had never himself walked the banks of the narrow river. The sedge rustled below where they looked and an ochre-coloured frog leaped out, springing from one clump to the next along the shallow rim of the water. He saw that Pat was bewitched by the frog, its golden skin pulsating like a loud gold watch; it seemed alien, larger than the small green specimens the kids had once brought from the banks. They watched the bright interloper go on with the river, thinning out towards Toberona and Castletown. Though it seemed hard for him to get the memories out of Pat, Brendan looked forward to the chats they were yet to have about all the great adventures.

Closer to home, Pat wanted to stop off at Cheever's. Brendan reluctantly followed Pat into the store, which was festooned on the outside with green and white bunting. A flag with WELCOME BILL stencilled on it protruded from the wall.

'That's a bitter day, Brendan,' Mrs Cheever said as she sorted through the newspapers. Brendan nodded then guided Pat towards the freezer at the back of the shop.

'But you have it lovely and warm in here, missus,' Pat shouted over to the stout woman. Brendan saw Mrs Cheever look up at them and move a fallen strand of hair away from her face, her fingers black with newsprint.

'I'm with him. Over from London for the visit,' Pat said.

'Very pleased to meet you,' Mrs Cheever replied, in her singsong voice. She walked over and put a copy of *The Democrat* under Brendan's arm.

'Here. The son's wedding is in that. Have another for safe-keeping.'

Pat picked out a pack of Galtee cheese, some rashers, a half-pound of lard, a sliced white batch-loaf, a copy of *Ireland's Own* and Kimberly biscuits. In the basket they looked like something from a 1950s tourist brochure, the type of provisions Brendan himself had bought years ago in Mandy's in Willesden when he was homesick.

'Pat, you're my guest. You're to spend nothing.'

'Always pay my way, you know that,' Pat insisted.

By Callan's Brendan heard harp music and stopped. It sounded loud and sad. He saw Joy seated at the table, staring stiffly into a hand-mirror. He saw her catch sight of him, then Pat, who was examining her winter flowers. He wanted to call out but she dashed from the room. He sensed they had stumbled upon a private moment, a low. His pace quickened. When he stopped he heard Pat laughing behind him.

'Now there's a woman in need of cheering up.'

'Can't tell you the times I've wanted to call in to her but never do.'

'You have to get yourself a reason, man.'

# The Visit

'She likes dancing, I drag my left leg. All I can think of is bringing things, flowers maybe.'

'All good, but it's not a reason. Ask her to come to Clinton with us.'

It had not even occurred to him to ask Joy Callan to go to the Square with them. One evening in Cheever's he'd spoken to her about the President's visit and had been impressed by her enthusiasm, by her belief that the visit would act as some kind of salve for what the town had been through in the last three decades.

'This is it,' Brendan said, opening the turquoise gates to the house. Pat gasped at the long, shrub-filled lawns. Brendan watched his friend hobble back to the gates, rest his hands on his hips and look up and down the bunting-covered road. Blue cigarette smoke swirled around Pat's head like a halo.

'How in the name of God do you manage?' Pat said, retreating towards him.

'I have a home-help. Her husband comes up, does the lawn in summer.'

'Good job you have such friends and neighbours.'

Brendan stopped. Surely Pat had seen how preoccupied and standoffish the people here were, and how different he was from them. Surely Pat had observed this.

'The people of this town never liked me, Pat. Nor me them. There's been no friends for me like the London ones,' Brendan said.

'Could have fooled me,' Pat replied, darting towards the woody fuchsia hedge. He broke a piece off, smelled the tiny buds. Shepherding him into the house, Brendan put Pat's assessment of his neighbours and friends aside. After all, what did Pat know?

Later, Pat suggested they bring their tea out onto the porch. Brendan followed Pat out with the teapot and an ashtray. The mauve dusk had begun to blacken. Small birds thronged in the elder bushes. Occasionally, passers-by saw them from the glow of the street-lamp and waved. He was determined to get Pat talking.

'Do you not remember all that carry on in Maida Vale in '74?' he said at length. Pat shook his head, hurled the end of his tea into the grass.

'You don't remember the police bulldozing into me, asking me about you?'

'No.'

'Came ramstaming into our digs in the middle of the night, said they wanted to question me. Took me to Harrow Road station, said someone the spit of you killed an off-duty soldier in Maida Vale. I said – well, ya know what I said. That you were with me up in White City.'

'I don't remember much of that time at all, Brendan, tell ya the truth.'

Pat seemed uneasy. Perhaps he should not have brought the incident up, but all evening Pat's memory had been hazy. He'd wanted to jolt Pat into remembering. Especially since the lie he had told had cost him so much: a precipitous move from London to this hardnosed border town, a move he hadn't wanted to make, had regretted all the years since.

He brought the cups inside. From the kitchen he could see Pat glaring meditatively out into the greeny-black of the garden, his hands cupped. It had been impossible to draw him back to the days of the Black Lion. Pat had just wanted to look out into the night and talk about the barely discernable shrubs: the mahonias, hebes, winter sweet. Surely this white-haired man with his apparent amnesia and love of plants was not the same Pat. Popeye Pat, who'd had the strength of a bear and may or may not have killed a man in a nightclub in Maida Vale. It dawned on Brendan then, that it had all changed, his London: the lads, the infamous Black Lion lock-ins, the dramas with the PTA. At nine, Pat said he was ready for bed, that abstinence had made a lark out of him.

At around five Brendan thought he heard Pat stir. When he

got up, the blinds had been raised, the curtains pulled. December glowed in the empty kitchen. He saw a folded note and a crisp twenty Euro bill under a cup on the table. He picked up the note. Pat's heavy spidery scrawl had almost punctured the page. He scanned it quickly. Something about Pat heading off to see his wife's people in Kilkenny, and that he would call in again next week. The note continued: *Once you said I'd die if I didn't stop drinking. You said you knew I could do it. You saw the best in me and it gave me hope to go on. Now, for god's sake man, would you ever give that town a chance. And give my regards to Bill and Hillary.*

Brendan opened the door to the backyard. The smell of sweet wort filled the room. He realised how familiar that smell was, how he'd smelled it daily now for almost twenty-five years. Perhaps, whilst he wasn't looking, he had entered the tapestry of this place after all. Trembling, he picked up the phone to ask Joy Callan if she would walk with him later to the Market Square to see the President.

# The Tribe

The American Dream has run out of gas. The car has stopped.
It no longer supplies the world with its images, its dreams, its
fantasies. It's over. It supplies the world with its nightmares
now: the Kennedy assassination, Watergate, Vietnam.

*J.G. BALLARD*

The images that came up on the screen were of a cold, forested
environment. Beside me the lake was iced over and wide as a
sea. There were trees all around frozen ponds and up and
down mountainsides. I wondered if there was human life here
at all. Nothing stirred outside, except for the unmistakable
shape of an owl flying across the almost-full moon. I wrapped
up in my boots and Gore-Tex and kept my gun close. Into a
compartment of my backpack I placed another, more lethal
gun and clasped the bag to my front. I secured my mask and
hood then exited the POD (shorthand for the small machine
that had brought me here, with its state-of-the-art Personal
Odyssey Drive® system).

Outside, it was freezing. I'd never known cold like it. Not even
on the coldest days in New York. In fact, it was not like any cold
I'd ever experienced on the earth, anywhere (including the
Northwest Territories where I had prepared for this trip). Yet it
was so clean, so *newly* clean. I could distinctly smell pine, and

the ice had a fragrant quality, close to mint. I knew that the tundra that covered the earth at this time had beneath it a multitude of flowers and plants, and it was as if the air now was full of the possibility of them. The season, of course, was spring.

I had begun to ascend the mountain when I saw what appeared to be a light. At first I thought my eyes were playing tricks on me. (I wasn't hungry but I was tired and had considered returning to the POD, though it would have been dawn before I got there.) I thought perhaps the moon reflected off the snow, but the light was orange. Within a few steps I saw that a fire burned just beyond a redwood copse. (The snow on the trees' laden branches made the copse seem like some outlandish installation, like those I'd seen years before in galleries in the Village.) My first instinct was to rush towards it. It had to signify human life – no animal as far as we knew had learned how to make fire. But what kind of beings had made this one? And what would they make of me? If they were the beings we sought, that I had hoped to find here, then could they *speak*? (We had presumed, perhaps conservatively, that I might encounter at best a protolanguage, and not, at this point, actual lexical structure.) I suddenly became afraid of what I might find, though I could feel the gun against my thigh, and it felt warm, as all security is warm, and that I was so quick to think of the weapons I'd brought with me gave me quite a jolt.

I gathered myself and tried to remember my purpose here. I checked that the vial was where I had packed it. It was. Cold and deadly as the modernity that had made it.

*

I saw them sitting around the fire, their backs against a circle of high stones. Some of their young ran from caves and were followed by females who evidently disapproved of them out in the cold air. I could smell something roasting on the fire and saw within the flames a long slim-headed beast. Suddenly, the group rose to their feet. They began to make sounds out of the back of their throats which reverberated throughout the hills. The sounds seemed to pass from being to being in a perfect choreography of polyrhythms; it was quite like what I'd heard of Flamenco music. They were covered from head to toe in taupe, grey and dark-red furs, which looked to be the pelts of rabbits, some kind of arctic-like fox, and bears. The group sang its song to the fire, to the beast roasting on the spit, and to the moon and icy expanse – and though I could not understand a word (in so far as their song was composed of words), I felt, somehow, that this was a song of praise, perhaps, even, of welcoming the spring.

After a while, one of the older males loosened the beast from the two thin poles it hung from and set it down on a long flat slab. He cut furiously into it with a hand-axe made of what seemed in the moonlight to be quartz or river-flint. He made many piles of meat, and only when he gestured did the group gather around the slab to eat. They were talking. The sound was unmistakable: laughter, grunts, jesting, the aural characteristics of human engagement, all the sounds that one might hear in any modern crowd. These hominids were clearly enjoying their food. It was then I realised that other than the energy biscuits and apples in my backpack, I'd no further supplies until I returned to the POD. The POD itself had enough food for a few more days of my explorations here; the rest held in reserve for the journey home (if I would, indeed, return). I slowly unclasped the pack and squatted down beside it. I was so hungry I devoured two of the three biscuits and washed them down with a small bottle of chemical-tasting water.

Within a few minutes I could hear a commotion. I stood up and saw a fight break out between two males, between them, a young female clinging tightly to a rock. The smaller of the two males was eventually trounced by the other and stole off like a honey badger into the woods. The tall, rangier male brought the female towards two older females who laughed as they walked her back to the caves. Quickly, the peace returned. After the meal, the taller male quenched the fire and moved the stragglers along. There was something civilised and quite authoritative, I thought, about this creature hanging back to tidy up the remains of his tribe's revels.

As I would need daylight in order to proceed with my task, I decided to remain where I was. Below me nothing stirred except three or four brindled dogs that looked like small wolves gathering in the centre of the valley to finish off the meat. There seemed also to be a constant rumbling sound, which I supposed was a distant ice storm (perhaps signifying some kind of metamorphic activity in the region). It was as I found an over-leaning bank of earth, under which I planned to sleep, that I heard the other sound. It was terrible and gurgling and instantly recognisable. I looked down and saw that the tall authoritative tribe-member stood in the empty valley below, a pole pierced through his chest, pinning him to the white earth. The others began to emerge from their caves and the sides of the valley. The young female and the group she had been with ran to him. They screamed and cried and pulled the pole from the tall male, at which he dropped to the ground. I heard a sound, if not an actual word, repeated again and again by one of the older females. 'Orvey! Orvey! Orvey!' she seemed to cry, as she continually tried to wake him. And I knew, somewhere in the depths of my being, that the sound – for how could I call it a word when I was yet to be convinced that this tribe was in possession of what could feasibly be called language? – meant: *child*.

*

My sleep had been fitful. My dreams full of images from my past: old friends, many already dead, the bustle of the city (before the Hudson disaster), nights at the theatre, candlelit dinners. All of it punctuated by the repeating image of the male skewered to the ice. I had reached for my gun a dozen times, and held my backpack close throughout the night. I deduced that what had seemed, at first, to be a harmonious scene from where I was perched had probably been some sort of projection of mine. Perhaps I had wanted to be surprised by the life I'd found here; had imagined I'd stumbled onto an icy Eden of sorts. But the night had ended as it does in any town or city in any country in the modern world, where, in my time, the murder of a man over nothing more than a piece of meat was a pretty common occurrence. I don't know why I was so surprised or saddened. What did I care about this group – with their backs to their high protective stones? I had not come here to care – not about this tribe anyway. Still, I could not get the older female's cry, or the younger female's attempts to shake the male alive, out of my mind. The sounds and images of the night weighed against any kind of meaningful sleep. These, together with the thought that nagged at the back of my mind, that the heavy-set, wilder male, who was probably the cause of the tall male's death, had not emerged onto the scene – and was now, no doubt, loose somewhere in the woods, which, in the dawn light, seemed to me to be comprised of a variety of pines, oak, hazel and pistachio.

I unscrewed the lid of my coffee flask and, though the remains were cold, I drank the liquid down. As I now had the day, and therefore the requisite presence of UV, I decided that this was as good a time as any: I would open the vial, release its contents then immediately return to the POD, hopefully without being intercepted by any member of this group, or others, though it hardly mattered, I reasoned, if I was. All the years of planning, the years put into the invention of and enactments with the POD, the meetings with world experts, all our predictions and conclusions on the modern world's predicament – that humankind had brought its own planet to the brink of destruction – would culminate in this single act. (One release and it was done. The earth would be free of us. There would be no 'man'. These early Homo sapiens would be wiped out. Whatever had brought about their leap in evolution, most likely the receding of the ice, would never again matter to archaeologists because there would *be* no archaeologists, no humans, no such concept, even, as evolution as consciousness itself would not exist.) I readied myself.

The sun rose magnificently. A hawk-like bird flew overhead. I had observed it come and go a few times and presumed it came for the remains of the meat in the valley. It was in tracing the bird's slow circular path that I noticed the intense brightness of the sky. It had so little sea to reflect off that it was as white as the ice beneath it, and the pale light dazzled my eyes. All the summits were the same giddying white, barely discernable from the vast opalescence above, except that here and there were thin lines of green, which were the trees. The winds had eased by morning, and the air was again full of the sweet minty smell. In this new light I could see also that horses ran wild from one end of a further-off valley to the other. A small, thickset species, mostly piebald, a couple of tans. But nothing else stirred in the valley of the tribe. The tall male's body had been removed, and I could not help but wonder what way the group would mark this, if at all. I cleared up my things. As I made a crude attempt to clean my teeth in the new snow, I saw a female walking with a couple of pitchers – adapted from gourds of some description – in my direction. I quickly leaned in against the bank of cold earth. She climbed only a short way up then was gone from view. I heard splash sounds. I edged closer, not far from where she was, just a ledge or two above her on the mountainside, and the thunderous sound I'd heard the night before, that I'd supposed was a nearby ice storm, was, I realised now, a river, a waterfall, white and heavy with ice.

As the female left the gushing river, I heard activity once more in the valley. I looked down and saw a crowd gathering. One of the group's elders led a small dappled-grey horse, tethered to what appeared to be a rope made from plaited grass. He brought the horse to the cave where the females had interred the tall male's body. Two males carried the corpse, placed it across the horse and fastened it to the horse's belly with more of the grassy rope. The elder yanked the horse and slowly walked it in the direction of a lower valley, and the small crowd followed as if in a funeral procession. Well, it was a funeral procession. What had I expected? We knew that many ages of hominids had held funerals of sorts; but this was so easy to recognise, so close to my own experience of funerals, i.e. following the dead to some place of rest, that, again, I found myself quite stirred by this group. Just as I watched the last of them leave their circle of caves and stones (the female who had drawn the water, children with dogs), intending then to turn to the vial, I heard something rustle behind me. I did not have time to see what thing or beast it was, for a jagged, coruscating piece of quartz flashed slantwards across my eyes. I felt the warm trickle of blood fall to my tongue and everything went black.

*

When I awoke I saw that I was inside a cave. The ceiling and walls were lined with leaves, straw and wood. In the gaps I could see a thick mud, a kind of adobe. Skins of various animals hung from the walls, together with an assortment of gourds (some of which seemed to be dyed or painted), and many bunches of pungent herbs and dried flowers. I could hear a fire crackling, the slow patter of the snow. I moved my head towards my body and saw that I lay on a bed of pelts – bear, goat, fox. Across me was a large fur – soft – perhaps from a big cat or bear. I went to put my hand to my face and saw that both my wrists were tied to pieces of flint impaled into the ground. I raised my head and saw the flickers of a fire at the place I had seen the beast roasting.

I was naked under the furs. Some ointment with a herby, sage smell was on my forehead and eye. I reeked of it. As the fire outside spasmodically lit up the cave, I saw to my right a stone mortar where I supposed the herby ointment had been prepared. I suddenly thought of my backpack. I looked around as much as I was able but could not see it. I began to fret. Over and over the same thought: what if someone, one of these beings, had opened the bag and found the vial. Of course, it occurred to me then that if that were the case my work here would be done: the virus would be released and within forty-eight hours this tribe and I, and eventually all the tribes of the earth, would perish (though the plants and animals would survive). This was all well and good except that I had not yet fully decided upon certain things – whether to return if I could, how to release the virus exactly, and when. So that the disappearance of the bag and the vial now did not at all strike me as convenient. I began to panic. I felt shame. Shame that they would intercept such a poison, and not when I intended. And that I should feel such things now also began to trouble me.

I seemed to be raving, could feel myself flailing about. I saw shadows move inside the cave and huddled figures gather at the mouth of the entrance. Something rustled constantly inside. It sounded at times like the fluttering of wings. And once, I thought I saw the shadow of a winged demon on the wall. Time seemed to converge into one interminable sweat. I awoke and slept, awoke and slept. One night I heard birdsong – a full and haunting sound. It caused a momentary break in my fever as I was suddenly brought back to a happier, more certain time. I recognised the song from recordings I'd once listened to, for this species of bird had been wiped out long before my time: it was the strange and splenitive song of nightingales.

A cool hand pressed down on my forehead, a cold, wet cloth placed on my neck. I looked up and saw the young female the taller of the two males had been trying to protect that first night. She went to the mortar, crushed and pounded herbs with a pebble; she mixed the powder with water and warmed it with her breath. After spreading the mixture on my forehead, she lifted my head and squeezed a liquid from a sponge into my mouth. It tasted sweet; like a diluted honey or sap. I saw that her limbs were long and sallow, her hair dark and plaited, her eyes, green. I dozed slowly off to sleep and had no thought of the whereabouts of my backpack or the vial. For some inexplicable reason I thought only of my mother.

★

What seemed like a few hours later, though it may have been days or even weeks, I was awakened by the creature. I could hear its light, erratic walk across stones and implements within the cave. When it squawked and flapped its wings I was relieved, glad at least that it wasn't a wolf or worse. It was tawny with some white through its chest, and stared with pewter-coloured eyes straight at me. It seemed tame enough. The female who had nursed me sat in a corner huddled up under fur. She had fallen asleep, and not even the loud cry of the bird had woken her. It was then I saw my clothes – my jacket and trousers, on top of which seemed to rest my gun, lying up against where she slept. I wondered where the other gun had gone, and hoped it was still inside the backpack – wherever that was. I struggled against the two shards of flint fixing my arms to the earth. I felt stronger than the previous time I'd awoken and, bending my neck towards my right wrist, bit myself free and untangled my other bind – which was a mixture of wool and grass, and very tough.

It was freezing outside the furs and my thoughts raced. I crept to the pile of my things. My neck and shoulders ached, though there was a numbness in the upper-left part of my torso, which, I deduced, was as a result of the herbs the female had applied. In two or three swift movements I retrieved the pile without waking her. I quietly dragged on my shirt and trousers. I found my boots close to the furs where I'd lain and put these on. Finally, as I went to put on my jacket, the bird, which I saw now was a hawk by its size and imperial poise, flew to the corner where the female slept. It rested on her shoulder and eyed me. Suddenly, the female dived out of the corner and I was thrown back. She pointed a long (and rather sharp-looking) piece of rock straight at me. She indicated to sit back on the bed, which I did, then picked up the one thing I had not yet taken up from the furs. I whispered, forcefully: 'please, no!' She laughed and, seeing my alarm at the sight of the gun in her hand, passed it from one hand to the other then tried to goad me by swinging it close to my face. I repeated: 'please, please, no.' I immediately saw that she was not young but an adult of perhaps twenty or twenty-five years. I kept my silence and made no further attempt to leave. Evidently puzzled by my new calm, she thrust the gun onto me and sat back. I was shocked, though damned glad, too, that the gun had not fired in the ruckus. I soon saw why: somehow the barrel and nose had been beaten down, rendering the piece useless. My heart sank as I realised I was now among these beings without a weapon (at least until I could find my bag). I tucked the battered gun into my pocket. As I zipped up my jacket the female gasped, evidently transfixed by the two pieces of fabric becoming conjoined. She came towards me but I pushed her aside, not wanting to leave the cave gunless *and* with a broken zip (and so risk dying of the cold). I shooed her as if she were a small animal and she backed off into her furs, afraid. With enormous effort, I got to the mouth of the cave, moved aside the large pelt that covered it. The moon was pear-coloured and full, the sky clear and immense with stars. I felt my head swoon. A new, stronger sweat broke, and I felt as hollow as the gourds that hung from the ceiling and walls of the cave. Then a sudden coil of hunger in my lower legs, and I fell over, weakly, back onto the bed of furs.

\*

# The Tribe

At first she fed me with crushed pistachios and a kind of sweet date. Later, she gave me flat, unleavened bread made from a cereal, perhaps wild wheat. As I gained strength there was meat – bitter, rough, gamey. As soon as I could move she bade me sit outside my dark asylum each day to take in the light and air. From here I would watch the tribe. Often I would see groups of males return with dead beasts; usually deer, boar, a bear once, two seals. And I remembered that the wide lake, huge as a sea, was not far away, maybe nine or ten miles east. I kept the backpack and the vial to the fore of my mind. That I and the others were still alive was a sign at least that the vial had not been found and tampered with, and was probably under several inches of snow somewhere. But where?

*

Sitting outside the cave, as weak as I was I quickly came to consider that perhaps we, my peers and I, had been wrong in our studies of these early Homo sapiens. They were as graceful as any man or woman I knew. Their facial bone-structure was wider than my own, and though the terrain I had arrived in was an ice-mass which, by my time, would become the hot and arid Middle East, they resembled, especially around the eyes, Inuits, or some tribe from the North, from Lapland perhaps. There were times I would look out at this tribe of snow-dwellers and consider that I was among a tribe very close in ways and appearance to my own. As they would pass, the tribes-people would acknowledge me, as if they were aware of how I'd come to be there. I did not see again the short, thickset male I'd seen fight with the tall male who, I now believed, had been my nurse's brother, though I could not be sure of this. (It was just that the older female who'd cried that first night seemed to be my nurse's mother by her absolute likeness and attention to me.) She (the older female) would work close by me as I sat snug in my bearskin outside the cave (usually scanning the sky for birds and wondering about migratory patterns), keeping her eyes on me like a sentinel as her quick hands skinned some animal, the entrails of which would gush a carmine-coloured river across the white snow. There were many females in the area of the valley in which I was domiciled, including my nurse, (though the males kept close account of my convalesence). Each day the women would comb down pelts, and from these make clothes and the caves' furnishings.

I was taken one day from my study of the sky above the valley when the younger female pressed firmly on my shoulder, as if urgently seeking my attention. One of the elders stood beside her, his face markedly wizened. He stared down at me with bright, suspicious eyes. He touched my head, examined the healing gash. I did not react or resist for I was well aware of my weakness, that my limbs were heavy and thin. The elder pulled my head from side to side, and somehow I knew he meant me no harm. He turned to the female and spoke. It was some miracle of language*, as fluent as my own. We had supposed language

---

* = In the late twentieth century the Nicaraguan government established the country's first drive to educate the deaf. A school was set up, and within a short time, over 400 deaf children were in attendance. However, the government could not afford to staff the school with trained sign-language teachers, so, instead of conventional signing the children were taught rudimentary Spanish, lip-reading and more everyday gestures such as finger-spelling and counting. Needless to say, the program was not a success. Though, within a few years an amazing thing happened. The children, left to communicate with each other, had begun to develop a sort of pidgin language (sign and vocal). Whatever they had learned from their teachers they would build on, developing their own combinations and permutations of the signs and words they had been taught. The teachers also observed that the younger children in particular absorbed the new pidgin so that it began to spread amongst this group (essentially, a controlled group) like wildfire in a dry forest. Researchers were invited to observe. The Nicaraguan government was alerted and in a few years the school became something of a scientific sensation. For it had accidentally become a laboratory for the study of the origin of language. An area of science, which, over the centuries, had caused endless debate, where no two scholars could agree and no theories were alike, to the extent that in 1866 the Linguistic Society of Paris thereafter banned debates on the subject, the effect of

the last of the major transitions towards modern man, and here it was, passing between these two primitive beings, perfectly musical and structured. It was as far as could be from the sound of apes and chimps (with their unorganised squeals and cries), and was rich and detailed, rather like the sound of Korean or Japanese with similar drawls and drags and, to my English-attuned ear, had irregular silences. It seemed to be a language that was rarely resorted to (each time I would hear them speak it I would be thrown by its strangeness and would be reminded of something William Burroughs had once said, that 'language is a virus from outer space'). For it was as if this tribe preferred physical action, as I myself had witnessed here. But this was different. The female and elder were trying to explain something to each other and, I realised, to me. (I could not help but feel sad that whatever language they spoke, it was lost now to my world, like an unheard symphony or story.) 'Mayga,' the elder said to me, over and over, while pointing to my gashed skull. He walked in front of me carrying a stick, and stabbed it into the snow. He

---

which set the solving of this mystery back hundreds of years. Research disseminated from the Nicaraguan Deaf School 'experiment' suggested to later scholars that language had most likely developed among Homo sapiens who were 'contained', settled, where trust could be developed and words held real and consistent currency. This skill – as opposed to mere vocalisation (which had originated with Homo ergaster) and genetic *propensity* to language, suggested by the presence in more recent hominids of the Foxp2 gene, occurred, it seemed, only when humans lived as a *tribe*. Scholars concurred at last that language was the last aspect of 'modern man' to develop because it was the most mysterious: the inside of a person exposed completely to another in sound and expression, and for H. sapiens to do this at all, there would need to have been around them a degree of peacefulness and trust. Otherwise, hominids may well have had to do with an unorganised system of ape-like squeals, or, perhaps, even a strange kind of silence. The tribe I was now observing had clearly developed real lexical structure, which I could not understand per se, but, as the days went by, I could, if I tried hard enough, follow its subject-verb-object word order. Watching the tribe 'speak' in this way, I wanted to scream down the funnel of time, to tell my own world that they had not taken care of what had been so beautifully, perhaps even randomly, born, and that had early H. sapiens been more nomadic (as earlier hominids had been) may never even have happened.

drew a circle, and within it an elementary map of the valley. Outside the circle he drew a shape, as common in my world as a symbol of evil and danger as it seemed to be in his. It was the body of a man with a maze of horns – antlers – on his head. He went from my head to the figure in the snow. His message was clear: someone was outside the tribe, and this someone had gashed my head open. Quite likely the squat figure I had seen kill the tall male that first night.

*

I began to gain weight and take walks to build up my strength, sometimes to the edge of the valley. This would also give me time to go over in my mind who I was and why I was here at all: I'd been elected to my task by my peers, the modern world's leading scientists – ecologists, paleontologists, biologists, environmentalists. In the end, the premise for our decision (which we, as a group, had made unilaterally, without the consent of corporations and governments) had been simple. By 2320 the earth's population had swelled to over thirty billion. Apart from polar regions, most rural areas had been urbanised. The world was dying from man's relentless anthropocentricity, and our conclusion was that if the modern world must die then best it not be born at all. Extinction at this point of the tribe's development would mean that a far lesser number of humans would perish, by some billions. (Because those billions would not have been born.) And with the combined invention of the virus* and the Personal Odyssey Drive® system, we had finally found a way to ensure the *earth* would survive. (Whereas, in my time, we were taking the earth

---

* = Developed in Milan University by a brilliant team who had arrived at an intense synthetic compression of the common cold virus, a virulent mutation with the power to rapidly corrupt the human immune system. The virus had been tested in freezing conditions, at around -40°C, proving itself ideally resilient and fit for purpose.

with us.) The task had fallen to me to come back to the snow and ice from which mankind had emerged, to Qal'at Jarmo, on the edge of the Fertile Crescent, from where we had begun our journey towards the destroyed planet I'd left behind. In these very mountains, modern archaeologists had found advanced implements – sickles, cutters. The tribes at Jarmo were considered the first sustained settlements on earth. Around them other tribes would watch and develop. Our hope was that from Jarmo the virus would circulate as coldly and quickly as an ice stream, with eventual global impact.

Had I doubts about the project? None. I had watched the most sophisticated societies on the modern earth implode. I'd visited extinguished cities as my forbears had visited Pompeii, walked their silent streets. (I'd seen the Hudson myself, the morning of the New Jersey chemical spill, had travelled by helicopter to see it from the air: a huge film of dead fish had covered the entire surface of the water so that it appeared like a vast bright Jello, stiff and unmoving.) As important animal species began to die out, it did not take my peers and I long to work out what would happen next: catastrophe, not just for humans but for the whole earth. And there was another, rather unpalatable, realisation: that we as a species were not unlike a virus ourselves in our modus operandi, one that could not conceive of its own toxicity. We believed we were divine, which was our trick; how we convinced ourselves to continue. In my age we had at last seen through to that trick. Therefore, throughout my trip I had been completely *convinced* of my task. I had seen the bee species die out from complex mites and plagues; observed with my own eyes the last of the Pine Island Glacier turn to meltwater. The world had not heeded the warnings of previous generations and was about to expire. I knew what needed to be done, and like some kind of Prometheus in reverse, I was prepared to do it.

But I was a suicide bomber without a bomb: I needed to find the vial. I had begun to wish that I'd shaken the virus loose when

I'd had the chance. If the earth was to have a future, I knew I had to do what I'd come to do, and soon: destroy this tribe and the tribes of the earth before Homo sapiens made their speedy and terrific leap forwards, which they were about to do. Soon, the tundra would leave much of the earth, now a great glacial plain. In a thousand years hence the New Stone Age would begin here and in Egypt. In less than four thousand years Mesopotamia would give rise to numerous towns and cities, Newgrange would welcome the winter solstice, Stonehenge would be erected and, soon after, the Pyramids would be built. Then the Chaldeans would map the skies. And all that came after would furiously devour the planet. Once I had cast the contents of the vial into the day, the earth would survive, though mankind would not.

I had lost time. Those I had left behind in the world would see it continue its rapid descent into a new dark age, and they would wonder why I had not put an end to it all; why they could not close their eyes on the devastated world and wake as atoms and molecules in the morning. Now they would awaken as they had always done, my beloved mother, those friends of mine – good people, scientists, lab technicians, cleaners, actors, poets. It had become obvious to them and me that hope had died for human beings, that the most dignified thing we could do was let the earth have the earth and exit gracefully, and that it would have been better for the planet if modern man had not been born, had not developed at all. Yet here I was, weak and doubtful in an ancient valley; my days spent watching young birds make their first flights across the spring sky. I could, if I tried hard enough, forget that the modern world awaited its ending, its swift unbirthing. I could. But I would not.

*

The air was milder than it had been, and across all the mountains I saw that the snow had melted in places. Patches of saffron-coloured gorse began to emerge across the hills.

# The Tribe

I called the younger female Dara. It sounded like the name I'd heard others in the valley call her. It seemed to suit her. Whenever I would wander away from the cave she would emerge from her own and watch me, her eyes beaming with pride in my growing strength. Once, catching me following the hawk's lofty movements, I thought she might have seen something of my plans to leave the valley (one way or another). She called to the bird with pursed lips; a loud, shrill sound. The hawk was her own bird and answered her immediately, landing on her outstretched arm. She brought it to me. The bird's speckled feathers heaved and vibrated as it beheld me with a familiarity that made me feel strange – as if I belonged here in some way.

A short while after the day of the snow-drawing, Dara urged me to walk with her into the mountains. We climbed slowly. As the air thinned, my legs felt weak and we rested on top of a hill. Below us I could see tribe members hunting, some gathered wood or plants, and the valley seemed to me as busy as any modern town. I saw, too, that where upland fields had begun to thaw, wild grain grew in abundance. Also emmer and einkorn and a primitive kind of barley. Goats and their kids roamed freely around the summits, and I realised that these animals were not yet farmed – merely killed from time to time for meat, or occasionally milked. This tribe was just at the beginning of its farming genesis; they took only what they needed. They buried their dead, danced and sang, had a primitive kind of art – but had not yet been so numerous in number that they would turn to the earth and command it to feed them. This had not yet happened. And with the (dark) plans I had for this place, I was loath to assist them with any kind of encouragement or instruction in animal husbandry.

We walked further into the mountains. The range was long and extended southwards for hundreds of miles, as far as the landmass known in the modern age as Iran. Dara let the hawk fly off and it circled above us making cackling sounds. She had a wide smile, and clearly saw the land she looked upon as precious and beautiful. She seemed to alter up here, became more contemplative and private, and this surprised me as I had not expected a break, a gradation, in the emotions of this tribe. I had already seen their pain and grief – why should I be surprised at this female's sense of repose? She caught my look, a strange mixture, I suppose, of surprise and admiration. (I could feel everything inside me opening up, like a ripening fruit. I was, bizarrely, coming alive in this place. In this place that was the cold, less-developed past, filled with a savage but also more innocent, child-like people, with their stones and fires and fur and herbs, and, I realised, feeling dead – as my world had more latterly caused me to feel – had had its uses. Now was not a good time for my heart, my – for the sake of argument – 'soul' to open, to thaw: because whenever I would find the vial I planned to use it.)

Our happy excursions into the mountains did not, however, last. One late-spring morning, the hawk having left us for its own fun and privacy, we heard below us in the valley an explosion of cries. Dara clung to me and I dragged her, weak as I was, to the ground. I gestured to her to be quiet as I peered over the bank. A group of about twenty males with blue and ochre markings on their faces and pelts, wielding axes and what looked like spears made from sturdy lengths of pinewood, had made their way down the mountainside. At the helm was a familiar figure: the short squat male, adorned now in beads, and necklaces of bones and teeth. There were antlers on his head. He was the male I'd seen the night I'd first arrived, and clearly the figure from the snow-drawing and, I realised, probably the same male who had gashed my head open. He led his group of marauders into the valley. We watched as the snow below us turned all shades of crimson. The antlered male searched where the women were. He looked perhaps for me, perhaps for Dara, whom he had fought over that first night. Some of the males threw stones – violently – in all directions. Then Dara let out an aching, breathless cry, as a burst of long, speckled feathers floated on the air, and the body of her hawk fell to the valley floor with a low but devastating thud.

*

Eventually, the invaders began to leave in the direction from which they came. I looked down to see nine or ten bodies lying scattered on the snow. I could feel Dara wriggle from my grasp and dart for the top of the ditch. When I pulled her down she began to cry and I urged her to be still. The floor of the ditch was soft and I saw that an oily, dark-red substance trickled underfoot. Even in the middle of all this mayhem, the environmentalist in me observed that the earth here was rich in fuel, and that this tribe had thankfully not yet learned to burn it. As I bent down to touch the resinous substance, I made my next extraordinary discovery: my backpack. I dragged it from its oily burrow and checked inside: the vial was still in the flask, and still inside its compartment was my gun – wet, but very much intact.

As members of the tribe began to return to the valley, howls of grief, loss, confusion echoed throughout the hills. Such sounds might have hailed from any modern war-scene: women and men screaming, long confusing silences, inappropriate laughter from children and the mad. As we approached, we saw that Dara's mother lay with the dead. Dara ran and flung herself down onto the bloody heap. More than ever, I could see the need to complete my mission here; our violent story had already begun. If there had ever been an Eden-like time on this earth, I was convinced it was not now and not here. Perhaps such a time had never existed on earth, at least not when hominids had been on it. It was clear that I needed to complete my task. I resolved to turn back and climb to the top of the mountain and release there the contents of the vial into the air. The day was bright and windy. The most perfect day on which to have found my backpack (and the vial). But I did not turn back.

The males of the tribe were gathering. They were pointing to the hills opposite. Dara was cradling her dead mother and hawk, her salty tears such that the ice around her had begun to melt. The males collected numerous long sticks procured from oak and pistachio trees, which they now flaked and made sharp. I thought they looked pathetic. The group who had come, led by the antler-headed male, was wilder, savage, far less domesticated, and so had less to lose. There was no match. Quickly, I had an idea. It was as if my modern self with all his cold clear thinking had suddenly awoken. I grabbed an oak branch, and, with a strand of grassy rope, I quickly made a crude-looking bow. The young males looked on, curiously. I took a smaller branch, sharpened its tip with flint – and this was now an arrow. I fired my crude bow-and-arrow at the snow and it went through at speed. The tribe quickly got to work. The females joined in, their deftness (as was evident from their work with the skins) bringing skill to the task, and production gathered pace. Within half an hour the invaders began to make their way once more into the valley. The tribesmen fired their crude arrows at the approaching gang. It was no use. Suddenly, the antlered male lunged at Dara. I did not think. I unzipped my bag, pulled out the gun, took aim and fired. The antlered male fell to the ground, his flesh desiccated onto the ice. One of the other invaders ran towards him. I fired again, and he too was blown aside. I fired two, three, possibly four more times. The gang rapidly dispersed, some on horseback. Others were captured by tribe-members and crushed with stones about the head, or impaled on their own spears. I ran towards Dara. She seemed dazed. The tribes-people flocked towards me, happy, elated, as if I was now their guardian or hero. I had interrupted a skirmish, something they had probably seen many times before (and which, without my interference, was likely to have resulted in far less carnage), and I should not have done. I felt sick. Surely it would have been better to have released the virus than to have shown them the gun and its power? But wasn't I going to release it anyway? (The truth was, I was confused. I had broken the number one rule in the mercenary's handbook and had become profoundly caught up, emotionally and otherwise, with 'the mark'.)

Dozens of bodies, blood, dead animals: I had brought this.

A group of males gathered from the tribe; I heard them speak in their primitive singsong language and knew by its tempo (and the males' physicality) that their anger was fierce, their intent equal to it. They split off into smaller groups and followed the last of the invaders. My standing amongst the tribe was different now. Old males and females bowed their heads; hunters met me with suspicion, as if I had somehow usurped their power. Dara sat sobbing with the hawk. Before dark, I walked her to her own cave. When she had fallen asleep, I took the bird and buried it up by the ditch with the harebells and wild violets and the melodious song of the nightingales for company.

*

One night, when Dara was sleeping, I walked up to the place of the hawk, sat and thought, my backpack on my back. I had made up my mind that I could not complete my task, after all. I would go this night and return, if I was able, to my own time. This ancient tribe of mountain people, who were mainly peaceful, who had treated me with immense curiosity and suspicion – but also kindness – did not deserve exposure to the unearthly microbes in my flask. The more I related to them, the more contact I made, especially since encountering Dara (and all that had come with that), the more I could not complete my mission. I realised now that militant as I had been, I was the wrong choice. I found that I could not be blind to them. I saw them as my own, and every instinct inside me would not let me spill that vial.

I sat on the edge of the bank and looked down at the valley, at the dark and sorrowful ice. The night was still, except for the low and constant rumble of the waterfall, the whinnying of horses in the valleys and mountains beyond.

I made a quick inventory in my mind of what illicit glimpses into the future I had given them: I knew I had been reckless in what I had chosen to teach the tribe. (I was well aware that each lesson, however small, could inestimably change the course of history.) Yet I could not bear to watch them suffer while in a position to help. I'd shown them how to make pottery from clay and water and how to fire it (the gourds being so utterly useless); shown them, too, how to make wine from berries and brew coffee from seeds and beans. But perhaps most reckless of all was the weaponry-making I'd taught them. I knew there was evidence of the development of bows in Spain around the same time, and I held tightly to this fact so as to allay my guilt.

The moon was yellow and full in the direction of the POD, and it cast a warm glow over the valley. I would miss this place. I made a mental note: if I did manage to make the return journey to my own ravaged world, I would, if I was able, come back one day to these very mountains and search for the valley.

Dara: the thought of her troubled me. Even so, I turned from the quiet place of the hawk and began my descent. I was stronger than I had been in spring, though I had gained much fat on my stomach so that I must have appeared pot-bellied. As I descended, I noticed that the ground was much grassier than it had been, for further down the mountain the ice had begun to retreat. I was certain as I went on that I could smell something fragrant and familiar: roses. Possibly some early wild-rose strain. I knew paleontologists had believed the rose older than man, older than the dinosaur (having found evidence of the flower from the tertiary period). I stopped, briefly, to look for a rose or rosebush, as if the flower stood for something, the hardy, determined spirit of the earth, perhaps, but I could not trace the source of that perfume.

# The Tribe

There was a natural staircase of turf-banks and rocks, though occasionally I had to hang off the edge of a sheer bluff in order to descend. (When I had first climbed these mountains they had been thick with snow.) There were numerous night birds chattering and singing. I recognised the hooting of owls and remembered the sweep of that first owl across the moon when I arrived. I sensed I was close to the POD. The air was saltier, and there was a new sound in the air, a hypnotic to and fro, a familiar crash and fall: the unmistakable sound of waves.

I felt a new hopefulness, an eagerness in every step. I realised how much I looked forward to seeing the modern brilliance of the POD, built by the men of my time. I felt my brain come alive, sharpen; the sleepy, fur-buried bliss of the valley begin to fall away like shed skin. I was both excited and sad, because I knew that the valley's comfort and quiet had healed me and made me happy, yet I was also happy to leave it.

Just as I saw the journey I had yet to make, I heard a scramble in the bushes behind me. I thought I was again under attack and reached for my bag. (Such was the sense of slumber in the valley these past months, I had forgotten to keep my gun close.) The bag fell to the ground and my assailant pounced, unzipped the bag and held me down, keeping the gun close to my mouth.

\*

From where she had found the strength to hold me down I do not know. Perhaps, it was that I was so weak, so much weaker than I'd been when I first came. The blow to my head all those months ago had been almost fatal. I had been impatient with my recovery, though realised now that it had probably been miraculous, due most likely to the herbs she had applied – plants about which we'd only folklore in my time (variations of burdock and cloudberry). Dara sat back in the Mesopotamian dark and held the gun out, as she had seen me do. Her hands shook, and I saw that her thick, long fingers were unable to grasp at the trigger. She knew I had come from very far; surely she suspected that one day I would want to return there.

'I'm going home, Dara.' I said. '*Home.*' I pleaded with my eyes for her to understand. She laid the gun on the ground and kicked it towards me. I could see she was furious and did not want me to leave. But I had to return; if only to inform those who waited for me that I was not the man for the job. I could not destroy the tribes, not even to save the earth I loved so much; a mercenary with more resolve than me would have to be sent. And even then, I hoped such a man or woman would set the dials a little further on, so that this tribe could live out their years, so that Dara could live out hers.

She stood up, and in the moonlight I saw she'd been crying. And once again in this ancient place, I felt shame. The kind of dark, twisted shame that is only felt by the people of my time. She gestured to the land around us, to the mountains, still cloaked in snow, as if to say, here was home. She took both my hands and laid them on her head, as if to say, here was home; she placed my hands and hers across her fat, protruding stomach, as if to say, here was home. 'Orvey,' she said quietly. (I had heard that word in the valley before, and knew very well what it meant.) I could not speak. I had never felt anything quite like it, this deep cloying certainty at the pit of my stomach. She was with child, and in an instant I felt as bound to them both as a flower is bound to its stem and root.

We walked towards the beach. Here, much of the ice had melted, and though in my time this was a large saline lake, here it was a real sea – tidal, blue, endless. The water crashed against the rocks and low cliffs. Great sheets of ice were washed up and dashed back again, and were eventually liquefied by the tide.

I turned into a wooded area before the low dunes. I saw the chrome and graphene shell of the POD shine out between the dark barks of the trees. I came upon the open space where I had landed. The POD looked magnificent. It had been a while since I had seen the beauty that modern man could create: we made these dazzling, miraculous machines, most of which we used in the business of killing. How had we imagined works at once so beautiful and cruel?

Dara was curious; she crept around the machine not knowing what to make of it. I pressed my hand on the locking device and the door opened. I indicated to her to remain outside as I entered alone. Inside, all was as I had left it. A pristine homage to a world that was addicted to control, yet completely out of control. I laid down my backpack on the small fibreglass counter. I took out the flask with the vial and placed it in its lead container and locked it: without a key the container could only be opened by some kind of terrific blast (nuclear would do it). I looked around, wondering if there was anything I needed. There was nothing I needed. I exited and re-sealed the door. I leaned all my weight against it and pushed. About the size of a small wardrobe, the POD toppled over the bank and onto the sand with ease. From the beach, Dara and I pushed and rolled it over three, four times, like a huge heavy beach-ball, until it reached the water. She watched her reflection bending and doubling in the chrome as the POD turned over, and we laughed.

The contents of the vial would remain inside the POD, possibly for eternity. I watched the machine float for a while as the tide took it further and further out to sea. At some point it would go under and find its way to the bottom, where, one day, thousands of years hence, Persian divers might wonder what strange aliens had come to visit these shores.

Dara joined me at the edge of the water to watch the bright machine, now half a mile out, sink beneath the white surf. Eventually it slipped from view. I would never go back now.

As the two of us ascended the mountain, I could no longer hear the waves, and the smell of salt was soon replaced by the sweet, minty scent of the pistachio trees. I thought of this tough dark-haired woman climbing beside me and of the child we would soon have. I decided then that I would tell our children to put their faith in the earth, but not to command it. To read it, work with it, share it. I promised my own age I would impart these things, and hoped as I walked with Dara into the mouth of the valley, the sea far behind us, that our children, and theirs, would remember.

# Trumpet City

*'if your theory about the chakras is true,*
*then every blue thing's a voice'*

*JEN HADFIELD, NIGH-NO-PLACE*

Joe tried to tap out his solo by the window in the bar at Connolly. It was difficult to concentrate as two men were arguing in the corner. He had noticed them arrive, befriend each other, then within twenty minutes and a few pints, lather each other with abuse. It had given him a dark feeling, as if the rough, pitiless voices of the drunks had stirred up something from his past. He glanced out at the North Star Hotel. Behind it a lone yellow crane moved across the skyline and it made him feel more hopeful. As Joe's attention drifted from the violent banter of the two men towards the rare sight of new construction happening off Sheriff Street, the tune came clearer in his head and he quietly tapped it out as far as the middle.

When his shift was done, he took down the case from his locker and slipped out of the station by the stairs. He hadn't told the lads about the band. He knew they knew he played, but figured that, like Ange, they considered his band days long behind him.

On Capel Street he checked his watch: fifty minutes early. He walked passed McGeogh's and stopped outside a white, glass-fronted building from which people were spilling out onto the pavement. Peering in, he saw well-dressed men and women holding glasses of wine. They were talking and looking at paintings, which, from the street, looked to be a series of depictions of the city. It occurred to him that he had spent his whole life in the city yet never been inside those walls. Of course he knew there were other worlds in Dublin, but felt apart from most of them, just as he did the trainloads of people that would pass him every day on the tracks at Connolly.

He went into the café that the band would sometimes take their breaks in. Seated, he tapped out his 'Flamenco Sketches' solo on the Formica-covered top of the café bar, but still he couldn't get right in his head what Miles Davies had played. There were other distractions now, the usual, more pleasant ones. For in each of the tracks on *Kind of Blue* Joe could hear (and see) what he loved about America. (For Joe, America was still a place where you could make the best of yourself. Not like Dublin, where, in recent years, horizons were so low for almost everyone he knew.) And in 'Flamenco Sketches', Joe heard and saw *rain*. Not the thin, malefic rain of Dublin, but rain that fell in long, full, open drops, like pieces of chandeliers. It was the kind of rain he imagined fell in New Orleans or New York or Chicago, where, in some parallel universe, he might now be living. He'd be joyously rehearsing in some tall building and he would look out and see this gloopy rain, and around the corner there would be a long, neon-lit café where people would be taking shelter. He could smell things in the tune, too: cigarettes, sweat, maybe something illicit like marijuana or morphine. There was a danger to what he could smell in the music, and he liked that. He liked that a lot.

Near seven, Joe entered McGeogh's, nodded to Sean at the bar, and headed for the stairs. He felt nervous, apprehensive; he knew the others had nailed the tunes. He walked along the narrow wood-panelled corridor, past the framed monochrome photographs of some of the city's best-loved musicians of the 1970s, the heyday of Jazz in Dublin, young men in black suits and wide gaudy ties who Joe had played with once or had seen play. He entered the room at the end. Kole was there already. He seems pensive, too, Joe thought, as he hung his coat up on the back of the door.

'Alright, Joe?' Kole asked.

'Sure Kole. You?' Joe glanced up at Kole's bright brown eyes full of their usual cheer behind the thick-framed glasses. But something was up. Joe could tell.

'Where's your sax?' Kole didn't answer.

'Where's Tommy and Des?'

'I wanted to tell you on your own. They're coming later. But I'll be gone by then,' Kole replied.

'Gone where?'

'Kyle Baxter. He's doing a tour.'

Joe knew what Kole meant. The Kyle Baxter band had won all sorts of awards. They were a real professional band; did all Duke Ellington, Count Basie, very little Miles Davis. Mostly real old swing. They'd even been in the French charts at one point.

'Where are you going?' Joe asked.

'Paris. Then the States. I get to go to New York, Joe.'

Joe looked long and hard at his friend. Five years before, Kole had come to Dublin from Nigeria aged fourteen with nothing but his gift: the ability to play the alto-sax in a way few can, skillfully and smoothly, with a distinctive lush tone. And now, here he was, soon to be among that 'going forwards' group of people that Joe had only ever read or dreamt about.

'When do you go?'

'Tomorrow.'

'That quick?'

'Someone dropped out.'

'More fool them,' Joe quipped. Kole smiled and nodded, but then quickly became solemn.

'You've been a good friend, Joe. One of the best in Dublin. I will miss you.'

Joe blushed. He sat down on one of the plastic chairs by the window and gazed out onto the street. He could see the edge of the Liffey, dark-green and swollen from the morning's rain. The day was brighter than it had been, the sky brushed through with orange and pink. They were the best moments in Ireland, he thought, those blazing pink-sky moments that came usually at the end of a terrible day, just in time to scupper any pipedreams he might have of leaving the place. It had been the undoing of him, he felt, this ability he had to see the beauty, the hope in everything. It had prevented him from making changes, leaving places, jobs, people.

'Suppose a shake is in order,' Joe said, and he stuck out his hand. Kole shook it and pulled Joe up towards him. In the close, gruff hug, Joe could smell the young man's crisp, watery breath. He felt a sudden pang of jealousy for Kole's youth, for the possibilities that lay before the young musician.

'You've been my good friend, Joe. You gave me confidence. More than my own father.'

'Players like you don't need confidence, Kole. You have your gift,' Joe replied.

'What I mean is, not everyone made me feel *inside*, Joe, you know? I've been outside a lot in Dublin. But not here. Not here in this room with you and the guys.'

'Where you're going no one's going to pass any remarks. Where you're going, you will be inside, as you say, all the time, wherever you go.'

'I don't know. America's just another place, Joe,' Kole replied.

Of course it was. Joe knew he had built the country up to a preposterous degree in his mind and to anyone green enough to listen. He had needed to believe in something. Yet he could have gone to the States many times over and didn't. Why not? Something always came up. A sick parent or child, a strike, a crisis of some sort. He'd wanted to visit Woodlawn Cemetery where Miles was buried, but he didn't go. After his sister had moved to Boston she'd invited him over many times, but still he didn't go. How he could have such a passion for a place he'd never been to and wouldn't go to when he'd been given the opportunity, he could not fathom.

'Come on, let me hear you play,' Kole said.

'Oh, I've been trying to sort out that middle section, Kole, and I get nowhere. You – well, you must be hot-wired to Cannonball's brain. You got that fat sound straight away. I just get bogged down.' Then Kole tilted his head right back as he always did when deep in thought.

'What do you think about when you hear it on the CD?' Kole asked.

'"Flamenco Sketches"? Well, I think what a genius Miles Davis was and how I know someone just like him.'

'What I mean Joe, is, what is it you *see*? What do you *see* when you hear the music?'

Well of course he saw things. Wasn't that his problem? An inability to concentrate on the notes due to being completely intoxicated with the tune and all it evoked in him. He closed his eyes and described what he saw to Kole. Velvety Edward Hopper-like greens and reds, steam rising from drains, yellow taxis, the concrete and glass of buildings, hardly the sky at all. He heard all sorts of things (other than the actual notes), too: the clatter of high-heeled shoes, people talking excitedly, the spout of an Espresso machine sputtering frothily into a cup, the legs of wooden chairs scraping across a tiled floor. But mostly he saw and heard: 'Rain. That's what I'm seeing and hearing the most, Kole. Warm, sticky rain and everyone is happy in this rain because it smells sweet or something. You know, it's probably just that high-hat and cymbal.'

'Concentrate, Joe.'

'Well, that's it. I see long and happy rain. And there's this café with rain-soaked people coming in and out of it.'

'Good!' Kole said.

'Now forget all those problems you had in the middle section. Miles was improvising, remember? Here's the trumpet. Don't open your eyes. Just keep seeing all you described to me, and play.'

Joe could not believe he was about to do this in front of his friend. It felt silly. But no sooner had he wrapped his lips around the tobacco-tasting tip than he began to feel something inside him yield and flow. He did not think about the music, about fighting his distracted thoughts, about Kole leaving, about his solitary lunch-breaks outside the hut on the sidings. He did not think of these things, only the sticky, warm droplets seeping through his shirt. It felt good to let himself loose in the images he saw in the music. He was outside. It was hot. New York or New Orleans at Mardi Gras. There was a sultry glow on the streets, from cafés, bars, passing buses and cars. Nowhere the windy sting of Dublin's rain, just imaginary *warm* rain. He felt alive, soaked through, invigorated. The rhythm oozed out of him. He could taste salt on his lips. Before he knew it, he had reached the middle section and could feel himself soaring, the sound taking flight out of his body like a seabird. When at last he opened his eyes, Kole had left the room, and Tom and Des were standing by the door, clapping wildly. Joe knew he had played in a way he had never played before. He'd played like Kole, free and lush.

On his way home Joe stopped by the white-walled gallery and glanced in. With only a few stragglers still inside, he could see more clearly the unframed paintings on the wall. He recognised in one a snow-covered Gardens of Remembrance, in another the silver sands of Dollymount Strand, and in the painting closest to him he smiled at two piebald ponies grazing on tall grass outside a block of flats. A man in an orange shirt moved towards the window. He beckoned to Joe with a glass of wine. Joe took a deep breath, entered the gallery and, declining the wine, sauntered cautiously towards the paintings.

'See anything you like?' the man shouted over, at length.

'Everything,' Joe replied, shyly, and drew closer to the wall.

'It's my father's work. He really only painted Dublin once he'd left,' the man said in a brash, well-spoken American accent.

'Really?' Joe responded.

'Oh yeah,' the man replied. 'He missed the place so much. He missed the way the light mellows over the Liffey in the evening, and that cold wintry rain you have here. Oh God, he totally missed that.'

# The Stonemason's Wife

At suction, Rose would sometimes go in too vigorously and pinch at the patients' gums, or let saliva build up in the hollows of their cheeks. She tended to be roughest with those who held tightly to her hand (even though she'd offered it). Rose said nothing about such compulsions to the dentist. He always seemed so interested in the patients' lives, especially those who were artistic or had travelled, and, she imagined, he lived a little vicariously through them.

On the whole though, Rose enjoyed her job. It had been difficult enough returning to it after her five-year break, a time during which, it seemed to her, the world had at last realised she was in it. By the end of the five years, however, life was as it had been before: a terrible, loveless struggle. Each day a confirmation that she was not in the world, not fully and deeply, but at best was a silent presence in it, forgotten at fourteen when Gemma came, and her life was taken up with another. In fact, at the end of the five years, Rose had wished she were dead. So how had it all come to this? She would often ask herself this question during her lunch-break, while glancing through the out-of-date women's magazines in reception. Declan Whately would sometimes find her looking up and out over the pages, sandwich by her side, thoughts back in the year she and her husband had spent building the house.

'You alright, Rose?' he would ask.

'Aye. I'm grand, Declan. Just thinking about Gemma,' she would say.

'How's she doing, Rose?'

'Flyin',' she would reply. And it, at least, was the truth.

Rose knew the dentist admired her because of Gemma. She knew there were quite a few people who did. And why wouldn't they admire her? At fourteen years of age she had, by herself, made the decision to keep the child; a decision her family had not wanted her to make, had been unwilling, at first, to accept or support. And she had persisted, becoming (either out of admiration or pity) something of a cause célèbre in the town. Of course, what people didn't know was that Rose had made such a decision because she wanted to show the town a valiant front: in appearing stoical she had hoped to restore something of her sullied reputation. Had she not kept Gemma (abortion not being an option for her in Ireland), and looked to a visible and busy motherhood, Rose was afraid people might detect her crushed hopes, her resentment, her wish that there had been no Gemma at all.

And so, up until the split, her marriage to Thomas L'Estrange seemed to her as a consolation for all the trials and difficulties of her younger years. It was what her brother, who was a follower of the Baha'i Faith, liked to call 'Karma'. For keeping Gemma that time, he would tell her, when everyone would have understood if she hadn't, she had been rewarded with this quiet stonemason. A man with whom she could take long walks along the beach in silence and still feel comfortable. *Somebody to do nothing with*, as *New Woman* had put it.

Thomas L'Estrange had initially come to the surgery for a root canal. He had not reached for Rose's hand though she had offered it. He courted her slowly and quietly and was attentive to her every change of mood or heart. He was also rich; had land at the back of his mother's house and, within a year of their marriage, had built a house on it from stone gathered illegally from the beach. He took the quartz-flecked granite from Templetown for the outer walls, the thick brown sand from Riverstown to render, the shale-coloured boulders at the back of Carlingford beach for the cornerstones. Rose agreed wholeheartedly with her brother: Thomas L'Estrange was her prize for keeping Gemma that time. For all the years lost, for the pitying looks from her friends. Friends who had gone into the world and come back to the town with its bounty – money, experience – while she had found a corner of it in which to keep her head down, rear a child, find a job.

Once installed in the tall stone house, yards from the shore, at the end of the sloping lane behind Mrs L'Estrange's white cottage, Rose would have her friends come to visit, and they would gasp at the view. They would wonder at the five ensuite bedrooms and the contemporary Italian kitchen; at her husband's building and architectural skills; at the smooth unpainted walls made from the stone he'd plundered from the beach. They would especially remark upon the stone, and how it still smelled of salt, and how standing in the house with its view of the curving shoreline one would think one was out at sea.

Thomas L'Estrange was a master craftsman. He had built their bedroom at the back of the house with a balcony so that at night they could watch the ships and trawlers pass slowly into the harbours of Greenore or Carlingford. He'd built a turreted roof for Gemma. Rose would beam with pride when her friends, home from London and Dublin and New York, would visit this 'castle' her 'prince' had built her. Most of them had left during the eighties, when recession had laid waste to the town, and, Rose believed, they had very much wanted to return, to have the life *she* now had. She would bring them on lengthy tours of the spacious sea-lit rooms, give detailed descriptions of her husband's meticulous building processes, list his ambitions for the property. It was, finally, as if it was *she* who had triumphed. And, if she were honest, this is what she had loved most about those five years in the house. She loved Thomas, she did. But she loved more the new and thrilling taste of triumph.

And it hardly lasted. For he had ruined it summarily, with something she could not in a million years have been prepared for. And whom could she tell? How could she turn to the once-pitying, now envious friends and tell them that after five years of marriage she had discovered Thomas L'Estrange was a – well, what was he? She hadn't the words for it. She was simply not ready for whatever vague and frightful thing her husband was. She knew only he was to have been her prince, not her princess.

Yet people did know. How, she had no idea; only he must have been in some kind of club or group. She had heard rumours; was told of a Gay and Lesbian Society in the basement of a building on Crowe Street in which there was a leopard-skin divan. Perhaps he had visited it. She wasn't sure and she hadn't asked. She saw what she saw and that evening left the house.

The image of him in the back room especially entered her mind during root canals. Again and again she would open the door, having come home early that day, and there he would be: walking towards the long mirror by the window, her tights stretched over his sinewy legs, ripped along his right calf, her Karen Millen dress a perfect fit over his slender back – while Supertramp's the *Logical Song* boomed from the stereo. She had wanted to laugh and thought he must have been joking until she saw his hands, those dry, stonecutter's hands, bejewelled and wafting through the air in an imaginary conversation with the mirror, his angular jaw jutting out from side to side. She stared in silence by the door for what seemed like an age, for she thought him beautiful: light and graceful, long and small-hipped. Surely this dazzling creature was not the man she'd married? It was as if he'd been set free from that person, like a butterfly let loose from a room. Then, as Thomas

L'Estrange's beauty began to conflict with what he stood for in her mind and in her life, Rose checked herself. She was confused. That she had found him so alluring like this deeply surprised and disgusted her. Her hands shook as she closed the door. She referred to the incident only once packed.

Declan Whately must have noticed something was wrong. She was aware she seemed more aggressive in the surgery, more distracted in her breaks, though he said nothing about this. She often wondered if he knew about Thomas, or if, indeed, the whole town knew. And it was thinking about the town's old condescension towards her that brought Rose lowest. Five years earlier she had transformed the 'tragedy' of giving birth at fourteen into a triumph. Now she was as before, her triumph reversed, like Cinderella's pumpkin, all due to Thomas L'Estrange's 'inclination'.

Declan was shutting up the surgery when she fainted. When she came to, she was on the sofa in the waiting room. The window was open and the dentist was making her tea.

'You fainted, Rose,' he said.

'I'm so sorry, Declan.'

'Oh no, you're grand. You've not been yourself at all lately, Rose.'

Then she told him. About the house, the stones from the beach, the discovery that day, about not telling a soul yet the peculiar sense she had that people knew. Though she neglected to tell him about the strange sensation that had passed through her as she stood watching her husband dressed as a woman. He would have asked her to describe it, and she did not want to explain how her eyes had softened and narrowed, how her legs had tingled.

'A terrible load of weighty stuff to keep to yourself, Rose. A person could explode with all that inside them. Or implode maybe, like you've been doing.'

She was glad of the dentist's fuss, and appreciated his kind and thoughtful words. Especially when he told her she was a treasure to the surgery, that her warmth was a natural gift, that her holding the patients' hands in their half-hour of need was proof of a large and indomitable heart, that any man would be mad to let her escape his life. He said that most people had secrets, and asked her to think again about the meaning of what she had seen her husband do.

'Is it really so bad now, Rose, to do a bit of dressing up?'

Rose noticed that in Declan Whately's eyes Thomas L'Estrange was not the monster she had made him out to be. He was much worse: a thing of pity. Rose did not notice, however, that the dentist listened intently, not only to all she told him about Thomas but to the musical tone in her voice, as if he himself would faint with pleasure; to her breathy pauses, her nervy intake of new breath. And she certainly did not see there was no triumph to be had in a time when no one was looking anyway, when no one cared, when pity might be the very most someone might offer another, when everyone in the town these days was busy not noticing anyone else. Rose, who noticed none of these things, walked into the dark and empty street wondering what the dentist meant by 'a natural gift'.

# Stitch-up

At least I'm still breathing. If I make small heaves with my ribs, I can just about get enough air: piney, laced with some kind of oil, perhaps Eucalyptus. Little to do except cast my eyes around the room's brushed chrome and steel; at the immaculate white and jade-green tiles and, poker-stiff, ponder my incredibly good fortune.

The room looks different. I know that, before, I was oblivious to its beauty. Before, I would never have marked, for instance, the sensitive design of that kidney bowl. How beautifully it curves and relaxes to one side. How it glistens in a file of pale, dustless light. And my drip: a clever, labyrinthine construction. If I had the wherewithal right now, I think I would kiss my drip.

There is no fruit in the room. No flowers, no fruit, no soft drinks. It is essential that I be sealed off from every kind of germ.

Caulked with sleep, I seem to have kept company with the figures of dreams for an aeon. Last night, for instance, I met a woman clad in thinly woven gloves – a sort of greeny Prussian blue. They hugged her fingers like net. She sat in profile, dark-haired, spindly. She tried to tell me something but I cannot remember what. This morning, I think I dreamt I was driving. Sometimes in my dreams, I drive a white car and sometimes an orange car. Anything orange usually indicates some kind of revelation. I love when I get orange. I love when I get the orange car. But usually I get the white car. The white car brings me through a lived experience, possibly so that I will examine it in some detail. I cannot remember if I drove the white or orange car this morning.

They will come in, I hope. When they realise the operation was a success they will enter. Perhaps I have woken up ahead of schedule. I like to be ahead of schedule. I am punctual to a fault. Hopefully, one of them will write a little something about me for the *Herald*: I am a miracle after all.

Plaistow described the procedure in detail. As a noted scientist myself I needed to understand what he would do. Let me explain: I was born with an exceptionally weak heart. I had open-heart surgery at two weeks old in Great Ormond Street Hospital in London where I was born. I was hailed the miracle boy: Anthony Blythe, saved by a radical new procedure. (It was the sixties.) I was expected to die at five, then perhaps fifteen; certainly, I was not expected to live past thirty. I am now thirty-four years old. Plaistow explained that after incision, my heart would be removed and packed in ice whilst a pacemaker was fitted, and a small, flexible metal gauze placed over the hole. The heart would then be replaced and reattached to the veins. It was to be, as has been my good fortune, yet another 'radical new procedure'.

Boston General is to all intents and purposes, a Victorian building. The cardiac annex however, is a state of the art addition – all gentle sheen, brushed chrome, glass bricks and steel. An architectural triumph, it was designed by Roya Foster, Norman's protégé and niece. It is a comfort now to guide my thoughts through the serpentine splendour of the place. Corridor floors consist of squares of sturdy, multi-layered, tempered glass with steel rivets; the wall-to-wall white tiles are sheets of small mosaic squares. All non-tessellated surfaces are wipe-able; there are no soft furnishings, no chintz. Standards of hygiene are second to none. The sense of clean, reductive distillation in this ward is tense, almost sexual. A sterile but nonetheless stirring place.

I have always been rather amused by the fact that the place where surgery takes place is referred to as 'the theatre'. It is as if the surgeons are the actors performing a rehearsed, intricate task; the nurses standing conscientiously in the wings the Greek chorus, and the patient the willing, trusting audience. Except that one can't get up and walk away from a bad operation as one can from a play. One has no choice but to endure. One wakes or one doesn't. Destiny plays the pivotal role. This is difficult: control of self given over entirely to someone else. Absolutely difficult.

Before they cut into my baby stitches, I asked Plaistow if I could inspect the wards. A colleague of my wife, he came with impressive credentials. Of course I take nothing for granted. One shouldn't. I wanted to ensure I was in the best possible hands and, in all honesty, wanted to allay my nerves by contriving to gain, via some modicum of understanding of his process, an element of control over my impending surgery.

We talked. I then went alone to Plaistow's Heart Theatre. Walked through, in the obligatory white coat with a hard, starched-linen mask secured tightly over my mouth. The instruments had been sterilised and placed elegantly in their white and dark-blue plastic pouches. They lay flush under sparkling glass. Containers of acetone lined a long white marble table. Sink areas were spotless; soaps made from bleached tallow were grooved neatly with a PLEASE DISPOSE OF AFTER USE emblem. I felt entirely at ease. Though I did happen upon one very annoying thing on my way out of the theatre. It had certainly not been there on my way in: on the long glass floor of the landing, where the tempered glass met the vinyl tiles of the Victorian block, lay a row of eighteen dead flies. They had half-mounted the verge of the glass partition as if they had attempted to crawl under, perhaps through.

# Jaki McCarrick

In a shaft of the blue-white Massachusetts morning pearling along the floor's rim, the flies both compelled and disturbed me. It has always been my particular idiosyncrasy to become rather electrically stirred by anything grouped: maggots, bees, rats, ants, sometimes even people. A strangely pleasurable repulsion that has been known to extend to inanimate objects. Once, I observed an April blossom in Krakow draped in a corolla of Christmas bulbs. The unlit bulbs appeared to me then as tumors devouring the tree, and it at once repelled and held me. Faced daily with sprawling, often mutated cellular formations under the microscope, my eye is drawn naturally to groups of anything; there is a certain magnetism for me, therefore, in swarms.

The flies had not been there before, I was certain. My sense of confidence in both Plaistow and Boston General, despite my peculiar fascination, had been undermined. How did they get there? Each miniature metallic body upturned, with black legs hooked, lying on the creamy floor. I put it down to a hatching from an imprisoned female that had probably made her way down the vents. There are no conventional windows in this block. The air is entirely controlled. Out of sheer courtesy, I felt compelled to mention the sighting. Plaistow confirmed the females came in search of heat and sustenance and, as there was neither sustenance nor means of escape once inside, the offspring would die. Boston had had snow for four long months; the warm mouths of the vents, he said, had clearly offered sanctuary.

I am looking forward to seeing them – my children, family and sisters. Even Mel. Such robust, vibrant people. I am lucky to have spent my days with them. I, a cobweb in this demandingly physical world, the runt of the litter, am miraculously still living. I have treasured my days more than I have expressed. It has been difficult to articulate one's love. People would have inevitably considered one's declarations determined by one's daily possibility of dying. But I rarely dwell on such things. I drink, I have smoked, I've played cricket and

# Stitch-up

football. I've also suffered a collapsed marriage, yet I believe I would do it all over again. Melanie loved the Boston Science world; the Harvard cocktail parties; the Cambridge soirees and charity evenings at American Rep'. She loved to spend her Saturday mornings on Newbury Street, then dropping by the Diabetes Clinic at the Evelyn Centre, where I still work, usually to dangle elaborate credit card bills in my face. There were scenes. To put an end to her vituperation I would usually capitulate. I think there were times she had hoped I'd turn blue and die. Perhaps she will be disappointed I have survived. Because of my condition, my insurance is enormous; cashed in, my premium could have made her a tidy sum.

If I could fling the kidney bowl at the door someone would come. There is now an awful smell in this room. A bad, bad smell. It stinks. Of oils, flesh.

The silence is shrill. I have been singing songs in my head in order to short-circuit the overpowering strength of it but this has been creating its own monotony, its own tyranny. I will just have to continue with these short rib breaths, and wait, though I do seem to have developed an ache from all this waiting and heaving. If only there was even the faintest hint in here of the efficient hive that is the cardiac annex, but nothing. The room is like a sealed container. The high, miniature glazed brick that serves as my 'window' an impediment to sound and air. Only, I do hear something. A tiny, flapping murmur. And it's been there for some time, merged within the shrill, rhythmic silence, not distinguishable enough for me to have hitherto singled it out. Something faint. What is it? To the left. I see it. It is a fly.

*

The fly. Its dark, silver-green body has been flitting along the upper tiles of the room for such a long time. Sudden flight and rest. Sudden flight and rest. Though I seem unable to sense the passing of time, I do think I've watched him now for at least an hour.

The door opens. Three men in orange uniforms brush past the side of my bed, disengage the pus and blood-filled drip. They bring with them the familiar smell of sweat. They do not catch my eye. I certainly cannot form words. At last, I think, I will soon be out in the clear air and the drip that has saved me, provided vital fluids and cleansed my blood, will no longer be required. Soon they will take me to sanctuary, to a light room with bay windows and fruit, views of the harbour; the iced-over pond where Canada geese will be screeching their rubbery heels to a halt on the ice; people skiing to work through placards of white fog, perhaps over parked cars as they had done the morning I arrived. Perhaps it has stopped snowing.

The fly lands on the crisp, white linen cuff of my sheet. Crawls a light, haphazard path up my pale, flaxen-haired arm. Hovers around my chest, lands on my raw pink stitches. I lightly blow him off. He springs to my wrist, where I notice I have a large vinegar-brown cloakroom tag dangling from a hoop of twine. My chest absolutely aches. From breathing and waiting and heaving yes, but also from something else. There is a frenzied buzzing inside my heart. It echoes the fly. The fly is wiping his pin-legs like paws. Licking and wiping and resting. Licking and wiping and resting. Hopping at intervals. His eyes drill. He watches with slow intent, like a basilisk. I see his eyes are lashed. I begin to wonder if he is a she.

The men in orange enter again, wheel me out. Talk about last night's game in hushed tones, stop. I want to ask about the cricket. England versus New Zealand. Who opened? Who bowled? Had it been Woods with his trademark parsimony? For a second I think of the Ashes in summer, and wonder will it rain at Lords. People are crying in the corridors. Melanie is crying. Melanie was always a terrible actress. Plaistow is plying the crying Melanie with white tissues from a blue box. His steady hands reach out for hers. My blue-eyed children are crying and shrinking from me.

# Stitch-up

They wheel me into a large red and black room, heavy with that smell, Eucalyptus, pine, flesh. I feel instantly marooned. The room is in the Victorian block. It is stygian, colder. They leave me alone. With the fly. Why is she so attached to me? Why does she wait? Ah. Eyelids weigh down on a throb, on a pitch-black breath. And finally, it dawns.

# The Hemingway Papers

As a boy her father had owned a mare called Nellie, whose skin, he claimed, was as dark as blackstrap molasses. Whenever he was sad or ill his thoughts would return to Nellie and what had happened to her; in the hospital he would tell and retell Nellie's story. He was eleven years old when he'd found the mare caught up in barbed wire at the top of the bog. He'd unloosed her and walked her home and he and his father hoisted her then in a sling to the joists of a barn, where, all summer long they lovingly nursed her back to health. Clare noticed how her father would always build the story up so as to make clear the message of *a good deed returned*: 'When she was well she bolted only once, with us out after her. And the second we left, lightning struck the barn and it burst into flames. Had Nellie not done that, me and my father would have died inside that barn.'

Now her father was asking for the stories he had written. He said they were in a red box brought over from London when the family had returned to Ireland. When he first mentioned the box Clare had thought him delirious for it had never arrived; he'd left it behind him years ago in their council flat in north London, the keys of which he had illegally sold to a friend of his for a thousand pounds. Besides, even if she were to find the box, she believed the chances of discovering anything inside it remotely resembling a written story were slim, for she'd never seen her father write more than a few letters. Certainly, no one in the family had ever believed him when he said he'd done a correspondence course in short-story writing with Ernest Hemingway.

'You probably mislaid them,' she said.

'No. They're in the box. No mistake about it. There's nothing wrong with my memory.'

'Why do you want to see that stuff now?'

'To read. For you to read, Clare. It's important.'

Every day, when she went to visit, her father would ask her had she found the box. And each time she would stop short of reminding him that it had never arrived. She felt it would be like reminding him of his enormous failure as a father. That he'd neither seen to the removal of their furniture from London to Ireland – nor to the transportation of his own things, that he'd hung back in London while her mother had reared her and her siblings alone and that he'd only holed up with them years later when he'd run out of money. That was the truth of it and Clare knew that somewhere inside her father, he knew it. But there was no point in going through all of that again. They had rowed about it for too many years – about his drinking, gambling, general abdication from all responsibility as a parent. Now, in the crowded ward, he seemed small and fearful, and she considered his persistency with the box to be really a means to distract himself, just as he had always managed to distract himself from some harsh reality or duty.

On his sixth day in the hospital she noticed that he appeared frail, more lost in himself, his voice light and unsure. So, that evening, beset by a stubborn compassion for him, Clare decided she would try to find the man to whom her father had sold the key to their London flat thirty years previously in the hope that she might also find the missing red box.

★

# The Hemingway Papers

She sat by the phone in the solemn front room of her dead mother's house. It was her father's house now, but neither she nor her siblings thought of it as such. He had never put a penny into it, and had twice tried to remortgage it. He really had been a passenger in their lives, getting by on his charm, his occasional deviousness and other people's pity. One by one, she jotted down the numbers for all seventeen Sean Igoes living in the Greater London area given to her by Directory Enquiries.

'Was it a *red* box by any chance?' the ninth Sean Igoe enquired.

'Yes!' Clare replied, and began to get excited as the gravelly voiced man at the other end of the phone described the box exactly as her father had done. He sounded nervous. She knew something had gone wrong with her father's friendship with this man but had not known what exactly.

She booked her flight to London for the following morning. It was expensive but there was no time to lose. From Heathrow, she took a black cab to where the ninth Sean Igoe lived in West Hendon. As she paid the driver, she silently questioned the costly trip she was making, all for a man who had never given her anything.

Sean looked younger than Clare expected. He wore jeans. He was tall and muscular and stared at her from the hallway of the pale-brick house in which he lived in an awkward, wide-eyed manner. From his gauche bearing, Clare thought him exactly the kind of man her father had always befriended. The kind of man – rough-edged, honest, gentle, shy – that her father could twist round his little finger and that she would always want to warn. He invited her enthusiastically into the living room of his flat, where she waited, stroking his calico cat, as he went into another room for the box.

'Here we are,' he said on his return, 'a blast from the past,' and placed the box, which was the size of a small cupboard, by Clare's feet. He swept back from his face a tuft of grey wood-shaving curls and began immediately to reminisce.

'Ah, your father was a great man. He'd light up a room,' he said.

'How come you lost touch?' Clare asked.

'Ya know how it is,' he replied.

'Not really,' she said, at which Sean's face coloured and narrowed towards her.

'The sun mighta shone outta the man's arse, but he did things. Enough said.' She didn't ask Sean what things her father had done to cause the rift in their friendship. She'd guessed it was to do with money, ripping someone off – quite likely Sean. 'But, 'tis obvious you're nothing like him,' he added, quickly, as if to take the sting from his earlier remark.

He left the room to make her tea. Clare sensed from his uncertain movements in the tiny kitchen that he was unused to visitors. As he rattled round, erratically going from cupboard to drawer, she found herself defending her father. 'You know, Sean, his own father died when he was twelve. My grandmother couldn't cope so they put him in a school. I'm sure you heard about those schools. God knows what happened him there. He never talked about it.' At that, Sean stopped what he was doing and speedily returned to her. He seemed annoyed.

'I know well the schools you talk of and the kind that ran them,' he said. Clare saw in the man before her then a small child. He had suddenly the same pained look she had seen often in her father: the open hurt face, the altar boy's grin, as if neither of them had moved on at all from some early part of their lives.

'But the thing about your father,' he sighed, 'was – I see it now but I didn't then – he made us all feel at home, us fellas over here so young and alone. And him with his stories. Ah, sure we adored him, as if it was his job to be adored and ours to adore him. I've often wondered why that was, and I think it was because he was all sort of hollow in himself – which brought out the best in others. We could forgive him anything and mostly we did. Most things anyway.' Sean's words shook her. They did not describe the man she'd lived with for almost half her life. Whatever her father's failures as a parent and husband, he had evidently been as a beacon to Sean and the men he'd known in London. Men who were damaged, perhaps, as her father was, or not long out of the fields of Ireland and so clueless as to how to behave in a big city. 'A man's man' her mother had always called him, and now, here in Sean's dark and Spartan flat, Clare understood something of what that had meant. Sean booked her a lift back to the airport with a friend of his from Cork who would do the lift for her cheap. She thought about asking the driver to make a detour, to go down the road where she had once lived, but decided against it.

When the plane touched down at Dublin the sky was still bright, shot through with orange and a stark watermelon red. She collected the box from the carousel, put it on the trolley and went to her car. She put the box on the passenger seat, drove towards the house. She couldn't wait to get home and open it. But she was also afraid. For there sitting beside her was a reminder of her parents' hope-filled dreams of returning and of the dreadful reality: their awful planning, their bungling, cobbled-together lives.

When she got inside the house, she placed the box on the kitchen table. She ripped off the duct-tape she'd taped it up with, and stared at the red leatherette veneer, torn and loose in places. In the corners there were tiny blue doodles, childish attempts at drawing the box, possibly her own. She lifted the lid. The smell was musty. After a while there was another smell, an undersmell. She recognised it immediately as her father's aftershave, Old Spice. She dived in, pulled out a bunch of notebooks. There were around twenty filled with his close, neat longhand. Beneath these were pages of typed text with sheets of metallic blue carbon paper between some of the pages. She found faded newspaper clippings. One featured a long poem with her father's name at the end. Another was about him winning a Biro for a parody he'd written of 'The Mountains of

Mourne'. The feature went on to say her father had a 'flair', that his style was 'crisp and succinct' and that the judges 'hoped he would carry on writing'. She rummaged to the end of the box and found a bunch of letters tied up in a dry coffee-coloured string, which easily loosened. The letter on top was dated February 1959, and printed in the top right-hand corner was an address: *Finca Vigia, Havana, Cuba*. The name, in type, at the end, was Ernest Hemingway. (Though the letter was just signed 'Ernest'.) She flicked through the letters: all were written on the same Manila paper, and all were from the American writer. They seemed to get briefer as she moved back through them, as if Hemingway and her father had had more to say to each other as the months rolled on. She returned to the letter on top, which, she realised by the date, was the last.

'Your last story is wonderful,' it read. 'You must gather all the stories you have written for the course and publish. Send to me and I'll see what I can do. This story, *The Light of the West*, recalls to me a story of my own, *Summer People*, which you mentioned you had read and enjoyed. I thank you for that. You place your young characters in an authentic setting, and the debilitating pain the boy experiences once he is removed from that beautiful bog-land place and sent to that evil school is truly moving. I remember summers like you describe. No adult summer is ever like the summers of our youth. Please continue to write me of your progress when I move to Idaho in the Fall.'

She rifled through the box but could not find the story Hemingway had mentioned. She stayed up till dawn looking and reading (stories about the deep snows of 1947 on the Ox Mountains; about a man lost in his own field; a musician whose gift is enhanced after an encounter in the woods with the fairies) but found no sign of *The Light of the West*, either typed or in longhand.

The next day she entered her father's ward and saw his bed was empty. She was scared. There were things she wanted to say: that she had found the red box, had travelled all the way to

London to get it. She wanted to tell him she'd met Sean, who had missed and praised him. She wanted to let her father know she'd read his stories and thought them superb. But most of all she wanted to ask what had become of the missing story, a story she suspected was more memoir than fiction, and that might, if she could find it, recover for her some of her father's past (and, perhaps, elicit some deeper understanding). As she stared at the thin and empty bed she felt so much regret, and so much love.

Frantic, she noticed a crowd gathered round another bed up by the window. She walked slowly towards the bed, half closed off by a blue curtain. The amber sun poured onto the corner where the crowd was. The windows were open and, for a change, the air in the ward smelled piney and fresh. She looked over at a group of men gathered round a yellow-skinned man propped up by pillows. They were playing cards and telling jokes as they threw their Euro notes down on the white sheet. One of the men, a bedside neighbour of her father's, in for a kidney-stone operation, was clandestinely drinking beer. Clare thought that the man looked happier and healthier than he'd seemed all week. As she went to ask this man about the empty bed, she saw that behind him, up by the yellow-skinned man's head, sitting in a wheelchair in his pyjamas and leading the group boldly on in the game, was her father, exalted-looking as he dealt out the cards in the sunlight.

# The Lagoon

She loosened her hand and walked towards the hedgerow. The holly berries were wizened, the haws dry and turning yellow. Smoothing her thumb across an ivy leaf, she thought of London, where there would be things to do on a Sunday other than walking and picking at hedges. At the turn for the Newry Road she could see the tide arriving in its horseshoe shape across the mud flats, after which, until Carlingford, there would be a five-mile stretch of beach; they had hoped to find a way down to it before the long walk to Riverstown or Gyle's Quay.

'Kate!' She hated when he hollered like that, as if she were his property or child. She ignored him, and continued: part reproof for the shout, part wanting to get on to the Ballymascanlon Hotel for a Coke. 'Over here! This way looks interesting.' She trudged back, and looked warily up a long dirt track.

'What's down this way?' she asked.

'I don't know. But it might take us to the sea.'

They had walked the Newry Road many times but not noticed this path before. Two ivy-covered stone pillars and an oxblood-coloured gate with a frayed green rope dangling from its bolt marked the entrance. Nick unloosed the rope and pushed the gate across the grassy path. She felt uneasy. There was probably a farmer up there, a farmer with a large loaded *gun*, for this land was most certainly a farm. Sheep dung dotted the fields (divided by swathes of barbed wire that had collapsed in parts), rusty implements rested haphazardly by plastic-covered bales of hay. Nick was undeterred.

'We'll say we're looking for our dog.'

'We don't have a dog,' she retorted.

'*I* do,' he replied. A joke, for which she slapped his arm. She'd heard them many times, these quips, yet always fell into Nick's trap. He seemed to enjoy his continual success with her, and she knew she had encouraged it by her feigned slowness.

She walked up the path with one hand in his pocket. The path ran through the centre of a steep mound. At the peak she could see the ruins of a limekiln. Ravens cawed from its jagged corners; ivy grew in tight v shapes across crumbling rue-red bricks; a lone elm presided eerily in the field opposite. On their descent a small redwood copse gave way to a dilapidated farmhouse. There were no cars or tractors, and no sign of a farmer.

'See, it's fine. We'll find a path down to some lovely beach now.' Just as Nick had uttered these words, a man appeared from behind the house. He strolled towards them, sat on the low blue wall of the house and lit up a cigarette. His white sleeves were rolled up, exposing his liver-brown, sinewy arms to the cold day. As he brought the cigarette to his lips, she saw that his nails were thick with dirt and tangerine tobacco stains. He did not carry a gun. He had a wiry frame, and with his cherub's face and flat side parting had the mien of a choirboy.

'Grand day,' he said, shyly, as they approached. She felt embarrassed by their blatant trespassing.

'We were wondering if there was a path down to the sea this way, maybe to Templetown,' Nick said, squeezing her hand.

'There was, but it's all mud and quicksand now. I don't think that'd be much use to ya.'

'No,' Nick replied, 'we'll have to wait till Riverstown then.'

'Be the guts of three mile, Riverstown. Are yous out for a walk?'

# The Lagoon

'Aye, that's it.' She glanced over at the house: the windows were covered with grime and bird-shit; the torn and yellowed nets hung as if at half-mast; the brown front-door lay open to a pile of detritus – newspapers, tins, bottles – all soaking up the pale sun in the hall. She thought, by his appearance, his yellow teeth, the state of the fields and house, the mustard shine to the embossed wallpaper in the hallway, that he was most likely a bachelor farmer. Perhaps his mother or sister had died and, like all the other bachelor farmers she'd ever met or heard tell of who were living out on the Cooley Peninsula, he'd done little or nothing with himself, or the house, since. His slate-blue eyes caught her poor opinion of his home and she felt her intrusiveness keenly.

'There's a good walk over there, down by that kiln.'

'Where's it get to?' Nick asked.

'You'll know when you see it,' replied the man. The morose and ominous way in which he said this frightened her. She wanted to turn back. On the other hand, she thought, *I have Nick*. If Nick turned out to be inadequate protection in this tumbledown place with the strange, child-like farmer, he'd be no good at all in a big city like London: continuing would be a kind of test. She squeezed his hand to indicate that they should do as the man suggested.

At the kiln, the road curled around the field with the lone elm. The land here was waist-high with sea-grass and vetch and samphire. If they did have to make a run for it, she reasoned, all they had to do was climb over the hedge bordering the field with the elm and head straight for the Newry Road. Just as she was beginning to wonder what exactly the man meant by 'you'll know when you see it', the path veered right, and there *it* was in front of them: a black lagoon.

The formation was glacial. A panorama of sheer, coal-black rock, the vast innards of a mound, loomed over two dark pools, one the size of a small lake. The water was absolutely still, the rim of both pools covered in a stiff, pale-green lichen.

'It's amazing!' Nick said, his voice echoing till it passed over the heather-topped peak. He walked along the rim of the bigger pool, then picked up a large stone from the undergrowth by the hedge and dropped it in. The splash made a thick black web, a heavy plop. After a few seconds the pool began to make loud gurgling sounds as if it had digested the stone. She watched Nick break a branch, about four feet in length, from a cherry blossom at the mouth of the path then lie down on his stomach towards the water and poke it in; the whole of the stick slithered beneath the surface. He hauled it out, and shook the dripping stick over the pool before discarding it behind him. How had she not known of the existence of this place in her own townland? Who had ever heard of such a hidden lake?

She gazed at their reflection in the water. She thought she looked younger and fatter, with more gold in her hair than she imagined she possessed. Her hair was dark, from where had the gold come? She looked happy and as bound up with this person standing beside her as she could ever hope to be with anyone. Nick was his tall, strong and boyish self. His eyes, though, were greener, and when she looked back at him, she saw that indeed his eyes were greener, and that they had more life in them than she had previously noticed. She began to see beneath the boy and girl in the water, beneath the reflected clouds and the overhanging calamine-pink blossoms, to the murk that wafted below. The stone and branch had disturbed the depths; grasses and brown things to-ed and fro-ed. She pulled back towards the hedge.

'There's probably bodies down there; if you wanted to bury someone where no one would ever find them, *this* is where you'd come,' Nick said. Again she slapped him. She did not want this thought, along with her suspicions about the doleful farmer, and her mother's skein of objections to her and Nick's imminent move to London (her mother had cried over it), all rattling around together inside her head. But Nick was right; here was a first-class hiding place; here, on the border, in the heart of high-octane IRA activity; and people *had* disappeared. Mountain caves and abandoned houses had been searched all along the Peninsula for any sign of them; even the newspapers had begun to refer to such people as 'the disappeared'.

She took a gulp of the icy air. The space seemed primeval; in a moment a pterodactyl might swoop down into this cavernous gloom and make off with the two of them. Yet Nick, oblivious to the extravagances of her imagination, persisted in walking close to the edge. He prowled, confidently, around the pools, vanquishing every rise and fissure before him. She watched him continue along the row of stones that divided the big pool from the smaller one, and perch precariously in the middle. Then, she noticed, just a few yards ahead of him, beckoning under the white full-bloom of a magnolia tree, a gate fixed to a charred wooden post. The gate was open and mercifully inviting them out of the place. She could see the tops of cars speeding along the road, and felt comforted by this.

Suddenly, Nick screamed. She looked around and there he was, hanging from the thin row of rocks that divided the two black pools. His voice shook: *it's pulling me down Kate, it's pulling me down*. She was dumbstruck. She rummaged around the hedge for the four-foot stick but could not find it. She glanced back at the pool: Nick was gone. She heard the same deep sucking sound that the stone had made in the water earlier, as if Nick had sunk so far down the pool had swallowed him. She turned, raced out towards the entrance, and screamed for the farmer. He did not come. She ran back to the second pool: all glassy, still as death. She cursed herself for wearing a dress then quickly hitched it up and tucked it under her knickers. She walked along the thin row of rocks, knelt upon their jagged quartzy tops, leaned into the black water, the rock edges cutting into her flesh, and plunged in her arm. It folded over her and clung to her like molasses.

'Kate!' she heard the voice howl from the direction of the gate. She stood up, steadily, furiously, walked back along the stones and, after loosening the dress, ran down the path in a panic towards Nick, who was swinging from the gate, head to toe in an oily black mud.

'I thought you were dead,' she said, slapping him across a wet leg.

'Come on, let's get out of here before yer man comes to chop us up.'

All the way across the damp, scratchy grass she thought of London; of the fun they were going to have far from the gloom of the border with its secret paths and neglected farms. Soon she and Nick would be in a brightly lit, bustling city, and their walks would never again have at the end of them, the possibility of disappearing – at least, not into an ancient black lake hidden behind a limekiln.

# The Jailbird

She had the same air about her, a goofiness sort of, and her teeth were the same, too, narrow and overlapping at the sides, so that with her dark hair and fringe she looked just like Patricia Arquette in David Lynch's *Lost Highway*. Whenever Martha would smile I had always a compulsion to lick her teeth. The caption said she was home.

'See Martha Cassidy is back in town,' my mother said, and I quickly closed the newspaper. She'd have something to say to me if it was I who peeped over her shoulder, there's no doubt. The customers in the shop looked up. I thought they were listening to the Joe Duffy show Ma had on head-thumpingly loud (as per usual) but obviously they weren't.

'They say she done well over there,' Biddy Hughes said.

'Josie will be pleased to see her,' Mrs Barrington said.

'Did someone die, Connie?' Coco Conway said, all offbeat, and everyone looked, as he was, and is still, a big thick. Ma turned down the volume on the radio.

'No one died, Coco. Just Martha Cassidy in the paper as she's home,' Ma said. If she thought I was going to stand there with the biddies gawping and waiting for a reaction she'd another think coming. I said, 'excuse me Ma, but I'm off now for my lunch,' and I took off the white shop-coat she'd make me wear as if we were a big shop when we weren't, we were a one-horse outfit, and sloped out from behind the counter with my lunchbox and stripy flask she'd got me the month before in O'Neil's in Dundalk. On my way out I heard Biddy Hughes say:

'I hear Michael is feeding the foxes, Connie. Jack Daly won't be too pleased, he has sheep up there.' Once out, I stopped to eavesdrop, but the biddies just went back in time to seventeen years ago, to the big dairy scam that Martha's father had been a part of, and one of the reasons the love of my life left for the big old US of A.

'He was in with *them fellas* that's why he done it. Watering down the milk! What a thing to be doing to make a bit of money,' Biddy Hughes said.

'Money for guns, too,' Mrs Barrington said.

'Indeed. And it's he *did*, Biddy. *Did.* Sometimes I wonder if you went to school at all.' Ma would correct other people's grammar no matter what the topic of conversation or how prismatic its flow. It was a way of reminding them all in Castlemoyne that she was a cut above, what with her shop, her background as a champion amateur actress who, as she liked to claim, had read all of Shakespeare, Shaw and Wilde.

I went up to the bog and waited for my foxes to emerge from their earth, which was deep beneath the over-leaning bank I would sit on. Straight away I thought about Martha and the band, and of the times we would come up here to talk about our futures. Our band was thought of as about the best thing ever came out of this borderland mire. Martha had a voice that sounded sassy, a cross between Patti Smith and the girl from Chromatics. We'd a big following and were raved about once in Hotpress (who'd said we were the 'Nirvana of the North'). All the Goths and interesting types would crawl out of the local woodwork to see us play. They'd loved us with a passion verging on the maniacal, or so it seemed to me then. I was full of hope that time. A real Pollyanna (or whatever the male equivalent is). Sometimes I wondered if that hopeful part of me would ever return. It seemed to me, as I sat eating my sandwich, no fox in sight, that the paradox of having retreated so far from the world as I had done, becoming nigh on a recluse in recent years, a veritable shut-in (discounting my visits to the foxes), was that during the years of the band I'd had a deeply hopeful and cheery disposition.

★

'Massage my feet, Michael, will you, Son, while I read this?' Ma said, seated beside the unlit fire. She already had her stockings off, her feet spread out onto a towel. She smelled powdery, beneath which I could also detect the sour undersmell of sweat. There were bottles of creams and lotions laid out beside her.

'Give me them,' I said, and I began to rub. And right there my night was ruined. Not just because there's nothing like massaging one's mother's feet (Ma's being all swollen and flaky) to quench any romantic feeling gathering in a man's body but because within seconds I could tell that what she *really* wanted to do was to reel me in, have a captive audience while she plotted out the course of our lives together:

'I was thinking, Michael, about what we might do in a few years when I get the pension. I'd qualify for a free travel-pass as well as one for a carer. You could put in for that you know, and you'd get a free travel-pass, and then we could travel the whole of Ireland if we wanted to on the train.'

'Who'd mind the shop?' I said, alarmed (to say the least) that she had me in her mind as her future carer.

'Well, the days we'd be going we could close up the shop. We wouldn't be going every day. You don't seem that enthused.'

'I am, Ma. I love trains. I am enthused.'

'Not like we can get off to Greece or anything. We're too busy now and by the time I get my pension I'll be too old for Greece. So the passes would be great to have.'

'I can't wait for you to be getting your pension, so,' I said. And all warmed from her dreams of availing of free travel, and from the Deep Heat I was rubbing into her shins, she took up her book again, flicked through the pages. I saw this as my opportunity: 'Do you think, maybe, you'd be alright if I was to go dancing one of these nights, Ma?'

'Dancing?' she said, 'what kind of dancing?'

'Just in town, maybe the weekend, maybe a disco.' Of course, I was planning/hoping to bump into Martha, thinking she might be inclined to venture out to one of our old haunts now that she was home.

'I'm afraid my dancing days are long over,' Ma said, 'them and the acting.'

'Well, I was meaning maybe not with *you*, Ma,' I said, 'with Noel I meant.'

'A disco?'

'Aye,' I said.

'It's not that you need my permission, Michael. Lord knows, but I'd be glad of a break from running round looking after you. But take a look at yourself, the cut of you, that leather jacket and the hair. And besides, you know yourself you wouldn't last five minutes with all the commotion around you. Not worth going out for anyway. All gone to hell out there. Drowning in a sea of drink we are and aren't there lectures advertised every week in the *Northern Star* for depression and suicide for young people?'

'Ma!' (It was ridiculous, I knew, that I should be pleading to do something twelve year olds were doing the world over. But Ma and me had history. And she never stopped reminding me of it.)

'After a few drinks wouldn't you be linking up with all sorts of dubious characters, might not understand how *fragile* you are, Michael,' she said.

'I'm not fragile, Ma.'

'Are. In your own way. My advice is to stay away from the

discos.' Clearly, if I wanted to accidentally-on-purpose bump into Martha I'd have to do it without my mother's permission, for it would never be given anyway.

'What are you reading?' I asked, trying to get her off the subject of me and discos and she turned the face of the book towards me: a Methuen School's Edition of *Macbeth*, probably Eugene's.

'Only for the memories,' she said. I told her she shouldn't be reading such books with all the blood and guts that was in them, especially considering what could happen if she were to get upset, but she got defensive, told me to go away from her, even after the excellent rub I'd given her. She said she wished Eugene was here because Eugene was the only one who understood her, and who could massage her feet properly also, as he was going to be a doctor in Trinity College and, naturally, he would be better at massaging feet. (Naturally.) Bad enough that I'd given up my evening of thinking and dreaming about Martha to massage my mother's feet but then I got shirked off for not being Eugene. I wanted to remind Ma that Eugene was dead seventeen years but I knew the whole thing would kick off then, so I left it.

'Don't forget to refill the crisps,' Ma said to me on my way out. I glanced back at her and saw she was ringing her hands and reciting *out damn spot*. I wished then I'd gone up to see my foxes for the entirety of the evening instead of having to suffer that old speech of hers (for which she'd won an award), which she would intonate in a sort of clipped and grotesque whisper, her face taking on an alarmed expression that always recalled to me Elsa Lanchester in *Bride of Frankenstein*.

*

McDaid's Grocery Store was left to my mother by hers. (When Ma married she changed the name from Soraghan's.) The apostrophe before the 's' was a reminder to all in Castlemoyne as to whom, exactly, the shop belonged. It also meant her husband and sons, if and when we worked in the shop, and we all did at one point, were, essentially, her *employees*. Constance Soraghan then McDaid was once a name to be reckoned with in these parts. Her trophies for acting filled the shelves of the house, a two-storey extension separated from the shop by a door. (And a very important door, too, for once I was in the house I was no longer her employee though she often abused that fact.) From within the shop could be seen a life-sized poster of her with golden, flocculent curls and Clara Bow lips, and the words *The Jailbird by George Shiels* emblazoned across her. There was rarely a day when someone would not comment on that poster. If they didn't, then she'd direct their attention to it somehow or stand close by so they would note the resemblance. Sometimes, if she thought she was alone, or I wasn't looking, she'd stare into it like a mirror. She'd find herself in the features, sweep down the loose skin of her neck, soften her curls, as if about to enter for her pivotal scene.

\*

The next day, Coco Conway called into the shop with a packet of fresh steaks sourced from his own private abattoir. This was more or less a weekly occurrence, and always he and Ma would haggle over prices, with Ma flirting, most disconcertingly, in order to get a reduction. Coco would lap this up, probably remembering her as she was in the poster. 'Moyne's own Meryl Streep,' he would call her, and I think she flirted with him not only to get the prices of his produce down but so he would call her Meryl Streep. When she went off to wash the blood of the steaks from her hands (before paying Coco the money) I knew he would take the opportunity to get all 'man to man' with me. 'A fine strap of a woman, your mother, the strength of an ox in her,' he said, lasciviously, one eye cocked at the poster. I moved over to the morning's pile of mail. Being no respecter of personal space, Coco sidled up to me: 'I hear you're up with the foxes again, Michael.' I nodded. 'Don't mind telling ya, but they're nothing but vermin.'

'I don't think so,' I said, and Coco laughed. 'Don't believe in "vermin", anyways,' I said, 'apart from the human sort. What's the point in shooting foxes for the sake of sheep and chickens you're going to get nothing for anyway? It's barbaric. Whole lives ruined just so some drunken gurrier can have a burger he's too pissed to taste,' and he laughed again, though I don't think he got what I was trying to say to him.

'I saw her today, ya know,' Coco said. I'd a good idea as to who he was talking about.

'A-ho!' he said, pointing at me, convinced he'd caught my blush. 'She'd be sure ta call in on ya boy.' (I hated the way they all called me lad or boy or boyo when wasn't I thirty-five years old?)

As Ma completed her dealings with Coco, I noticed a brochure newly arrived from the Postcard Company. I quickly scanned the cover letter. They'd new postcards to send us. Did we want to order a postcard carousel? Have cards with famous faces of Monaghan on them, excerpts of poems by Patrick Kavanagh? The brochure read:

*Contemporary & Vintage Postcards*
Kavanagh Country images (Inniskeen village; D. McNello's Bar; Kavanagh's headstone; the banks of the River Fane; Kavanagh's portrait by Patrick Swift; excerpts from *The Great Hunger*, with the poem's protagonist, Patrick Maguire, depicted sitting on a wooden fence, *Tarry Flynn*, *The Green Fool*)
Carrickmacross Lace images
Fishing in Lough Muckno images
Retail price: 50 cent each.

Coco had gone two minutes when the doorbell rang out again. Thinking it was him who'd entered I went to chide him for calling my foxes 'vermin' when I saw an apparition, the midday light bouncing off her hair so that it looked silver-streaked. Thinner than before, like in the *Northern Star* photo, Martha seemed even more beautiful than the mental image I'd been dwelling on for the best part of seventeen years.

'Hello Michael,' she said. I hoped that Ma, who'd gone upstairs after Coco had left, hadn't heard the bell.

'Hello,' I replied. It wasn't the right way to say it. But I could see she knew, Jesus, she knew I was glad to see her.

'Been a long time,' Martha said.

'It has.'

'You look great.'

'Not so bad yourself.' I wanted to take off my shop-coat right there, walk out of the place with her, but then Ma clattered down the stairs. When she came into the shop I saw she'd half the contents of my father's wardrobe in her arms.

'Here now,' Ma said, without bothering to look up and see who it was I'd been talking to. 'Been thinking, Michael, these suits of your father's should fit you. You should give some thought to wearing these.' Embarrassed by such talk in front of Martha, I replied:

'Don't bloody-well want to be wearing a dead man's suit, Ma,' and sort of threw a laugh out of myself and Martha laughed in return. Then Ma looked up, saw who it was I was laughing with. It was sheer pleasure watching the blood drain from my mother's face. Ashen she was, ashen.

'Hello Connie,' Martha said, soft and clear.

'Well, if it isn't Martha Cassidy,' Ma said, with the utmost disdain in her voice. Even for her it was a pretty low, sarcastic tone. I was embarrassed for Martha, but also for myself, for it must have been plain as day that in all these years nothing much had changed with me: I was still living under my mother's thumb. In fact I was sure I could see in Martha's face something of the look I'd seen on all my friend's faces, on the face of every girl I'd ever been out with since. The look that said: Norman Bates is alive and well and living in Castlemoyne.

She swept her fingers through her hair. Oh that soft, cold, wavy hair… the bright eyes… the pale skin… the full, pillowy lips…

'How have you both been?' she said. Ma was just about to reply with something cutting, haughty. I could feel it coiling round her brain, dipping down into her sack of bile for some relish, working its back legs into the ground, ready to burst out of her mouth, but before it did it was I who answered this apparition on the doorstep of our shop: 'Everything's grand, Martha. We've been very well.'

'I heard about your father, Michael.' I nodded at this, and out of the corner of my eye saw Ma retreating behind me, sort of sadly. When we were alone Martha made a face, her eyes following Ma as she made her way upstairs with my father's suits.

'God, I remember the band practices up there!'

'Do you, Martha?'

'And her banging on the ceiling at us to be quiet!'

'There by the grace of God, says you,' I said, before I knew it. Of course, had we got hitched, as had been the plan all those years ago, there'd have been no chance in hell Martha would have ended up living above and working in the shop. But, standing there, seeing me for the first time in an age, she was polite enough not to question the daftness of what I'd just said.

'I see the hair's the same.'

'Aye. Dirty blonde,' I said, and she laughed.

'It's good to see you, Michael.' And suddenly seventeen years fell away and we were back to the comfort and effortlessness of each other's company. We arranged to meet that evening and already my mind was ticking over about what I'd wear, how I'd smell, like some lovesick puppy. I could hear movement again upstairs, the sound of pacing, followed by an impatient shoe-tapping sound on the wooden floor of the landing. Martha heard it too and I could see she wanted to get out before Ma returned.

'Right then,' she said, 'by the bog road at seven.' Then Ma's voice echoed down the stairs, all polished and pointed: 'An *awful* busy day I reckon it's going to turn out to be, Son. And a *big* trip to the Cash and Carry we need to be making, too.'

'We'll be grand, Ma,' I shouted, and waved to Martha as she left. I could hear Ma move to the window, probably so as to watch Martha (with middling-to-strong hatred, no doubt) as she walked away from the shop. When she came down Ma seemed sniffy, busied herself with the newspapers.

'She's brave, Ma,' I said.

'Who's brave?'

'Martha,' I said.

'How d'you make that out?'

'To have come back here after all this time.'

'Tie back your hair will you, Michael?' she said, as if she sensed already that she was losing her grip on me with Martha's return, and I, feeling bizarrely sorry for her – and for the loss of that grip – tied back my hair as she requested.

\*

Martha stood on the highest hill. The evening was fine, the sun fat and low in the sky. Before us the bog simmered. Everywhere bees and flies swirled about plants that had been growing there for as long as I could remember: foxtail, vetch, purple moor grass, bog-cotton, tormentil, deer sedge, bog-asphodel, bindweed, ling, sundew. The land below us was covered in lush-looking crops and the haze of them breathing filled the air. The rushes shook by the stream behind us. The gorse throbbed with light. Out on the heather I'd lain a flask of tea, the leftovers of Coco's scraps (for the foxes), and my cigarettes. I lay back and watched the fleet bog wind blow through Martha's hair, as if pulling it up and out by invisible marionette strings as she leapt from rock to rock. It could have been twenty years ago; it was like no time had passed at all, as if it had been breeched somehow, folded back on, by this tryst at the top of the bog, like those we had had many years before.

'Lady's Brae, Devlin's, Pat May's, Daly's, Keady, and over there – Dundalk, Dundalk bay…

'That's cheating,' I shouted, as she was naming places that could not be seen with the naked eye.

'Fermanagh, Loughill, Mass hill, Shercock, Shancoduff, Ballybay – Cassidy's and McDaid's.

'What's the biggest hill?'

'Mass hill.'

'Who owns the blue sheep?'

'Henrys.'

She plucked a stem of bog-cotton and said she'd missed the bog flowers. I couldn't believe how much she'd remembered. Once I'd have won this game we were playing of naming places that could be seen from the bog (which divided McDaid's land from Cassidys') but it seemed the place names had stayed more alive in Martha's memory than in my own, and me living all this time beside them.

'It's the details help you hang on to a place, Michael, when you're away as long as me,' Martha said.

She had wanted to see the spot where once we would have our chats, our 'private liaisons'. And I agreed to show her my foxes. After an hour or so, it was clear there would be no detail of our history here together that she would leave untouched. To deflect, I asked her about herself, how life had been in America, but she was vague about it, said her friends had helped her and that she'd ended up in some weird town in California (near Roswell) where she'd had some brainwave-slash-epiphany thing which had launched her forward. The details of this she was not talkative about. I presumed it was only as she didn't want to be yammering on all the time about how successful she was. Martha had always been a most modest person.

'Where was it you did it, Michael?' she said then, as I sort of knew she would, eventually, and I felt my bones chill. I looked at her and knew from the wide earnest eyes of her exactly what she meant.

'Over there,' I said, and pointed to a flat stretch of lichen, close to the stream. I was sort of annoyed she'd brought the matter up. I wanted to ask did she want to erect a fucking plaque there or what but of course I didn't. She turned away.

'You were a god, Michael. Do you know that?' she said, her back to me.

'A wha'?' I said, mock-incredulously.

'You heard. Remember you drove into that gig on a motorbike?'

'Sort of,' I said. And I started thinking again of our days in the band.

'Where was that?'

'Riverside Inn,' I replied.

'That's it. You see, you've not forgotten. Like fucking Kurt Cobain, you were, remember? You were so...' Martha didn't finish her sentence. She didn't have to. I knew what she meant.

'Things change, Martha,' I said. 'After Eugene... I couldn't let Ma down... she was... well, she was a bloody mess after it all.'

'You tried to kill yourself, Michael. And I totally blame her.' To this, I said the words: *it wasn't because of Ma at all...* well, I mouthed them, without volume, because I was nervous, had felt I was hitherto coming across like I suffered from Tourette's Syndrome so I held back, possibly on the one thing I should have said outright to her. I realised that in all the years we'd been apart she still did not know why I'd come up to the bog that day. She'd thought it was to do with my mother's usual prodding and poking. I saw, too, that Martha still had the old confidence in me; still saw in me that 'god', as she put it. So how could I tell her I'd come up here like a ninny, missing my dead brother, pulled this way and that by my mother's attempts to wreck my life as she had Eugene's, stuck between love and guilt and sick with the indecision, at once paralysed and overwhelmed, and taken a blade to my own arms – because of *her*, because she was going to leave me, here, alone, in this closed and sodden tomb of a county.

★

That night I arrived home to find Ma had bolted the door. I'd had a few jars with Martha in town and had walked her back on the balmy night to Josie's, her aunt's place. (In the pub, we'd bumped into a few old faces, including Noel, who ran his father's butchers on High Street. He'd drummed with us for a while. Everyone was glad to see us. In fact, the whole evening had been rather wonderful. And I was closer to feeling like a god this first night with Martha than I'd felt in a long time.)

'Open the door, Ma,' I shouted up at the window. No sound. Then the curtains were wrenched back and I could see her staring down at me, glasses on, chocolate-brown hairnet pinned to her head, no doubt to protect for Coco Conway those grey-golden Meryl Streep-ish locks of hers.

'Come on, Ma. Open the door,' I shouted. I could hear her footsteps then, heavy on the stairs, and eventually she unlocked the door making a big ceremonious deal out of the whole lot – the bolts, the mortice lock – and opened it, slightly, with the chain still on, and looked straight at me, her own and only living son: 'Who is it?' she said.

'Jesus fuck, you know it's me, Ma! You just looked down at me from the window.' And then this long, black shotgun was being pointed at me, and I screamed. As soon as she pulled back I burst clean through the door, breaking the chain. When I stumbled in, Ma was up against the stairs, pointing the yoke straight at me. I honestly thought she would fire. I could see something dark and cruel in her. In all the years we'd been cooped up in this house together (which was bad enough after

Eugene and worse after my father died) I'd never *directly* encountered this look but I had felt it. In every sarcastic comment, in the way she'd no tenderness for me, not at any time or in any situation, in how she would mock the music I listened to and denounce my fox-feeding to the worst animal-haters that would come into the shop. Now, in the half-dark of the room, I saw her for real, sort of maskless. I saw with alcohol-derived clarity that there was something caught, trapped between us, that was almost creaturish, like an albatross – weighed down and entangled in net: it was *blame*. I fucking knew it, I said to myself, as she stood there in her long white nightdress that was shamefully flimsy and bare feet with the rough-skinned toes all painted up in a brash persimmon-coloured nail varnish, her eyes ablaze and narrow like a snake's, or a fox about to pounce on a rat. She blamed *me* for Eugene. (I had always the sense that because I was in a band she thought it must have been me who'd dragged Eugene into the scene he was in. But he was well capable of finding his own trouble.)

'You were out with that one,' she said.

'Who's that one?'

'That hussy. The Cassidy one.'

'Don't talk about her like that,' I said, quite viciously, near enough forgetting about the gun, though, like I said, I'd had a few jars. I pulled back then, just to be on the safe side. 'Put. The gun. Down. Ma. For fuck's sake.'

'She was never any good.'

I let out a big sigh, went to the door, saying I'd sleep in the barn as I couldn't stand to listen to her any more, nor be in the same house with someone pointing a gun at me.

'Come back, Michael,' she said, seeing me go to leave. When I stopped, she went to the cupboard under the stairs, lodged the gun inside, covered it with a few coats and closed the door.

'Pretty bloody handy with that gun aren't you, Ma?'

'Never know what scum'd be calling these nights,' she said. 'And besides, wouldn't a mother need a gun with a son like you comes in stocious drunk with the big foul breath on him?' Well, I couldn't resist. It was like those articles I'd read in the shop when I was bored, which was most days, about people in northern England or southern America who supposedly had 'out of body experiences.'. That's what it felt like as I lunged at my own mother and let out an enormous stinky breath directly into her face. She screwed up her eyes and mouth with the repugnancy of it, turned away.

'Oh, this is what she's done to you. What she's always done to you. Makes you belligerent. That's what it is.'

'It's not belligerence! It's fucking freedom. That's what she gives me, Ma. Freedom to be myself. Li-ber-ty!'

'Liberty!' Ma said, mockingly, and stood there shaking her head, a crafty smile spreading across her face. I was annoyed that she could come so quickly back from the disgusting thing I'd just done to her. I think I would have halted in my tracks, thrown myself down at her feet, begging her forgiveness had she, say, started to cry. But no, she'd gotten a taste for a row and was going to stand her ground, and she did, and she looked just like she did in the poster on the wall by the shop door, and it was then I realised she fucking loved it, the drama, the operatic proportions of things, the rows between us.

'Come on, Ma, let's go to bed,' I said, afraid for the thing to get out of hand and all too aware that both of us had easy access to a gun.

'I've heard a few things about Martha Cassidy and her fabulous singing career. Oh, I've heard plenty.'

'Like what have you heard? And from whom? The biddies round this way? They'd make muck of a saint,' I said.

'It wasn't a biddy who told me,' Ma said.

'Who told you?'

'Never you fucking mind who told me.'

'Don't swear, Ma, it doesn't suit you. Told you what?'

'Just how your precious Martha Cassidy's been making a living over there, and it's not by singing. It's by lying on her back, best way she knows how.' I looked at my mother, at her mouth all foamy and thin and twisted, and all the horrific stories I would read in the newspapers each day came suddenly into my mind, instantly metamorphosed as stories with me and Ma in the starring roles: *Son bludgeons own mother to death in row; 'Meryl Streep' mowed down in Castlemoyne; Son of woman-who-ruined-his-relationship-with-the-love-of-his-life-and-caused-her-firstborn-son-to-stop-taking-his-insulin-in-order-to-get-the-fuck-away-from-her turns nasty and shoots his mother's head clean off.* All this zipped through my brain (along with the words Ma had just said about Martha earning her keep in a supine position), as the two of us stood there, simmering with rage in the alcohol-scented room, and way way way back towards my spinal cortex a little thought started up, that just maybe my mother was right (about Martha). This was the terrible, insidious hold Ma had on me: that even when she was spiteful and wicked, a part of me thought she was right.

I could hear her wandering around upstairs. She had the radio on and was pottering about, probably working herself up into a tizzy (as she was prone to do), probably coming on all Elsa Lanchester and launching into Out Damn Spot. Why is it you like that speech, I asked her once and she said it was because she could relate to her, Lady Macbeth. Well, just let her fucking sleepwalk, I said to myself. Ever since my father died it was me who had to watch out for her so she wouldn't be getting upset and go sleepwalking into the bog behind the house, like she did a few times, after Eugene's death especially, and went spraining her ankle once with it, too. So I went to the door and undid all the bolts in the *hope* that tonight she *would* go out and sleepwalk. I'd a good mind, too, to empty all her Clonazepam and bottles of sal volatile down the sink. I was in such a mood I was inclined to lure her up to the bog myself.

Instead, I went to the long sideboard that housed my stereo and old LPs and took out my favourite album. It felt damp and dusty in my hands. I removed the vinyl from the *Nevermind* sleeve: between the two hovered the mildew-y, tobacco-y, vaguely semen-y smell of my youth. I placed the needle on 'Something in the Way'. I turned the volume up, loud, then louder still. I jumped onto the sofa and violently thrummed my air-guitar, louder in my mind than Kurt Cobain had ever played it and sang directly up to the ceiling so she could hear. I had not forgotten the words, which had quartered themselves somewhere in my DNA, like a long-abandoned prayer:

> *Underneath the bridge*
> *the tarp has sprung a leak*
> *the animals I've trapped*
> *have all become my pets*

When the song was done, I flung myself down onto the sofa to catch my breath. I lit up a cigarette, rested my two feet on the coffee table (something Ma hated me doing), and started to laugh. Between jumping around to the song, meeting Martha and having a good night out, I was beginning at last to feel more *in* the world than out of it. I was all sweaty and stinking from the jumping and air-guitaring so I took off my jacket and shirt. And immediately I was hurled back seventeen years, as my eyes followed the curling paths, first on my left arm, then on my right, of the long, deep, milk-white scars.

\*

The next day, Ma had me plagued in the shop, giving me this order and that return for the Cash and Carry. I'd been sneezing all morning but Ma was pretending the whole episode of the night before hadn't happened.

'Keep some of this chocolate in the fridge, nice and cool it is then. Always the mark of a sophisticated shop when you can get a cold Turkish Delight,' she said, sort of distant and falsely

chipper, as if I was not her son, but a sales rep. or customer.
But I wouldn't let her off with her aloofness; I was determined
to cheer her up.

'See Ma, you're a hostess type of woman.'

'I am not. But I might have been a hostess type of woman,'
she replied, 'if I'd gone to the Abbey, who knows.' This was 'the
great tragedy' in our family, the one, at least, that *was* allowed
to be spoken of. That Ma had turned down the Abbey Theatre
when they'd asked her to join them due to the pressure of her
own mother. Ma always told this story without any words of
regret, claiming her mother had been right. Though the regret
was nonetheless palpable. It may not have contained a single
*word* of regret but the way Ma would tell the story, it had the
delivery of Tragedy in which she became St Joan, and so it was
for others, her family mostly (of which I was now the last), to
observe the terrible wrong that had been done to poor
Constance.

'A family of entertainers we all were,' I joked, ever so slightly
hinting at my own lost career, but Ma did not hear this in my
voice. Instead, she took my surface-joviality as permission to
hightail it back to the past, once more to Eugene.

'When he was younger, he used to like sneaking into the shop,
stealing away with the sweets.'

'That was me,' I said.

'No. It was Eugene.'

'No, Ma, it was me used steal the sweets. You have it mixed
up. Eugene couldn't have sweets on account of…' I stopped
short because I could see what she was doing. Changing the
past so Eugene would emerge the perfect dead son. Just as she
had whitewashed the events that had led up to his death.

'No. That's it. He couldn't. But I used to catch him in here
all the same.'

'That's because he was at the till,' I replied.

'Shut the fecking hell up,' she said.

'He was never after the sweets, Ma. But he *was* after stealing money and you know it, too. I'll say no more, Ma, but get it right.' By now she had her hands over her ears.

'No, *you* get it right. Eugene had the big brains that would take him to Dublin to Trinity College to be a doctor with the best Leaving Certificate results a boy could get in the whole of Ireland, and coming out of this wee dot on the map of the world. MOYNE BOY WONDER, the papers said, knocked down in his prime by a weakness in his blood. That's it, Michael, and that's all it is with Eugene.' I wanted to vigorously argue this but I hadn't the energy or courage so I let it go.

We spent the morning stacking and pricing tins in silence. People came and went, and we kept the radio on loud so no one would notice we weren't speaking. After lunch I thought I could hear the far-off purr of an engine, increasing in power as it came close to the shop. Eventually, the doorbell rang and Martha came in, head to toe in bike leathers, a glossy black bike helmet hanging out of her hand. She looked unbelievable.

'Connie,' she said, greeting my mother, who grunted a reply and went to tear the plastic off a new delivery.

'I found your motorbike, Michael. The Norton,' Martha said. 'I was wondering if you'd like to give her a test run.' I felt a combination of adrenalin and lust course through my veins and was unbuttoning my shop-coat before I knew it.

'Sure, look at the cut of him. Hasn't he a cold from being out half of the night?' Ma said.

'We won't be long,' Martha said.

'I'll get you a jumper,' Ma said, and was almost off to get it and me letting her when I saw the horror at that sentence on Martha's face.

'A jumper? Don't be getting me a jumper. My jacket's fine, sure,' I said. I took off the shop-coat, threw it on the counter, took my jacket off the coat-hanger and put it on. 'I won't be long, Ma. I just want to see the bike again, that's all, ' I said. To which Martha added, 'aren't we only going for the wee *ride*, Connie,' and she winked at me in quite an alarming, exciting way, and I turned and saw that Ma was not disgusted by this, but sad, and so help me I felt sorry for her. Then Ma had to go and spoil even my ridiculous pity.

'Tell me this, Martha.'

'Tell you what?'

'How is it, if you're so big in America, no one's heard of you here? You've never been on the radio, or in the *Irish Times*. *Northern Star* is the only place I've ever seen you. And sure Josie could say anything to them and they'd print it. Josie's always bigging you up. Ever since your father, she…' and then Ma stopped short. Martha did not look happy.

'"Ever since your father" what, Connie?' Martha said. I tried to sort of push Martha out the door then but she was determined to get to the bottom of Ma's dig.

'Ma meant nothing.'

'Oh yes she did.'

Martha probably didn't know it but this is what Ma had been waiting for. Ma would always want to be led up to the big dramatic speech (the précis was never her forte; she needed expansion, brewing room for venom). It was her modus operandi. I should know. And sure enough, Martha had pressed the right button and Big Dramatic Speech was delivered: 'I meant, when he was caught mixing the milk with the water, and the dairies were all closed. Do you remember that, Michael? Of course we know now it was because he was thick with *them fellas* with their big politics and bigger drug rings. A lot of people lost their jobs over that scam; lots of retailers got caught out by it, too. Do you not remember, Michael, when we were shocked to hear the likes of *them fellas* would even think of bleeding money from a clapped-out Monaghan dairy when they could be at your glamorous, lucrative crimes like, I don't know, robbing banks or post offices.'

'You fucking bitch,' Martha said.

'Didn't I always say she had a foul mouth?' Ma said, looking at me. I squared up to Ma and made a ZIP IT gesture to my own mouth. Then Martha burst across me, her years in America ringing out in the cadences of every sentence.

'I bet you were glad to see the back of me, Connie, eh? And you know what? I still didn't get an explanation. What reason do you have for stopping Michael and me marrying that time, huh? You'd think you'd have backed off by now. Because didn't he have to go and pay a heavy price for it, and hasn't he paid up big time, Connie?'

'He's got a good life,' Ma said.

'Eugene had a good life too and looked what happened to him! Seems the action in this house is so fucking spectacular all the men can't wait to be getting away from it! And now we're on that subject, I'm sure you know about Michael's little heart-to-heart with Eugene at the hospital that time. I'm sure by now Michael has told you all about it...' and then she looked at me, at my big *vacant* face. She looked from me to Ma. It must have been obvious I'd not told Ma a single word of my last conversation with Eugene.

'No more, Martha!' I said.

'Whist, will you, Michael,' Ma said, as if I wasn't even in the room.

'So you listen to me,' Martha continued, 'because me and him are going on that bike right now and we're going to tear up this fucking road, do you hear?' Ma backed off. I grabbed Martha, pulled her out of the shop. Outside, I revved up the Norton for the first time in nearly two decades, and sped off with Martha sitting behind me, her arms wrapped tightly around my waist.

\*

The last time I'd seen the Norton was the summer of 1993. It was the last night Martha and I were a couple; the night she said it was her or Ma and that she believed I would never get up from under my mother's feet, and that after Eugene died, Ma had me good and proper and it was crucial I get away from her ('cut the fucking umbilical cord' were Martha's exact words); the night she said she would be leaving for America, leaving the band, leaving Castlemoyne, and that if I wanted her I should go with her; the night I ran like a frightened little girl into the bleak bog, running for home. And so the bike stayed all these years at Josie's. Because I'd not had the courage to go back for it. Not after the split with Martha, and not after I'd split open my two arms and near enough emptied them of all life up on the bog. I was glad to be on that bike again. I was ecstatic. But despite Martha's hair blowing forward into my face and the black softness of it, I could not get Ma and her sad, defeated look in the shop out of my mind. I dropped Martha off at Josie's and rode as if I'd never been off that bike – straight for home. I reckoned then that I was a hopeless case, and was probably much worse than Norman Bates, who at least had madness as an excuse, whereas mine was a warped, utterly misplaced and unrelenting sense of filial fucking duty.

\*

There's a picture in Ma's room of me and Eugene as kids. She's in the middle, sitting in a chair in the garden. He's sort of behind her, like he's in charge or something, and I'm standing beside her, chest out, grinning, my legs apart like John Wayne. Eugene is holding a turquoise-coloured ball. The way he holds the ball always would pull me into that photo. Up to his chest, firmly, as if he'd been fully involved in his game of ball-playing before being called to sit for the photo, probably by my father. Most kids would have let that ball go, run off to the new adventure of having their picture taken, but Eugene was never like most kids. He brings the ball. It's his thing. The call to the photo has interrupted *him*. He is saying, as he stands there behind my mother, his already manly hand around the ball, that he is a private person with his own world, that he is *not available*. I look different. Though only a year younger, I don't have that sense of purpose, of self-possession, of interest in anything other than smiling stupidly at the camera. Three or four years after the photo is taken, Eugene is diagnosed with Type 1 Diabetes. And everyone says it was then we sort of lost him. First, he would retreat into his books, then show up late for the shots (in the days of hypodermic-administered insulin) that my mother would give him, and when he was older he'd stay out with his glue-sniffing friends in the town (a crowd worse even than the grunge-heads I knew, who at least were making music, creating stuff). But I think differently. In the photo I can see it: the distance from us has already started. I can see it in the way he holds that ball; he's apart, chosen his own company. And I sometimes wonder how my mother and father could not have noticed this earlier about their strange but beautiful boy, that he was always playing *his own game*, and would never let anyone else in.

\*

It was Josie's birthday. She was sixty-five. Martha said that this was why she had come home: to do something nice for her aunt, who had looked after her all those years when her father was busy with his 'politics' (since the scandal with the dairy he had moved to Dundalk and Martha had seen little of him). Martha invited me to the bash which, she apologised, was to consist of a séance of some kind followed by drinks and snacks al fresco. She said she thought I might think the affair too hokey. I didn't think it too hokey at all. It wasn't as if I'd been to anything much that wasn't hokey in about seventeen years. Josie was glad to see me. I had bumped into her a few times in town, always making my excuses, rushing off somewhere. In seventeen years we'd not had a proper conversation, and I never once asked her how Martha was doing, though I'd read all the features about Martha's singing career in the *Northern Star*. Now, sitting out on the long lawn in front of Josie's cottage, the sky's blueness fading to the grey bruised colour of early moonlight, I turned and saw Josie, Coco Conway, the large bleach-blonde medium, a few others, all gathered round the table in Josie's front room, and I was sorry I'd not been friendlier all those years.

Martha and I were sipping slowly at our glasses of wine, our seats placed before a crest of blue hydrangeas and southernwood while we listened in to the séance. (It sounded like a lot of fun that séance and I half wondered if I should go in myself and ask for Eugene to be 'got in touch with' so I could tell him what a cunt I thought he was for doing what he did.) It felt fine to be out in the moonlight with Martha. I looked at her sitting in her deckchair, her legs crossed, her top leg swinging slowly back and forth, so that when it was forth it was nicely inclined towards me. Sometimes she would look up at the sky, trying to make out the constellations, and this would give me occasion to consider the situation. For I kept having to remind myself that no matter what strange notions I had about time, about not being able to feel correctly its passage, knowing other people could feel time more correctly, more conventionally somehow, but that I could not, seventeen years *had* actually passed since we'd been 'a couple'. Because I was tempted to believe that what had really passed was just *one* continuous *day*. This *one day* where I open my eyes in the morning, get up, brush my teeth, work, eat, go to bed, sleep – with her not there. And as I more or less did that every day for seventeen years, it did not feel like 17 x 365 days, it felt like one day. Which is why I could not fully feel that it was over between us. Because the thing that had separated us, time, I was not able to experience. Of course, I kept such thoughts to myself.

'This place you said you went to in California, where you had your *awakening* thing, what did you say it was named after?'

'A TV quiz-show.'

'Jesus. Strange name that, *Truth or Consequences*.'

'It is, I suppose.'

'Who wouldn't have an epiphany in a town with a name like that?'

'It has these lithium-rich waters. Maybe that's what did it. The lithium,' she said. I smiled at that, thinking of 'Lithium', the Nirvana song we'd both loved once.

'Roswell is due east, close to the Mexican border,' she said. 'Now that's a really interesting place. Still dining out on the whole alien thing, of course, and why not? People move there for the dry air. It's good for the bones. Unlike the Monaghan damp which makes cripples of everyone. Josie's destroyed with arthritis.'

'What else do you remember about life here,' I asked, sort of hoping she might think of the old days, or else maybe remind me again what a 'god' she thought I was.

'I remember our gigs,' she replied. I nodded. 'I remember Dalty O'Hanlon sleeping in a coffin, jumping off the balcony of the Adelphi Cinema, thought he was a vampire. At *A Fistful of Dollars* and wearing a cape.'

'He broke his legs doing it,' I said.

'Castlemoyne was like the Wild West back then,' Martha said. 'Remember Dinger?'

'Dinger Ward?' As she tried to put a face to the name, I got up and did an impersonation of Dinger Ward's walk, which was like that of a tight-arsed penguin.

'He walked with his fists clenched, like this.'

'Just in case?'

'Just in case.'

'They were violent times,' she said, shaking her head.

'Hard young men with no jobs on the borderlands. That's what it was, Martha.'

'I thought there'd be better people, better men. You know, not long after us, me and men didn't work out, Michael.'

'There must have been someone,' I said. Martha shook her head. And just as things were starting to get interesting, the séance party broke up. I could hear raised voices. I glanced back at the house and saw Josie and Coco on the porch but ignored them as the moment between Martha and me was far too electric to disturb.

'Mother of Jesus,' Coco said, rushing towards us. Dogs were barking from the yards of nearby farms so eventually I stood up to see what all the commotion was about.

'By the roads, look,' Josie said, pointing to the lane. A female figure was walking towards us with her arms out. It was a startling and unsettling sight, for the woman was completely naked. Across her legs were wisps of grass, bracken, cuds of the thick black mud of the bog. Her figure was strong and full, her breasts heavy, the nipples dark.

'Oh Jesus, oh Jesus, oh Jesus,' I said, upon recognition.

'Oh dear Christ,' Martha said, upon recognition.

'Jesus, Mary and Joseph,' Josie said, as the figure of my mother came towards us.

'Is that… is that…' Coco asked, his jaw dropping further and further so that if he had finished that sentence and said my mother's actual name I would have punched him.

'Get some slippers for Christ's sake,' Josie said, 'and some clothes. Coco! Stop gawping will ya and get Connie some slippers and a blanket!' Coco hurried to the house. Martha looked at me, nodding. I knew what she was thinking: there she goes again, Constance McDaid and her marvellous acting, about to hijack the show, wreck the party she has not even been invited to. This was the kind of thing Martha had often thought, and said, about my mother.

'Did you ever see such a thing in your entire life?' Josie said, with utmost compassion in her voice.

'She should get an Oscar for this performance,' Martha said, with none.

'She's sleepwalking. Usually only does it when someone dies, or she gets nervous,' I said. I went to my mother, wrapped my jacket around her. She shrugged it off.

'Wake up, Ma. You're out. At Josie's. It's her birthday,' I said.

'I'm looking for my son,' Ma said, plaintively, so that I wanted to hug her, tell her everything would be fine.

'Here I am, Ma. Come on now and we'll go home.' But then she looked at me with a great sourness in her face.

'No,' she said, 'my son *Eugene*.' Her words stung me with a scorpion-like precision, not least because they had been heard by all present.

'Come on,' Josie said, 'I'll drive you both home.' I turned to explain to Martha, to let her know that I'd to deal with this, bring Ma home, give her her pills (get some clothes on her at least), and to communicate that I was sorry to leave the wonderful reminiscing we were having, but Martha had left already, was about to enter the house, her head bowed, evidently no longer prepared to give my mother any more of her time, probably as she considered Ma had taken up enough of it. As I watched her go in, more slumped, more the Martha who had lived here before, unfree, smaller than the apparition who had entered the shop a week or so before, I knew then that I'd lost her. For the second time.

Now it was Ma who was sneezing and going round the place all sheepish. I had still not worked out what had caused her to go so far with the sleepwalking, or why she'd had no clothes on her at all, except that with the warmth of the night she had probably gone to bed without them. These were not thoughts I wanted to dwell on. Anyway, I didn't tell her where I was going. 'A fag break,' I said and she nodded. When I got to the bog road, Martha was waiting, all zipped up in her close-fitting jacket. As we walked, both a little breathless, I sensed a tension between us. Eventually she came out with it: 'I changed my booking, Michael. I'm heading back Friday.'

'Right,' I said, coolly. I could straight away feel myself shutting down a little inside (due to the thought of returning to that Norman Bates-type creature). But I'd no claim on Martha, no claim on her whatsoever. 'You should go back,' I said. 'There's nothing for you here now.' Then we walked quietly up to the bog. What we saw when we got there knocked all thoughts of Martha leaving out of my head. For lying in a great awful heap by the rock where we would sit, were three, four dead foxes. I recognised them immediately as the mother and her cubs that I'd been feeding. The sight of them there, bullet-riddled, was something to behold. They lay slack-jawed, their eyes closed, side by side, as if they'd clung to each other in their final minutes.

'What. The. Fuck.'

'Oh, it's awful!' Martha said. 'Who would do such a thing?' I could think of several people, their faces immediately collapsing in my mind into a single face, a single set of cruel dead eyes peering down the barrel of a gun.

'Oh God!' I kept repeating. 'They're supposed to get permission. The gun clubs. This side of the border alone there's Castlemoyne, Tullycorbe, Castleshane…'

'*Gun* clubs?'

'Or Jack Daly, worried about his bloody sheep.' As soon as I said Daly's name it was he I saw (in my mind) shooting the foxes. 'Bastard! He's been saying he wasn't happy I'd been feeding them up here. I'll fucking kill him!' I was about to run down to Daly's cabin when Martha held me back by the arm. Just her touch seemed to make everything melt inside me and so help me I started to cry.

'Oh, Michael. Don't make it worse.'

'I loved them, Martha.'

'There'll be no sympathy for you here, Michael. Not with foxes.'

'Aren't you the only one ever understood me here?'

'How do you live in such a place? You, who's so sensitive, the sweetest man. How do you live with these people who don't, won't, understand you? Who would kill your foxes, *knowing* they were yours?'

'It was probably the gun club.'

'It was probably your *mother*, Michael!'

'She wouldn't.'

'She fucking would. Oh, when will you wake up? Eugene couldn't stand her. Everyone bloody knows he stopped taking his insulin on purpose except her.' Then I turned from her, my head (and heart) reeling, and scooped up the plump bodies. I brought the fox and her cubs to a small bog pool, thick with duckweed, and buried them in the dank and stagnant water, covered the mass of fur with stones. As I placed the last stone on the pile, Martha sighed and went and sat on the long rock. After it was done, I wiped my hands in moss and lit up a cigarette. Martha was looking out at the land below, and I could tell by the way she looked, with a strange blend of love and disgust and rage, that when she would leave here she would never return.

'Your mother will be wondering where you've got to, Michael,' she said. I got the sarcasm.

'Come on, we better go,' I said.

'Look, I haven't been entirely honest with you,' she said.

'How d'you mean?'

'I didn't just come home for Josie. I thought, maybe, here, I could... Josie's been exaggerating my success, is what I mean, Michael. At singing. I did a few good gigs, got good reviews. But you see...' and I noticed she seemed again as she had the night before, smaller, less angelic.

'You see, Michael, that town I was in... the epiphany thing... I'd been at music for years, not getting anywhere. And then I was invited to do a gig in this hotel, and when I got there, about two people showed and the gig was cancelled. But it was there, I suddenly realised something. That it was all a sort of con. Ambition. Getting where? Where's the top? *Where* is it? And that's the moment I started to relax. To sleep properly. A lot of the cares I'd had before just vanished, and I'd bathe in the healing waters they have there every morning. In 38 degree centigrade, lithium-rich water. I made friends there, too. One of these – we call her the Countess – has bought a bar. Not far from Truth or Consequences. Between there and Roswell. She wants it to be a music-orientated bar, a few alien dummies, maybe, but she wants me to run it. For a couple of years. I think you should run it with me. You'd be good at that, Michael. What do you say?' Martha lay back on the rock, facing the sky. I wondered if I should mention the thing that Ma had hinted at, the rumours about how Martha had been earning her living (i.e. supinely) but suddenly I didn't care one way or the other. 'Michael,' she said, 'just think about it, OK?'

'OK,' I said. I saw in her eyes then that her life in the States had not been easy, and I felt pity for her. I could see, too, that maybe this Roswell bar thing was, as far as she was concerned anyway, her last shot at a vaguely interesting life.

'Once I asked you to choose,' she said, 'between me and Connie. It was probably too much to ask, after Eugene, I see that now. So I won't ask you to do that again. But this day, Michael, after all that has happened: your beautiful foxes, herself ruining the party, give *me* this day and not her, will you? Before I go back, huh?' For a split-second I did actually think of getting back to the shop. Then my eye drew up on something lying in the grass. I kicked at it, picked it up: a two-inch, cinnamon-red, gold-rimmed cartridge shell. I brought the shell to my nose. The former liveliness of the foxes I had come to know and love haunted the cold, indicting smell of sulphur. I put the shell in my pocket and walked towards Martha who was lying back on the rock like some kind of terrific ancient sacrifice. I went to her, my face wet with tears, cupped my hands around her hair and she came towards me.

\*

We were to leave the following week. Martha made all the arrangements. She changed her booking, made a new one for me. I spent three days sorting myself out with appropriate clothes, suncreams, US dollars; filled several rubbish bags with junk and in so doing revealed a bedroom that looked to have been the room of a child or teenager. (Posters of Bruce Lee, skateboard-themed wallpaper.) It felt enormously gratifying to take all that old stuff from walls and drawers and plunge it into rubbish bags. Also into the bags went my comics, my stash of Men Only magazines and all the touristic tat Ma and I had bought on our trips to Donegal, Cork and Kerry. (Including the framed photo of us outside Blarney Castle, where Ma had refused to trust the man responsible for holding visitors as they bent backwards to kiss the Blarney stone, saying she could smell alcohol off his breath and that he was bound to drop us all to our deaths down the unguarded opening, and a ruckus had broken out so they'd asked us to leave. As well as the watercolour from Letterfrack where, in a corner of that lonesome wilderness, we had bumped into the British MP, Robin Cook, the year before he died.) So by the end of my dumping session all that was left were my more modern clothes, a few books, CDs, select mementoes. My old life was over and my new life was about to begin. So why did I feel so confused? Was it because I had secretly (really secretly) loved these days in this house with my mother? The years of our sometimes-humorous bickering; watching rented films and bringing the two of us cocoa; blackberry-picking in September so she could make jam; meals on the first Sunday of the month in the Shercock Hotel and everyone knowing me and Ma, knowing she was once Meryl Streep and had a great talent and that I wasn't so bad either. Hadn't it secretly made me feel all sort of safe and warm inside? And what was this I was about to do anyway? Take a one-way flight to L fucking A. Not Boston or New York or Chicago, but LAX, California, to shack up with Martha in the desert. Thoughts of all of this *new stuff* jingled around my head like loose change. I started to sweat. Maybe, I should hang on, a day, two. I'd boasted (a lot) about the new life I was about to have with Martha and the plans we had to do music again (slight exaggeration) but still I sensed Ma did not believe me somehow. As if she could read my mind and see my conflictedness and understand it better than I could myself. Not once did she ask me to stay. And though I'd spent an entire day trying to get it out of her: was she sleepwalking or 'acting', was it her who killed my foxes or some other, I believed her when she said she *was* sleepwalking and that she'd never kill my foxes. She was my mother for God's sake, no matter what Martha thought of her.

We were both in the shop when Josie entered. I could tell something was wrong.

'Martha's gone, Michael,' Josie said.

'What do you mean "gone"?'

'She didn't wait. Went this morning. She asked me to give you this.' I took the envelope. As I opened it I could feel the tension between Josie and my mother, once pals, once passionate participants in the local am-dram scene. Ma had said terrible things about Martha's father, Josie's brother, all those years ago, and Josie had not spoken to Ma since. And Ma had maintained the moral high ground on the subject, though this had been largely conceded since she had somnambulated without a gobbet of clothing (in front of several witnesses) across the bog to Josie's.

'Shop's looking good, Connie,' Josie said.

'The work never ends, Josie,' Ma said, and I returned to Martha's letter, which was not strictly a letter, more a one-way ticket to LA with a Post-it note on top that read: *only when you're sure.*

'That girl's not changed,' Josie said. 'As impulsive and flighty as ever.' I put the envelope in my pocket, carried on refilling the crisp boxes. I was at once relieved and annoyed with Martha that she had read correctly my hesitancy.

'So what did it say?' Ma said, nodding away to Josie, both of them bug-eyed, trying to divine by my movements what

Martha might have communicated to me. When I shook my head, Josie pressed her lips together and looked at Ma as if to apologise for her wayward niece and the effect she'd had on my life. On her way out, Josie turned and said: 'Connie, guess what they're putting on in the community centre this year?'

'What's that?'

'*The Jailbird.*'

'That'd be a bit dated now, wouldn't it?'

'I hear they're looking for an actress to play Mrs Kelsey. You should give that group a call.'

'My acting days are long gone, Josie.'

'You were the finest Mrs Kelsey ever seen outside Dublin. They couldn't judge you unless it was by professional standards, you know that. You should call that group.'

The bell rang out after Josie and a heavy silence followed between Ma and me. I knew she was embarrassed for me, but she needn't have been. Martha had detected my uncertainty and was giving me a chance to be sure. That's how I saw it anyway. To be sure I wanted to run a bar with her in the desert, a life I might come to hate soon enough. So before Ma had a chance to grill me about the letter, I said, 'it's a ticket. To America. One-way and open. She says I'm to use it when I feel like it.'

'And do you feel like it?'

'I do.'

'Do you feel like it now?'

'Ma,' I said, exasperated, 'show me that postcard brochure that came in, will you?' And I could feel her step quietly, like a bird, towards the place where she kept the brochures and catalogues.

★

Days and weeks passed and I didn't hear again from Martha. Meanwhile, I established a mobile shop, two fellas driving a van selling our goods up and down the housing estates of

Castlemoyne and its environs. I put chairs outside so people could sit and eat what they'd bought in the shop. I placed the carousel of postcards by the door, took charge in a way I'd never done before. And Ma let me do it. I had a one-way ticket to LA hanging over her and I could have done anything I liked with that power. She didn't resist, even seemed to enjoy letting me have the upper-hand. She never once asked me to massage her feet and I wore what I liked in the shop. When the biddies came in they nodded. They had respect for me. They spoke quietly to Ma and didn't stay long, as if they were a little afraid of me. Coco would come in and nod so much I thought his head would drop off.

Autumn arrived, this time wet and damp. The junk from my room remained in the black bags. Though things had gone well (with the changes I had made) at first, I nonetheless began to think that Ma took no particular *triumph* from having (more or less) trounced Martha Cassidy. It was me who seemed happy, not Ma. In fact, she seemed less flirtatious with Coco, generally more distracted, a little slow and depressed in the manner she would be before she would sleepwalk, like they say the warning sign is of one who has epilepsy. One day, when we were in the shop, the rain pelting down outside, I could see Ma looking sort of dejected, a raggedy piece of paper in her hands.

'Not that bad is it?' I said.

'What?'

'The weather.'

'?'

'The weath… look, what's wrong with you, Ma? What's with the bit of paper?'

'Oh. Just the number for the community group.'

'What community group?' I said.

'Group doing *The Jailbird* in the centre. Apparently they still haven't found their Mrs Kelsey.'

'Oh, is that it?' I said, assuming she'd wanted to apply and hadn't.

'Give them a call,' I said, and for a second or two her mood lifted. But the furrowed brow remained. She had the look of someone who had left something very important undone.

'Michael,' she said, then, ominously, sort of spitting it out, 'time is dragging.'

'What do you mean?' I said.

'Well, the ticket, is what I mean. You're still here.'

'I know I am, Ma. Isn't that what you wanted?' And as I scanned her face I saw to my horror that maybe I was wrong, maybe she hadn't wanted me to be at home with her at all.

'Well, maybe you should have gone *before*, is what I meant.'

'Before what?' Now I was getting panicky, probably because I knew deep down that she was right. Wasn't she always?

'Aren't we doing well now?' I said, and she nodded.

'Michael, I've something to tell you.' She went to the door, closed it, pulled the shutter down, turned the sign to CLOSED. She stood suddenly taller than usual, her hands folding over in rapid ODS rinsing movements, and she was all breathy.

'About the foxes.' The mention of them hit me with force. I'd not gone up to our bog or thought of my foxes in weeks. I had only to think of them and I'd feel sick and my hands would shake.

'What about them?' I said, unable to hide the emotion rising up in my chest. I watched the colour drain from my mother's face. Without replying, she turned and kept her back to me.

'Ah you... don't say you... you didn't, Ma... did you...? don't say it...' and as if from nowhere I started to sob, deep hungry sobs, and from the rattling of her shoulders I could tell she was sobbing too.

'I'm sorry, Michael. I'm so sorry. It was an awful business and I wasn't in my right mind.'

'Why are you telling me now for fuck's sake, why now?'

'Because I don't want you to make a mistake.'

'Mistake about what?'

'Martha. America.'

'Why Ma?! Why?! I loved them cubs, the fox. I loved them.'

'How else was I going to get you up from under my feet, Michael, huh?'

'Doing everything to keep me one minute and the next – everything to make me go! Make up your fucking mind will you, Ma?'

'It was a drastic step, and no doubt one too far, but I was just trying to give you a little push,' she said. I looked at her then, the paper trembling in her hand.

'A little push?' I said. She nodded. Straight away I took off my shop-coat (which, I am ashamed to say, I'd begun wearing of my own volition), and ran upstairs. I went to the place where I kept the envelope and saw I still had time on the ticket. I lay down on the bed, scoured the room for the few things I'd bring. I'd go as soon as possible, in the morning, for I felt now that everything was ruined with Ma and me. I could never travel around Ireland on the trains with the person who had killed my foxes (whether she was my mother or not).

The next morning I was ready to leave. I was tempted to go without saying a word. I looked around the living room, at the shelves with all her plays, books, trophies, my ancient stereo, then over towards the shop where I could hear her clicking away at the calculator. The shop door was open and I could see the poster, all leathery and swollen-looking in the soft morning light. I saw for the first time, I think, that Coco was right: she had a strong, haughty look, just like Meryl Streep, and an intensity, an immersiveness in her role that suddenly reminded me of Eugene (and his turquoise ball). She was talented. As he had been. As I had been. How had the entire talent quotient in one family gone down the toilet, I wondered? How had that happened? As I looked at her, so poised and fierce and direct, I wondered if she could possibly have been *lying* about my foxes. I wasn't sure she was capable of such an act. Not really. (And not *my* foxes.) I had every intention of leaving via the front of the house but I didn't. I went into the shop. She was by now starting to get the coffee and sandwiches ready for the truckers who would be passing. The radio was off and I could tell she was deep in her thoughts. She looked up at me and smiled.

'What time's your bus, Son?'

'Eight,' I replied.

'Well. Good luck. Here, have a few plums and sandwiches for the journey,' and she took up a small paper bag that she had filled, rolled it down by the cuff and handed it to me.

'Good-bye, Ma,' I said, and I was about off when she called me back.

'Michael?'

'Yes, Ma?'

'There's something I want to ask you. Something Martha said when she was here. About what Eugene said to you in the hospital.'

'It's nothing. You don't want to hear.'

'Tell me, won't you?'

'You know.'

'Tell me yourself, now you're going. Please.' Her voice sounded weak.

'Ah, you do know. You do. It's not like you always say, Ma. Eugene didn't *forget* to take his insulin. He knew what would happen if he missed that shot. Eugene wasn't ever going to be a doctor, Mam. It's not what he wanted. Tell her *it's not for you*, I said. But he couldn't hurt you, he said. Couldn't let you down with all you'd sacrificed. He was hanging round that crowd in the town, drinking the head off himself, and I worried because if he wasn't careful he'd miss the insulin. He knew what would happen if he missed that shot. The kidneys would fail and he'd go blind. And it did happen. And he told me it was because he saw the rest of his life before him and none of it belonged to him. So he let it slip. Do you have any idea what it's like not to own your own life, Ma? Well, I'll tell you. All there is ahead of you is time, and for Eugene it was endless time, time and needles. He felt he had no life. And I knew he would do that one day.' It felt good to tell her the last words Eugene had said to me. She had no clue, I think, just how much her own squashed dreams had shaped, and warped, her sons. No fucking clue. Until, maybe, she saw that I would not take my last chance out of Dodge.

'Good cut on you that suit.'

'I'll send it back when I get settled.'

'No need.'

'Don't want to be wearing a dead man's suit, Ma. Only it's a change. I'll send it.'

'Did Bucky Lawless cut your hair?' I nodded.

'Stylish it is.'

'I'll go out the house way.'

'Good luck to you, Son.'

'Goodbye, Ma,' I said. I did not kiss her.

*

It was a dark, frosty morning as I walked to the bus stop. There was a long queue already formed. A few men in suits; some women, one in an ultramarine stewardess' uniform; quite a few young men in twos, mostly with big duffle bags; a whole family (all of them quiet and downcast) with a ton of suitcases. Every man and his dog is getting out of Moyne, I thought to myself. Once the bus had left the towns and was onto the motorway, I gazed out the window at the bumpy Monaghan landscape. It looked just as it did in our postcards. Lots of sheep and cattle and big houses (though the postcards, naturally enough, missed all the houses I saw that were now empty, or for sale, or unfinished, some of them almost fully returned to nature) all surrounded by lush deep-green fields. And until we reached Louth, a scattering of lakes, some covered in a thick blue mist with swans on them. The hay in the fields was all still and sort of smug-looking from having been recently gathered and baled. The hay done, the farmers were now at the barley and it was short and blunt where it had been cut already. The land was busy with autumn activity and was full of harvesters and tractors. Some of the farmers I saw I knew. I felt a lump in my throat as I looked out at the morning light, all frail and black-tinged over the fields, and I tried to tell myself it would be the death of me that land (I knew well that Maguire in Kavanagh's *Great Hunger* ends his days a 'hungry fiend' who 'screams the apocalypse of clay' and that if I were to remain I was destined to have much the same kind of half-buried existence; even Kavanagh himself had gotten out and he'd loved the place) and not to get too upset about leaving it, though tears rolled down my face nonetheless. As the bus approached Dublin airport, I felt a shift, a loosening (my breathing deepened), as if all of a sudden I could *feel* time and its passing, and those years with Ma in the house and shop, when I thought I'd be stuck forever in Moyne (and half wanting to be stuck there), were somehow laid to rest, and I felt ready for whatever lay ahead.

# Notes

**The Badminton Court**
The central image of this story is based on the painting 'The Badminton Game' by David Inshaw.

**The Visit**
In 2000, President Bill Clinton and his family visited the town of Dundalk on the Irish border as part of the Good Friday Agreement.

**The Lagoon**
There were sixteen people who 'disappeared' during 'the Troubles' in Northern Ireland. The Provisional IRA admitted responsibility for thirteen of the sixteen, while one was admitted by the INLA. No attribution has been given to the remaining two. To date the remains of nine victims have been recovered.

# Acknowledgements

Thanks to the editors of the following publications, where some of these stories, or versions of them, have appeared: *The Dublin Review, Irish Pages, The Warwick Review, Wasafiri Magazine, Cyphers, Brace: A New Generation in Fiction* (published by Comma Press), *Verbal Arts Magazine, Wordlegs, The Frogmore Papers.* 'The Congo' was shortlisted for the 2009 Asham Award. 'Blood' won First Prize in the Spinetinglers 2009 Dark Fiction short story competition. 'The Visit' won First Prize in the 2010 Wasafiri New Writing Awards and appears in the 2012 *Best British Short Stories Anthology* (published by Salt, edited by Nicholas Royle). Thanks to Penny Thomas for reading and editing, to C.V. for his careful reading, and to my sister, Tracey McCarrick, for her observations on 'The Tribe'. All characters in *The Scattering* are fictional, and though some places and events are real, for the purposes of fiction-making they are often depicted without geographical veracity.

# About the Author

Jaki McCarrick lives in Dundalk and studied at Trinity College, Dublin, gaining a Master of Philosophy Degree, Creative Writing – Distinction. Before this Jaki gained a BA Performing Arts, First Class Honours Degree at Middlesex University. She has also completed an RNT Directors Course, 2001, and has studied for a PhD thesis on the work of Patrick Kavanagh.

Jaki has won many awards for her work including: Winner of the 2005 SCDA National Playwriting Competition for *The Mushroom Pickers*; Shortlisted for the Sphinx Playwriting Award 2006, Bruntwood Prize 2006, Kings Cross Award 2007 for *The Moth-Hour*; Winner of the 2010 Papatango New Writing Award, Shortlisted for the 2009 Adrienne Benham Award and the 2010 Yale International Drama Award for *Leopoldville*; Shortlisted for the 2012 Susan Smith Blackburn Prize, Winner of the Galway Theatre Festival Playwriting Competition for *Belfast Girls* (developed during McCarrick's attachment to the National Theatre, London in 2012). For fiction her prizes include first prize in the 2009 Northern Ireland Spinetinglers Dark Fiction competition for **'Blood'**, shortlisted for the 2009 Asham Award for short fiction for **'The Congo'**, winner of the 2010 Wasafiri Prize for New Writing for **'The Visit'** (also selected for *The 2012 Anthology of Best British Short Stories*). For poetry she won the first Liverpool Lennon (Paper) Poetry Competition, judged by Carol Ann Duffy, for her poem, 'The Selkie of Dorinish' (2010), and was shortlisted for 2012 Patrick Kavanagh Award and Cork Literary Review Manuscript Competition (in which she was placed 2$^{nd}$). Jaki has recently been awarded a writing residency at the Centre Culturel Irlandais in Paris commencing April 2013.

# SEREN

## Well chosen words

Seren is an independent publisher with a wide-ranging list which includes poetry, fiction, biography, art, translation, criticism and history. Many of our books and authors have been shortlisted for – or won – major literary prizes, among them the Costa Award, the Man Booker, Forward Prize, and TS Eliot Prize.

At the heart of our list is a good story told well or an idea or history presented interestingly or provocatively. We're international in authorship and readership though our roots are here in Wales (Seren means Star in Welsh), where we prove that writers from a small country with an intricate culture have a worldwide relevance.

Our aim is to publish work of the highest literary and artistic merit that also succeeds commercially in a competitive, fast changing environment. You can help us achieve this goal by reading more of our books – available from all good bookshops and increasingly as e-books. You can also buy them at 20% discount from our website, and get monthly updates about forthcoming titles, readings, launches and other news about Seren and the authors we publish.

## www.serenbooks.com